A BIBLIOPHILE MYSTERY

Murder Under Cover

Kate Carlisle

WHEELER
CHIVERS

This Large Print edition is published by Wheeler Publishing, Waterville, Maine, USA and by AudioGO Ltd, Bath, England.
Wheeler Publishing, a part of Gale, Cengage Learning.

The text of this Large Print edition is unabridged.
Other aspects of the book may vary from the original edition.
Set in 16 pt. Plantin.

LIBRARY OF CONGRESS CATALOGING-IN-PUBLICATION DATA

Carlisle, Kate, 1951–
Murder under cover : a bibliophile mystery / by Kate Carlisle.
p. cm. — (Wheeler Publishing large print cozy mystery)
ISBN-13: 978-1-4104-3945-1 (softcover)
ISBN-10: 1-4104-3945-3 (softcover)
1. Books—Conservation and restoration—Fiction. 2. Murder—Investigation—Fiction. 3. Large type books. I. Title.
PS3603.A7527M87 2011
813'.6—dc22 2011018217

BRITISH LIBRARY CATALOGUING-IN-PUBLICATION DATA AVAILABLE

Published in 2011 in the U.S. by arrangement with NAL Signet, a member of Penguin Group (USA) Inc.
Published in 2012 in the U.K. by arrangement with The Penguin Group USA Inc.

U.K. Hardcover: 978 1 445 83832 8 (Chivers Large Print)
U.K. Softcover: 978 1 445 83833 5 (Camden Large Print)

Printed in the United States of America
1 2 3 4 5 6 7 15 14 13 12 11

This book is dedicated with love
and affection to my brother,
Timothy Michael Beaver. Tim honey,
thanks for always letting me steal your
best lines.

And to my beautiful sister-in-law,
Pam Tsakirgis Beaver. Your vitality,
joy, and spirit inspire us all.
Love you, honey!

This book is dedicated with love
and affection to my brother,
Timothy Michael Beaver. Thanks
for always letting me steal your
best lines!

And to my beautiful sister-in-law,
Kari [illegible] Beaver. Your vitality,
joy and spirit inspire us all!
Love you, honey!

CHAPTER 1

"You're having sex!" my best friend, Robin, cried as soon as I opened the door. "I mean, not currently, thank God, but recently. Oh, I'm so happy for you!"

"Say it a little louder, why don't you?" I yanked her into my apartment and quickly shut the door behind her. "I don't think they heard you up in Petaluma."

She dropped her bags on my worktable and pulled me into a hug. "Your closest neighbors are two lesbians. Do you really think they'll judge?"

"It's nobody's business," I grumbled. "I'm not even going to ask how you can tell."

"It's a gift." She patted my cheek. "Besides, just look at you. You're glowing."

"Don't be ridiculous," I said, feeling my cheeks warm up. So maybe she was right; maybe I was glowing. Did she have to point it out to the world?

Robin Tully had been my BFF for years,

ever since we were eight years old and our parents joined the same spiritual commune in the hills of Sonoma County. We first bonded over Barbie dolls, Johnny Depp, and a mutual disgust for dirt. Now all that dirt has transformed itself into the upscale town of Dharma, a wine country destination spot for Bay Area foodies. But back in the day, it was backwoods enough to make two fastidious little girls go berserk.

Robin grinned, amused by my reaction. Then she scooped up her bags from the table. "I brought wine and presents."

"I ordered pizza," I said, leading the way down the short hall to my living area.

"I'd kill for pizza."

"No need. I'll share." I pulled two wineglasses from the kitchen shelf and set them on the smooth wood surface of the bar that separated my kitchen from the living room. "I missed you a lot. How was India?"

"India was exotic and wonderful and smoggy, and I missed you, too." She pulled the bottle of wine from one of her bags and handed it to me to open. "And I missed showers. And ice cream. And hamburgers."

"The pizza's got sausage and pepperoni."

"Oh, God, meat." She closed her eyes and sighed. "It sounds like heaven."

"I have ice cream, too."

"I love you. Have I told you that lately?"

With a laugh, I poured the wine and handed her the glass. "Welcome home."

"Thanks." We clinked glasses and she took a good long drink. "You have no idea how happy I am to be back."

The doorbell rang and I ran to pay the pizza deliveryman. After piling pizza and salad onto plates and pouring more wine, we sat at my dining room table to eat.

Besides Robin's work as a sculptor, she owned a small travel company that specialized in tours of sacred and mystical destinations all over the world. In the beginning, she had catered mainly to fellow commune members, but her client base was growing. It seemed there were more and more people interested in stone circles, pyramids, Gothic cathedrals, and harmonic power centers. And who better to guide them than my friendly and gifted pal Robin? Her tours catered to the adventurous seeker of esoteric knowledge who had tons of cash to throw her way. She had just returned from leading a group of four couples on a three-week tour of India.

So for three long weeks I'd been gnashing my teeth, unable to share my exciting news — specifically, the news about me and my mysterious British boyfriend — with my closest friend. And Robin had guessed it the very first second she saw me. I supposed that's what the whole BFF thing was all about.

We opened another bottle of wine as she regaled me with the highlights of her India trip and I filled her in on all the news about me and Derek Stone, the hunky British security expert I'd met a few months back during a murder investigation. Yes, we'd done the deed, as she'd shouted to the world earlier. And yes, he was opening a San Francisco branch of Stone Security. And yes, our relationship was so new that I still tingled every time I thought of him, and yes, I'd boldly offered him a place to stay — with me — until he found a home in San Francisco. So yes, he was staying here, but no, he wasn't home at the moment. Right now, he was flying back from Kuala Lumpur, where he'd provided security for an installation of priceless artwork from the Louvre.

And yes, I'd been threatened by another vicious killer. Robin had been packing to leave for India at the time and wasn't around to hear the entire story, so I filled her in on all the gory details. The killer was safely tucked away in jail now. And that was my last three weeks in a nutshell.

As we cleared the dishes, I figured it was time to ask Robin the burning question I'd avoided long enough.

"So, did you see your mother?" I asked cautiously.

Robin scowled. "And we were having such a lovely evening."

"Sorry."

"Not your fault," she said with a sigh. "Yes, I saw her. I left my group in New Delhi and flew down to Varanasi to spend some time with her. And yes, she's just as annoying as ever."

That was no big surprise. She and her mother, Shiva Quinn, had always had issues.

Shiva's real name was Myra Tully and she was raised by missionaries. Suffice to say, Myra had a real savior complex from the get-go. In the 1970s, Myra had accompanied the Beatles to India to see Maharishi Mahesh Yogi. While there, she changed her name to Shiva Quinn. No one was sure where *Quinn* came from. As for *Shiva,* Robin always thought it was telling that her mother had named herself after the supreme god of Hinduism.

When Robin was really irritated with Shiva, she'd call her Myra.

It didn't help that her mother was tall,

glamorous, and model thin. She was also sophisticated and interesting and everyone loved to be around her. Her missionary upbringing gave her an awareness of the world and its problems, which led her to become the spokesperson for a humanitarian organization called Feed the World.

By the time Robin was ten years old, her mother was traveling constantly, returning home every few months for only a day or so. But that was okay with me, because when Shiva left the commune, Robin would stay at my house. We had a slumber party every night. I would've been happy if Shiva stayed away permanently, but I could never say that to Robin.

"How long did you visit with her?" I asked as I started the dishwasher.

"Three excruciating days." Robin laughed drily. "She's such a drama queen. She couldn't settle in London or Paris. No, she had to go live in Varanasi. I swear she thinks she's Mother Teresa in Prada. She shows up at the marketplace and women beg for her advice on everything from child care to fashion. Child care. Are you kidding me?"

"That's a little surprising."

"You think?" Robin shook her head. "But you know she loves it all. Never mind. I promised myself I wouldn't bitch about her, but it's always so tempting. Anyway, the city of Varanasi itself was awesome. I'll probably return with a tour group sometime. I saw the Monkey Temple and walked for hours along the Ghats overlooking the Ganges. It was amazing. I took lots of photos. I'll send you the link."

The Ghats were the flights of steps that ran for miles along the Ganges River. "It all sounds fascinating."

"It was. And I have a surprise for you from my mother."

"For me?"

"Yes." She held up one of the bags she'd brought with her. "Do you want to see it?"

"Of course I do."

"Let's go to your workroom."

My curiosity piqued, I picked up our wineglasses and followed her to the front room of my loft, where I did my bookbinding work. We pulled two tall chairs close together and sat at my worktable. Robin turned the shopping bag on its side and slid the contents out onto the surface. It was a worn leather satchel made in the style of a courier bag, with a long, wide shoulder strap, but it had to be decades old.

"It's . . . a bag," I said. "How thoughtful."

Robin chuckled. "Wait for it. You know my mother. We must build the suspense."

She unbuckled the satchel and pulled out something wrapped in a wadded old swathe of Indian print material.

"Um, is it a scarf?" I said, touching the pale, woven fabric. Once, it might've been dark green with burgundy and orange swirls of paisley, but it was faded now. Colorful beads, tiny brass animals, and chunks of mirrored glass were woven into the fabric and tied into the braided fringe at each end. "Is this really for me?"

"Hell, no." Robin wrinkled her nose at the matted material. "That's my mother's idea of wrapping paper, I guess."

"Ah."

"She told me I could keep it and wear it. She just doesn't get me. Never did." Resigned, she flicked one of the silvery beads.

"No, she never did." The threadbare fabric had an ethnic style that was intriguing, but I knew Robin wouldn't be caught dead in it. I stroked the worn leather of the satchel. "This bag is nice."

"I suppose it is, if you're a camel driver."

I laughed, then fingered the old scarf again. "Maybe Shiva's been in India a little too long."

"You think?" She shook her head as she gingerly unwrapped the cloth. "Okay, get ready." She pulled the last of the fabric away. "This is for you."

"Oh, my God," I whispered.

It was a book. The most exquisite jeweled book I'd ever seen. And possibly the oldest. It was large, about twelve inches tall by nine inches wide, and almost three inches thick. I suppressed the urge to whip out my metal ruler.

The heavily padded leather binding was decorated with intricate gilding and precious gems. Teardrop-shaped rubies were affixed to each corner. Small, round sapphires lined the circular center, where a gilded peacock spread its tail feathers. Tiny diamonds, emeralds, and rubies were encrusted in the feathers. The thickly gilded borders of the cover and turn-ins were reminiscent of the patterns used by royal French bookbinders of the eighteenth century. Some of the gold had flaked off and the red leather was rubbed and faded in spots.

"Peacocks are the national bird of India," Robin said. "Did you know that?"

"I had no idea." I picked up the book and studied the fore edge. With the book closed, the pages were deckled, or untrimmed, for a ragged effect. I could tell that the paper itself was thick vellum.

I checked the spine. It read, *Vatsyayana.* I

looked at Robin. "What is this?"

"Open it and find out."

"I'm almost afraid." But I lifted the front cover and turned to the title page. "You're kidding."

"Nope."

"The Kama Sutra?"

"Yes." Robin grinned.

"From your *mother?*"

Now she laughed. "It actually belongs to one of Mom's friends who's been wanting to have it refurbished for a long time. Mom insisted there was no one better for the job than you."

"That's so sweet."

"I thought so." Robin sipped her wine as she watched me ogle the book.

"Who's her friend?" I asked.

"His name is Rajiv Mizra and she's known him forever. Nice man. Wealthier than sin, naturally, or why would Mom hang out with him? I think he's been in love with her for ages, but she always says they're just good friends."

"Very interesting."

"Yeah, I wonder if maybe they'll get together eventually. Anyway, he wrote a letter of authorization and tucked it inside the book. That's to let you know he's consented to let you do whatever is necessary to make it sparkle and shine. So, you think you can clean it up?"

"I can take it apart?"

She laughed. "I guess, but you don't have to sound so excited about it."

"Are you serious? I live for that."

"Good times." She took another sip of wine.

"It is for me." I stroked the corded spine, counting the ribs.

"Once it's cleaned up, they'd also like you to have it appraised."

"Sure." Opening the cover, I studied the dentelles, the lacy patterns of gold that were worked into the leather borders. Some dentelles were so intricate and unique, they were as good as a bookbinder's signature. I couldn't wait to study this pattern more closely. "I wonder why your mom recommended me to do the work."

"Apparently, Abraham visited her a few years ago and talked you up."

"Really?" I smiled softly. "Isn't that nice?" Abraham had been my bookbinding teacher for years. He'd died a few months back and I still missed him every day. I turned another page with care, unwilling to disturb the binding too much. The book was more than one hundred years old, and I was amazed to see that it was written in French.

I turned to a page near the middle of the book and saw a hand-painted illustration of a couple having sex in a most fascinating style. I closed it quickly. Then I couldn't help but sneak another peek.

"Wow, it's painted by hand," I said after clearing my throat. "Isn't that interesting?"

"Yeah, it's all about the strokes." She snickered. "Paint strokes, I mean. Beautiful."

We both began to giggle. It must've been the wine.

Robin let out a deep breath. "Well, hey, speaking of sex . . ."

"Were we?"

She laughed. "Sort of." She waved her hands as if to get rid of that thought. "And I'm not talking about the sex you're having. It's about me. I met a man."

"Oh." That got my attention. "In India?"

"No. Here in San Francisco, just last night. I was on my way home from the airport and I was starving, so I stopped at Kasa to get some food to go. He came in right after me, so we were both waiting for our orders and struck up a conversation."

"You went to Kasa after coming back from India?"

She laughed again. Kasa was part of a small, local chain of good Indian restaurants. "I still had a taste for the food. But that's not important just now."

"You're right. So who is this guy?"

"He's . . ." She looked baffled. "He's . . . wonderful."

"Okay," I said slowly. "What's his name?"

"Alex." She smiled dreamily. "He's an engineer. Can you believe it? He was born in the Ukraine, but he's lived here forever. His full name is Alexei Mikhail Pavlenko. Isn't that cute? He's great. Really handsome and funny. And smart."

"You found out all that while waiting for to-go food?"

"We ended up grabbing a table and eating there together. It was his idea. He said he didn't want to be a ship passing in the night, never to see me again."

"That's sweet."

"He really was. I'm feeling very sappy about the whole experience." She even shook her head to wipe the sloppy smile off her face, but it was useless. "Anyway, we had a great conversation and found out we actually have a lot in common. He's wonderful; you'll see. We're going out tomorrow night."

I stared at her in surprise. "Oh, no, you're blushing. You never blush. You really like him."

"Give me a break." She rolled her eyes. "I blush sometimes. But yeah, I like him."

Disconcerted, I glanced down at the Kama Sutra and decided that further inspection could wait. I closed the book and looked up at Robin. "Okay, he sounds great, but I have to ask why you're seeing Mr. Wonderful when you're in love with my brother."

Her lips curved into a frown. "Austin hasn't made any moves in my direction lately."

I frowned, too. "Well, it's not like you live in the same neighborhood anymore. He's going to have to make an effort to come after you."

"Yes, he is," she said pensively. "Look, he traveled and partied for years and now he's ready to settle down back home in Dharma and run the winery. But I'm not ready to do that yet. Not that he's asked me to."

I sighed. "I don't want my brother to blow this."

"I don't want him to, either." Her chin jutted out stubbornly as she added, "But I'm not going to sit at home waiting for the phone to ring."

I wanted to kick my brother sometimes. Robin had been in love with Austin since grammar school, but he had always considered her too young for him. That had all changed a few years ago, when he finally settled down in Dharma and realized that Robin was perfect for him. That was right around the time she moved to San Francisco and was beginning to be recognized as a talented sculptor and artist.

But instead of pressing Robin to move her work to Dharma and live with him, Austin had decided to back off and give her space to have fun and enjoy her life as he had been doing all those years before he moved back home. Now, every time she suggested that she might come back to Dharma, he brushed her off, telling her she should experience the world and live every moment to the fullest.

With all the mixed signals, Robin had decided to let Austin make the next move. But if he didn't move soon, he would lose her.

Timing was everything, as they say.

She looked like she could use a hug, so I jumped off the chair and wrapped my arms around her. "You know I love you, no matter what happens. So I hope you have a good time with Mr. Wonderful."

"Yoo-hoo!"

We both jolted in surprise. I turned and saw my neighbors, Jeremy and Sergio, poking their heads through my open door. I guessed I hadn't locked it earlier.

"Hi, guys," I said. "Come on in. You remember Robin, right?"

"Of course," Jeremy said, waving both of his hands at us as he walked in.

Sergio gave me a hug, then said, "Hi, Robin." Then he handed me a small white paper bag. "I brought you some cookies from the restaurant."

My eyes widened as I opened the bag. "You brought cookies? Did you make them yourself?"

"Of course," he said modestly. Sergio was a world-class chef whose pastries and desserts were the stuff of dreams.

"Thank you," I whispered, overcome by the sight of the half dozen tiny, chocolate-laden, delicate puff-pastry circles all bundled up in plastic wrap. In a separate packet were fragile pastel-colored macaroons. I opened it up and handed one to Robin, who reverently placed it on the tip of her tongue and closed her eyes.

"We're sorry to bug you," Jeremy said, pacing around my workroom, staring at the shelves, "but I'm preparing for my performance-art debut at the Castro Street Fair in a couple weeks and I'm on the hunt for accessories. Do you have a boa or any girlie hats or big jewelry?"

"Big jewelry isn't really my style," I said, "but I probably have a hat you could use."

"I have lots of pretty things at home," Robin said, wiping a tiny cookie crumb from her lips.

"Your stuff is probably too nice for what he wants," Sergio said, then whispered, "He's presenting an homage to the homeless."

"Yeah, the tackier, the better," Jeremy said with a grin. "Ooh, what's this?" He grabbed the funky Indian scarf and wrapped it around his neck. "Is it me?"

"It's totally you," Robin said.

"I love it," he said, holding the material out and studying it. "It's so scruffy."

Sergio nodded in approval. "Very ethnic, with a touch of grunge."

"It's yours if you want it," she said.

"And I have other stuff you can look at," I added.

"No, this is perfect. Shabby but colorful." Jeremy scurried over to the small mirror hanging near the front door and tossed the length of the scarf back and forth and over his head. "I love the sparkly beads."

"Take it," Robin insisted. "Consider it an even trade for the cookies. Besides, I'll never wear it. My mother is insane to think I would."

"Thank you," Jeremy cried, and clapped his hands. "I want you both to be there. It's two weeks from tomorrow. Write it in your calendar."

"I love the Castro Street Fair," Robin said. "I go every year."

I got up and found a pencil, then wrote the event in my office calendar. In one of the cabinet drawers I found a clean white cotton cloth, and as I wrapped the Kama Sutra up to protect it, I asked, "Would you guys like a glass of wine?"

The men exchanged a look; then Jeremy waved his hand with indifference. "Only if you insist."

"I'll get the wine," Robin said, laughing. "You show them your sexy new book."

"You have a sexy book?" Sergio said, moving closer to the worktable. He was fascinated with my bookbinding work. I unwrapped the cloth and pushed the book his way.

"Is this it?" He touched the spine of the Kama Sutra.

"Yes, and wait till you see it," I said, excited all over again. I opened the book and turned to the page Robin and I had been peeking at earlier.

Jeremy began to squeal and slapped my arm. "You naughty girl."

"This is fantastic," Sergio said in awe, as he carefully ran a finger over the outer edges of the page.

"I know. I can't wait to take it apart."

"Ooh, that does sound exciting. Maybe I should sign up for that bookbinding class you teach after all."

Later that night, I read the letter of authorization from Shiva's friend Rajiv Mizra. In the same envelope, he'd included the original sale document from the Mumbai bookseller who sold him the Kama Sutra. The document indicated that the book, though undated, was thought to have been made in France between 1840 and 1880. That would be easy enough to verify once I'd examined the ink and paper and gilding style. Rajiv had paid 1,801,200 rupees back in 1997. I had no idea how much that was in U.S. dollars. I would calculate it in the morning, but I had no doubt the book would be worth much more in today's market.

In his friendly note, Rajiv gave me full authority to do whatever it took to increase the book's value. He also included his e-mail address in case I had any questions.

I smiled as I tucked the letter and documentation back into the envelope. The only question I had at this point was, How soon could I get my hands on that incredible book?

The following night, Derek returned from his Kuala Lumpur trip. Ever since he moved in, I'd been experimenting with cooking, so I made pasta with a creamy tomato vodka sauce, and we drank an Etude pinot noir I'd been saving for a special occasion. Our relationship was new enough that Derek's coming home after a short trip definitely qualified as a special occasion.

I guess he felt the same way, because he'd thought to bring me a gift from his travels. It was a stack of beautiful Asian fabric samples for me to use as book cloth in my bookbinding work. It was the loveliest and most thoughtful gift a bookbinder could dream of receiving.

After dinner, we snuggled on the couch. In my wildest imagination, I never would've used the word *snuggle* in regard to the ruggedly masculine Derek Stone. But there we were, snuggled. And I felt completely satisfied with life.

Naturally, I couldn't allow that blissful feeling to just exist. My mind rushed to scrutinize and worry over it. Call it human nature, but if I was this happy with a man, I had to wonder why. After all, I'd made mistakes with men before. I wasn't always the best judge of character. So now I forced myself to ponder some key questions: Was he the right man for me? Why were we together? How did it happen so fast? And there were follow-up questions: Where would we go wrong? How would I screw things up?

The fact was, I'd never dated an ex-spy from another country. Were there issues I should be aware of? Was he a bad risk? Had he done things in his past that would come back to haunt him and, therefore, me? He seemed remarkably well-adjusted, and his level of self-esteem was the healthiest I'd ever encountered. But had he done things in the past that would someday cause him to hate himself? Would he have flashbacks? Would they develop into full-blown post-traumatic stress disorder?

And speaking of his former lifestyle, what exactly had he done? I imagined he must've played many roles during his time in British intelligence, but he rarely spoke of them. He still worked in that world peripherally. Did his current job of providing security to his wealthy clients ever entail role-playing? Suppose a rich young widow required someone to play her lover in order to uncover a blackmailing scam. Would Derek play that role or would he send an associate? Did I have the right to ask? Should I trust him to be faithful? Was I being ridiculously naive?

Or was I just imagining monsters in the closets?

To be fair, he had every right to ask himself similar questions about me. I was raised in a commune. How weird was that? And let's not forget that we'd met under the most bizarre circumstances: over a dead body. Since then, I'd been involved in several murder investigations in which I'd played the role of number one suspect. My strange connection to murder had caused some of my colleagues to wonder if they should risk being in the same room with me.

Nevertheless, I had been relentless in my quest to find the true killer in each case. Derek had been right there beside me, and I was elated to know that we shared a passion for justice.

Still, I wouldn't blame him for harboring doubts about my own ability to sustain a healthy relationship. I figured there was no time like the present to discuss it.

"Derek, I was wondering if you've —"

He emitted a soft snore and I realized he was sound asleep. Jet lag had hit him hard.

"Okay, we'll talk later," I murmured, then roused him enough to drag him off to bed, where he continued to sleep like a dead man.

It was five o'clock in the morning when the pounding began.

"What the hell is that?" Derek muttered.

"I don't know," I said, sounding whiny as I punched my pillow. Were they cleaning the streets? Or digging holes through concrete? The pounding continued, so I finally tossed the covers back and sat up. Throwing on my flimsy robe, I stood on wobbly legs as the pounding grew louder. By standing, I had a better grasp of the direction the noise was coming from. It wasn't outside the building, I realized. Someone was pounding on my front door.

"I hope it's not the little kids who just moved in," I mumbled. "That won't make anyone happy."

That was when the screaming began.

Derek jumped out of bed and yanked on a pair of jeans. "Stay here."

Ignoring his command, I raced after him down the hall, through the living room, and out to the workshop. I skidded to a halt behind him as he threw the door open.

It was Robin, wrapped in a trench coat and screaming as tears rolled down her cheeks.

She was covered in blood.

Chapter 2

Derek reached out, grabbed Robin around the shoulders, and pulled her inside.

"Oh, my God," I cried, enfolding her in a hug. "What happened?"

"She's in shock," Derek surmised. Shoving the door closed, he led us both through the hall to the living room. Robin's shrieks had faded to muffled whimpers and sobs.

I hadn't noticed whether any of my neighbors were staring from their doorways, but was there any doubt that everyone in the building had heard the screams?

"Wait," I said, when we reached the living room couch. I ran and retrieved my big old yellow blanket from the linen closet and threw it over the couch.

"Can we take your coat off?" I asked.

She twitched, then shook her head and wrapped her arms around her waist in a protective gesture.

"Okay, coat stays on. Sit down, sweetie."

Derek helped Robin sit on the blanket, and we both tucked the soft fabric around her. I grabbed some socks for her to wear, because she wasn't wearing any shoes.

Why was she barefoot? I didn't ask. She was incapable of putting the socks on, so I knelt to slip them on her feet for her. But when I lifted her heel, I gasped. The bottom of her foot was caked in blood. Robin didn't notice my reaction. She was still shuddering and crying and seemed unable to speak.

I ignored my own dizziness as I stretched out the socks and managed to pull them onto her feet without touching the blood.

There were also dried streaks of blood on her hands and across her face and forehead. The trench coat was relatively free of blood, so I figured she must've thrown it on at the last minute to drive over to my place. Was she wearing anything underneath the coat? I was just too plain scared to ask any questions yet.

I sat down next to her and angled myself so I could stroke her arms to get some warmth back into her. She was so cold.

Derek sat on the coffee table directly in front of Robin and pulled the blanket tighter over her legs, then patted her knees to keep them from knocking together. Her teeth began to chatter and I thought she might be sliding deeper into shock.

"I'm guessing the blood isn't yours," he began.

She blinked and tried to swallow, then licked her lips.

"Let me get her some water," I said, pushing myself off the couch and running to the kitchen to fill a glass. I grabbed some tissues while I was there and returned to the living room.

I helped her take a few sips; then she closed her eyes.

"Honey, what happened?" I asked. "Can you tell us?"

"Blood," she managed, then sucked in a breath between hiccuping and shivering. "Blood."

"Whose blood is it?" I asked warily, glad that I'd thought to wrap her in the blanket. The fact was, I had an unfortunate tendency to pass out at the sight of blood. It's not my finest quality, and it was a testament to my love for Robin that I didn't shriek and drop like a tree when I first saw her.

Robin ignored my question and stared bleakly at Derek.

"Robin, love, we're going to have to call the police," he said gently.

"No," she whispered. She turned and appealed silently to me. She tried to reach for me, grab my arm, but she was wrapped like a mummy in the blanket. I watched her struggle for a moment before I thought to pull her hand free and grip it in mine. I refused to think about her bloodstained palms.

"It's okay," I said. "We won't call the police." I gave Derek a look that said, *Not now, but soon.*

He seemed to understand, and turned to Robin. "We won't call the police yet, but you must try to tell us what happened."

I helped her take another sip of water.

"Alex," she uttered finally.

I thought for a moment. "Mr. Wonderful? The man you met at the Indian restaurant?"

She nodded slightly. "I . . . We . . . um, we went to dinner. Then he came back . . . to my place. We had some wine . . . and . . . you know . . ." She paused and met my gaze.

"Yes, I know."

"Then . . . we went to sleep."

"He spent the night at your house."

She nodded, then signaled for more water. It was slow going, but she was beginning to come around. Her skin wasn't quite so pale and damp, and her eyes seemed clearer than before.

"I slept," she whispered. "I've never slept so well. It was . . . it was wonderful. So deep. Peaceful."

I looked at Derek. "She's always been a really light sleeper. If she wakes up in the middle of the night and can't get back to sleep, she'll get up and start working on her sculptures."

Even when she was young, Robin didn't sleep through the night. My mom used to think it was because she was worried about her own mother.

"I woke up," Robin continued slowly. "I needed to use the bathroom. I was so sleepy. Groggy, you know?"

She sought our acknowledgment after every other sentence, so at this, Derek nodded. "Yes, I know."

"I came back to bed. I was so sleepy, I almost tripped over a pillow on the floor. I picked it up. There were marks on it, like . . . like dirt streaks. It was weird. I could barely keep my eyes open, but you know how I get a little anal retentive about things."

"Yes, I know," I said, relieved that small pieces of her personality seemed to be returning.

"I didn't want to wake Alex by turning on the bedroom light, so I took the pillow into the bathroom to look at it."

She swallowed, started to sniffle; then one teardrop fell, followed by another as she continued. "It . . . it was blood. I thought maybe he'd cut himself. Then . . . then I happened to look in the mirror. I screamed. I had blood on my face. Clumped in my hair. On my hands."

She stopped to try to swallow again. For a second or two, I thought she might throw up. I felt close to it myself.

"I ran back to check on Alex and saw more streaks on the sheets. There was enough light coming in from the street that I could see dark streaks and . . . and blotches. Everywhere. I yelled his name to wake him up, then shook him. I flipped the light on and that's when I saw . . ."

"What did you see?" Derek asked with remarkable calm.

She covered her face with both hands. "I was so afraid. I hated to leave him, but I had to get out of there. I ran. I'm so ashamed."

"Tell me what you saw before you ran," Derek said evenly.

"Blood. Everywhere." She shuddered uncontrollably. "Alex. Dead. Blood trickling down his face, on the sheets. On the wall above the bed. On my hands, my stomach, my legs. I was covered in his blood."

"Did you see a weapon?" Derek asked

carefully. "Was he stabbed? Shot? Could you tell?"

Grimacing, she said, "No. No weapon. Just . . . b-bullet holes. In his . . ." She couldn't say the words, just covered her eyes again.

"Robin?"

She nodded, then managed to rub her forehead. "Here." Then she touched her chest. "Here." She closed her eyes and bowed her head and rocked slightly back and forth.

"Somebody shot him in the head and the chest?" I exchanged a quick, apprehensive glance with Derek. "While you were sleeping?"

"And I never woke up," she whispered on a sob. "I was curled up next to him, holding him, but I never woke up."

"It's okay," I said, and wrapped my arm around her shoulders.

We sat like that for a long moment, rocking slowly. I watched Derek, whose eyes were narrowed in thought.

Finally Robin eased away and looked at me, then Derek. "Who would do that? Why? In my house? How did they . . . ? Oh, God. They were in my house." Her face contorted into a mask of disgust and pain and dread. Her entire body shivered as more silent tears fell.

"I'm sorry, sweetie." I squeezed her hand, wishing for things I had no control over. "We really need to call the police now."

"Yes," Derek said, standing. "We've already let too much time pass." He was clearly anxious to get the police involved. He couldn't help himself, having been on the proper side of law enforcement his entire life. "We'll put clothes on, get Robin bundled up and in the car; then I'll call Inspector Lee on the drive over."

Robin grabbed my hand. "They'll think I did it. But I didn't do it. You believe me, don't you?"

"Of course you didn't do it," I said indignantly. "You're the victim here." And there was Alex, I amended silently. I met Derek's gaze again to telepathically convey the message that I expected him to make sure the police didn't do something stupid, like arrest Robin.

His mouth twisted into his version of a determined grin as he telepathically assured me back that he would do his best. His best was pretty darn good, so I was satisfied with that.

Robin's gaze darted around my living room; then she stared at her hands in dismay. "Can I take a shower first?"

"No, honey," I said gently. "You might destroy evidence, and the more evidence we destroy, the worse it'll look to the police."

Derek's expression of surprise almost made me laugh. Believe me, it was a shock to hear myself say that, too, because, you know, been there, done that, tried to wash off the evidence. But I guess I'd learned a little something from being involved in so many murders over the past six months. I wouldn't say I was starting to think like a cop, but at least I was no longer doing the kinds of stupid things that invariably led to my name being put at the top of the suspect list.

"There's one thing we can do," Derek said, looking at me. "If you have a clean cloth to spare, I'll wipe the blood off Robin's hands and give the cloth to the police."

"Thank you," Robin whispered.

"Perfect," I said, flashing a grateful smile at Derek.

He took care of washing off her hands, then left the room to change into street clothes. I took his place on the coffee table and leaned forward to grab hold of Robin's arms. "I want you to know you won't go through this alone. Things will get better eventually, but it's going to be slow and awful for a while."

"I know you'll be there for me," she said softly, her voice tinged with sadness. "That's why I came here."

"Oh, come on," I teased. "You came here because you knew Derek would be here."

"Well, that, too. I'm really glad he's here."

"Me, too."

Her smile faded. "You know what's awful?"

"What's that?"

"I was too flipped out to put on shoes. My feet are filthy. I hate that."

"I'm sorry. As soon as we talk to the police you can shower everything away."

She giggled. I wasn't sure why. It was a sweet sound — or it would've been, if not for the fact that Robin rarely giggled like that for no reason. Was this just another way of dealing with the stress and shock? Or was she coming unglued?

I couldn't say it to her face, but I was going to need her to snap out of this soon. I couldn't take it when she wasn't strong and firing on all cylinders. It was as if the balance of power in the universe was askew, and I didn't like that one bit. And when had this become all about me and my wants and needs?

Robin rested her head against the couch, and I felt my eyes mist up as I contemplated the hell she'd be going through over the next few days.

Derek slowed the elegant black Bentley, then pulled into an available parking space two doors down from Robin's flat on Elizabeth Street. The police had not arrived yet.

I got out of the car and stared up at Robin's building, wondering what the police would see when they got inside. Everything looked deceptively calm and quiet from here, but I knew that wouldn't be the case for long.

The Noe Valley duplex was designed in the classic San Francisco style, with a small two-door garage on the street and a set of stairs on the side that led up to a wide outdoor landing with two doors. One door opened into Robin's flat on the second floor, and the other door opened to another set of stairs that led up to her neighbors' apartment on the third floor.

Robin's friends Gilbert and Sharon lived upstairs. They all had access to a tiny rooftop patio, where they'd thrown a number of legendary parties. The view looking out toward Twin Peaks was a great perk.

Robin liked to claim that Noe Valley, with its upscale urban professional population, had more baby strollers than humans. It was a scary statistic, if true. But I think she had a tendency to exaggerate the facts after being clipped in the ankle one too many times while out walking.

Derek held Robin's arm as we walked to the stairs.

"Do I have to go inside?" she asked.

"No, you wait here," he said, "but I'd like to take a quick look before the police arrive."

Robin handed him the key and he jogged up the stairs, then disappeared inside. Robin and I clutched each other's hands as we sat down on the bottom steps.

It was barely seven o'clock in the morning, still cold enough for our breath to be frosty. I'd thrown on jeans, boots, a sweater, and a down vest, but I felt the chill. I'd loaned Robin a pair of ill-fitting sneakers, some sweatpants and a shirt, along with a wool scarf and another jacket, but she was still shaking. A jogger raced by; then a dog walker strolled down the walk. Both checked us out as they passed.

"Let's get off the sidewalk, okay?" I said.

"Yeah, good idea." She grabbed my arm and we walked up to the landing outside her door. It was spacious and filled with plant stands, two directors' chairs, and a small table along the side rail. I steered

Robin over to one of the chairs and helped her sit. I knew she often sat out here with her neighbors, drinking wine and watching the world go by. There wouldn't be much of that going on today.

"Sorry for being such a wimp," she said.

"You're kidding, right?" I took the other chair and scooted closer to her. "Give yourself a break. You've been through hell — plus you're covered in . . . you know. You're nowhere near being a wimp. Don't forget who you're with. I'm the queen of the fainting couch, remember?"

"Oh, God, I forgot all about your thing with blood." She started to reach for my hand in sympathy, then shrank back. "I've been touching you. You must be totally flipped out."

"I'm not." To be honest, I hadn't thought about it in a while, but now I shuddered at the memory of touching her bloody hands and feet.

She shook her head in self-disgust as she stared at her own hands, mostly clean now. "It's so awful to think . . ."

"Stop thinking about it."

She sighed. "You're a total hero to put up with all this."

"You'd do the same for me," I said, and resolutely grabbed hold of her hand again.

"Maybe. But I'm glad I don't have to prove that right now." She leaned her shoulder against mine. "And can I say again how glad I am that Derek's here with us?"

"Yes, you can. I'm glad, too. He knows what he's doing, and his connections should get us some answers a lot faster than if it were just you or me."

She stared at her front door. "I don't know how he can go in there, though."

"He wants to check everything out before the police show up. Once they get here, he might not have the chance."

"Better him than me," she murmured.

"Or me," I said. "I love you a lot, but there's no way I would go inside your place right now."

"There's no way I would let you." She shivered again and I put my arm around her. I knew it was crazy, but I was actually dying to know what Derek was doing inside her place. Robin had described a horrific scene. I wondered if it would help if I could see it and be able to relate to what she'd been through last night.

Who was I kidding? There was no way I could walk in there and not pass out within ten seconds. And wouldn't that be fun for everyone? No, I just wasn't a good enough friend. But I could live with that.

Less than a minute later, two police cars arrived. One of them stopped while the other made a U-turn to grab a parking place. I jumped up and pounded on Robin's door to alert Derek. I knew he wouldn't want to be caught at the crime scene. When he didn't respond, I opened the door ever so slightly.

"Derek?"

He didn't answer, so I pushed the door open a little more and stuck my head inside. I wasn't about to step beyond the doorway. "Derek?" I called out louder.

"Right there, love," he said from the bedroom.

I could see Derek from where I stood. He was standing by the overstuffed chintz chair in Robin's bedroom, where it looked like the man had thrown his clothes. Derek held the man's jacket as he checked the pockets.

"The police are here," I said with more urgency.

"Good," he muttered. "Be right with you." He threw the jacket down on the arm of the chair and walked quickly but cautiously to the front door.

But now that he'd moved, I could see what he'd been blocking before. It was the view of Robin's bed. And the dead man lying there. And the blood. And his eyes, open, staring at nothing. And the small, dark bullet hole in the middle of his forehead.

Derek caught me as I slid to the floor.

Chapter 3

Swearing ripely, Derek dragged me out the door and pushed me back into the chair next to Robin. Then he shoved my head between my knees to keep me from passing out altogether. I knew he did it lovingly.

"Oh, no," Robin cried as she grabbed hold of my hand. "What did you see in there?"

"Nothing, nothing," I said when I could breathe again, then waved away her concern over my idiocy. "I'm okay."

"Why in God's name did you go inside?" Derek demanded as he paced back and forth in front of my chair.

I sucked in one big gulp of air and sat up. "I didn't go inside," I insisted weakly. "I had no intention of doing so. I *looked* inside. Big difference. I was just trying to get your attention."

"Well, you got it," he said, scowling.

"I'm sorry," I said, humiliated by my weakness. "I was just worried the police would find you and arrest you or something."

He gritted his teeth, then drew a heavy breath. "Thank you, love. That was very thoughtful. Unnecessary, but thoughtful."

"I know. Sorry."

He nodded and smoothed my hair back from my forehead. His jaw was clenched but he said nothing more. He didn't have to. We'd both seen something awful inside Robin's apartment.

SFPD Detective Inspector Janice Lee stopped at the bottom of the stairs, looked up, and shook her head. "Wainwright, we've simply got to stop meeting like this."

"You're telling me," I said as I stood up to greet her. Janice Lee had been assigned to the first murder investigation I'd been involved in, when my old bookbinding mentor, Abraham Karastovsky, was killed. Then just last month, she'd investigated Layla Fontaine's murder at the Bay Area Book Arts Center. I'd been working at BABA at the time of the killing and was able to give Lee some help with the suspects. So we were like old friends, only not so much.

"How are you, Inspector?" I asked, shaking her hand.

"Can't complain. Nobody listens," she said with a shrug. Her voice wasn't as husky as usual, and I took that as a good sign that she'd managed to break her smoking habit. She'd gained a few more pounds, and with her exotic Asian-American features and long, shiny black hair, she looked prettier than ever. I could learn to hate her if I didn't respect her so much.

"Hello, Inspector Lee," Derek said cordially.

"Always a pleasure, Commander Stone," she said, her tone a bit lighter. I suppose she had a soft spot for Derek — along with every other woman on the planet.

Four uniformed officers climbed the stairs in Inspector Lee's wake. With eight people standing around, the normally spacious landing was starting to feel claustrophobic.

Derek passed Robin's house key to Inspector Lee, then asked, "Will Inspector Jaglom be joining you?"

"Yeah, he should be here any minute. Why?"

Derek smiled. "Just curious. You two work well together."

"Yes, we do," she said, casting a wary glance his way. "Once we've seen what's going on inside the apartment, I'll have my uniforms canvass the neighborhood and watch things here until the ME and the lab folks arrive."

He nodded. "Sounds good."

"Yeah, thanks," she said with just a touch of sarcasm. "What's going on, Commander? Have you already been inside the premises?"

"Yes," he said succinctly.

"Care to share your thoughts?"

"Of course." He lowered his voice. "Body's in the master bedroom. Blood has been tracked throughout, especially in the bedroom and attached bath. It's a bloody mess, you'll pardon the expression. Walls, sheets, hardwood floors. Victim was shot once in the head, once in the chest. Death appears to have been instantaneous. Ms. Tully was asleep in bed with the victim when he was shot."

"Good to know," she said, sliding a curious glance at Robin, who noticed her looking and shrank back into her chair.

Inspector Lee turned back to Derek. "Thanks for the info."

I figured a rundown like that from a civilian would normally grate on her, but coming from Derek, Lee took it well. She was no fool, and Derek was no run-of-the-mill witness. As a former Royal Navy commander who'd gone on to work for Britain's MI6 before starting his own private security company, he knew what he was doing, to say the least.

But with his brief recap of the crime scene, I could feel my eyes goggling as my brain painted some really gross mental images. There went my stomach again.

Derek noticed and swore under his breath.

Lee turned and looked at me with interest. "How you holding up, Wainwright?"

"Not well, thanks." Seriously, with as many times as I'd landed in the middle of a murder scene, you'd think I'd be getting better at handling the sight of blood.

"Did you go inside the apartment with Commander Stone?"

"Not exactly." I stood on unsteady legs, grabbed hold of the landing rail, and took deep breaths. It was getting bad when even the mere thought of blood made my stomach clench.

"Then what, exactly?" Inspector Lee asked, tapping the toe of her shoe against the wood floor.

I turned. "I just poked my head inside for a second or two."

"Yeah, sometimes that's all it takes," she said philosophically. "Guess you got an eyeful."

"Guess I did."

With an evil chuckle, Inspector Lee turned from me to Derek. "Since you've been inside, we'll need a print of your shoes for comparison. Probably be a good idea if you took them off right now."

"Certainly," he said.

She caught the eye of one of the cops and jerked her chin up. That was all it took for the officer to hurry downstairs to the squad car. He was back in less than a minute with an evidence envelope large enough to carry Derek's shoes.

Finally, Lee turned to Robin. I was pleased to hear her use a gentler tone than she had with me or Derek as she said, "It's Robin, right? We've met a few times."

"Yes, hi." Robin stood unsteadily and shook her hand. She tried to smile but it was a shaky effort. "I'm glad you're here."

"This your place?"

"Yes."

"Okay, good. So what's going to happen is, as soon as my partner arrives, he and I will go inside to look around. In the meantime, I'd like to get some preliminary information from you. I understand you've been through a bad time, so we'll take it slow."

"Thanks."

"Now, I assume that since the commander and your good friend Ms. Wainwright are here, you called them first and they came over to keep you company."

"No, I . . ." She glanced at Derek and me, and I noticed she looked as though she might fall over any second now. Lee seemed to notice the same thing.

"Let's sit," the inspector said as she maneuvered Robin down onto the director's chair.

I watched Robin more carefully. I'd never seen my friend so wiped out before. It wasn't just shock or grief. Her eyes were unfocused and she seemed unstable whenever she was standing. I was beginning to wonder if maybe she'd taken a sleeping pill or something. Was that why she'd slept through Alex's death? But as Inspector Lee questioned her, she seemed to rally and was able to repeat the same story that she'd told us earlier, going into even greater detail than before.

As Robin finished, her upstairs neighbor Sharon, still wearing pajamas and a plaid bathrobe, opened her front door. She glanced around, her forehead lined with concern, until she spied Robin. "What's going on out here?"

"Oh, Sharon, I'm sorry we disturbed you," Robin said. "There's been a . . . an accident in my apartment. The police are here to look into it."

"An accident?" Sharon said, taking a step

out onto the porch. "Are you all right?"

Robin waved her back as if she didn't want her neighbor to get too close. "I'm okay."

"Good morning, ma'am," Inspector Lee said, standing up and pulling a business card from her pocket. "You live upstairs?"

"Yes."

She handed Sharon the card. "We'll need to ask you some questions in a little while. Will you be home all day today?"

"Yes, I'm off on Sundays." She stared down at the card, then back at Lee. "You're a homicide detective?"

"Yes," Lee said. Before she could say anything else, she spied Inspector Jaglom strolling down the sidewalk.

"Nate," Lee called, and waved. "Up here."

He glanced up, saw me and Derek, and his eyebrows rose in mild disbelief. "What's all this?"

I was grateful Inspector Lee didn't shout something pithy like, *If it's Wainwright, it's murder!* Just because that little declaration was becoming uncomfortably true didn't mean I wanted to hear the police stating it as fact. I wouldn't be surprised to see them printing it up on bumper stickers one of these days.

As Jaglom walked toward Robin's building, Lee turned to finish her conversation with Sharon. "As soon as one of my officers is free, he'll come by and get some preliminary information from you."

"Of course. I need to take a quick shower first. Then I'll be available."

"Appreciate it."

Unsure what else to say or do, Sharon gave Robin another anxious look, then went back inside and closed the door.

"Commander, Brooklyn," Inspector Jaglom said in greeting when he reached the top of the stairs. "This is quite a surprise."

Was it a good thing or a bad thing that I was on a first-name basis with a homicide inspector?

"Good to see you, Inspector," Derek said, shaking hands with Jaglom.

After introducing her partner to Robin, Inspector Lee said, "Ms. Tully, I'd appreciate it if you would remain on the premises for a while."

"Sure."

As Jaglom and Derek spoke with each other in hushed tones, Lee pulled two pairs of disposable rubber gloves from her bag. She handed one pair to her partner, cutting short the niceties. "Let's do this, Nate. Watch where you're stepping."

"Lead on," Jaglom said, and the two disappeared inside Robin's flat.

Within forty-five minutes, the medical examiner and a number of crime lab people were crawling all over the property. Robin's neighbor Sharon invited us to hang out at her place while the police combed through every inch of Robin's home.

After one of the criminologists swabbed Robin's bloodstained skin and hair, she was allowed to take a shower in Sharon's bathroom. Nervous to be alone, Robin begged me to sit in the bathroom with her while she showered. We both relaxed a bit once she'd washed all the dried blood away.

Derek spoke to the police a while longer, then left to go back to my place to shower and dress for work. It was Sunday, but since he'd been gone all week, he'd arranged several meetings that couldn't be canceled. Once he was gone, I dozed on Sharon's couch.

At some point, Inspector Lee took Robin into Sharon's kitchen to ask her a bunch of questions. After an hour or so, Lee went back downstairs and Robin curled up on Sharon's recliner. She slept soundly, but not calmly as she tossed and turned and moaned every so often. Poor Sharon didn't know what to do to help, and truthfully I didn't either. We commiserated in her kitchen as she made a pot of soup. She said she always made soup when she was worried.

We'd been there for over three hours and I had thumbed through most of the magazines on the coffee table when Inspector Lee walked into Sharon's apartment again. Robin was still stretched out in the chair, but I stood and watched the cop as she folded her arms tightly across her chest and flexed her neck muscles. I could tell something was up.

"I have to ask you to come downtown with me for further questioning, Ms. Tully."

Robin blinked, then looked at me in confusion. "What does that mean?"

"Wait." I jumped up from the couch. "No. What for? She's innocent. You can't arrest her."

Inspector Lee thrust her hand out in a gesture of understanding. "I'm not arresting her, Ms. Wainwright, only taking her in for further questioning."

"That's just one small step toward county," I said, angry now. "This is unacceptable."

"Calm down, Ms. Wainwright," she said in a patient tone she probably used with lunatics.

"I won't calm down. This is Robin we're talking about. She's a victim here."

"Ms. Wainwright, please."

I hated that she was calling me *Ms.* Wainwright, all formal and patronizing. It was not a good sign, and it didn't bode well for Robin's future. I was feeling all kinds of betrayal, because Inspector Lee should've been on our side. She and I were practically friends, we saw each other so often.

Okay, maybe not friends exactly. More like crime scene buddies. Why did she need to question Robin any further? Why wasn't she out trying to find the murderer who'd killed Alex and ruined Robin's life?

Meanwhile, Robin could barely move the recliner up to a sitting position.

"Look at her," I said indignantly, pointing at Robin. "She can barely sit up. Oh, crap." That was when it finally hit me with both barrels. I'd wondered earlier if maybe she'd taken a sleeping pill. It had been bothering me off and on for hours, but I kept getting distracted.

"Robin, did you take a sleeping pill last night?"

"Huh?" she said, taken aback. "No, I never use them. You know that. I hate the hangover. I'd rather just get up and work when I can't sleep."

"Why do you seem so groggy?"

She swiped her forehead and scratched her head. "I don't know. I just can't seem to snap out of it."

I'd thought it was the trauma she'd been through, but that couldn't be the only reason Robin had been so out of it all day. I whipped around to Inspector Lee. "Have you considered giving her a blood test? I wouldn't be surprised if that guy drugged her last night."

"If he drugged her, she wouldn't remember having sex," Lee pointed out. "That's the point of Rohypnol, after all."

"I know, I know," I said, pacing the floor between Robin's chair and Inspector Lee. "But maybe he drugged her *after* they had sex. And maybe it wasn't Rohypnol. Maybe it was just some kind of strong sleeping pill." I turned to Robin. "Did you have anything to eat or drink after . . . you know."

"*Sex*, Wainwright," Lee said. "They had *sex*. Jeez, don't get all puritanical on me now."

I shot her a dirty look, then went back to Robin. "After *sex*, did you have anything to eat or drink?"

Robin had been watching Inspector Lee and me go back and forth like a tennis match. Now she had to think for a moment.

"Yeah, we shared the rest of a bottle of wine."

"Oh." My shoulders sagged in disappointment. "You shared it?"

"Yeah." Her forehead creased in concentration. "He went into the kitchen and poured two glasses and brought them back to bed."

"Aha." I turned to Lee in triumph. "Some of these drugs stay in the system for only twenty-four hours, right? I want a blood test taken right now."

"What are you, a lawyer?" Lee asked, her eyes narrowing dangerously. "You don't make demands of me."

I usually enjoyed trading barbs and quips with Inspector Lee, but this wasn't funny. This was Robin's life we were talking about.

"No, I'm not a lawyer," I said as my irritation escalated. "But I can get one over here faster than you can shout *benzodiazepine.* Just say the word."

She folded her arms across her chest and tried to stare me down. I stared right back.

"Fine, Wainwright," she said finally. "We'll run a damn blood test."

"Thank you," I snapped.

"I was going to do it anyway." She found her cell phone.

"Then why didn't you say so?"

She gave me a sideways glance. "And miss the fun of watching you go all F. Lee Bailey on my ass? No way."

I tried to channel my mother by concentrating on keeping my breaths even, my thoughts positive, my dosha aligned. But I was still riled. "I was beginning to think you were playing good cop, bad cop. Without the good cop."

"I'll take that as a compliment."

I snorted politely. "You would."

She chuckled. "I really like you, Wainwright."

"Jeez," Robin muttered. "I'd hate to see you with someone you don't like."

CHAPTER 4

It was past eleven a.m. when the assistant medical examiner ran up to Sharon's to draw Robin's blood for analysis in the lab. He also recommended a urine test and handed her a small plastic cup.

Robin made a face. "You're kidding."

"No," he said. "Date-rape drugs can be detected in urine and hair follicles a lot longer than in the blood."

"Good to know," I said.

Normally, the medical examiner wouldn't run a test like this, but he'd agreed as a favor for Inspector Lee. It made it a lot easier for Robin, but she was still a little grossed out as she took the plastic cup from him in front of all of us.

As far as I was concerned, she could be as disgusted as she wanted to be, but I was reassured. If they could find drugs in her system, I knew it would exonerate her completely.

As she disappeared into the bathroom, Derek walked in the front door. My heart stuttered as I watched him stride toward me, looking ridiculously gorgeous in a navy pinstripe suit, crisp white shirt, and the most beautiful burgundy tie I'd ever seen. The tie alone probably cost more than my entire wardrobe. I glanced down at my turtleneck sweater, jeans, and scruffy boots, then back at him. It was sad to realize that he was a far better dresser than I was, but he didn't seem to notice or care.

In fact, he seemed just as pleased to see me as I was to see him. So I guessed I didn't have anything to worry about, wardrobe-wise. Not yet, anyway. The relationship was still young. Besides, I was capable of cleaning up quite nicely when the occasion called for it. This one just happened to call for jeans and old boots.

"You're back already?" I asked, my voice betraying my happiness.

"I was able to cancel my afternoon meeting," he said, wrapping his arm around my waist. "I couldn't concentrate on work, knowing you were here having all the fun."

I frowned at him. "Fun?"

"No," he said soberly. "This has definitely not been fun for you. But except for Robin's involvement, you can't pretend you're not in your element."

I pressed my forehead against his chest. "What does it say about me that a crime scene has become my element?"

He lifted my chin up with his fingers. "It says you're endlessly fascinating."

I gazed up at him and knew I could lose myself in his dark blue eyes. "That's very sweet."

"Oy, take it somewhere else, you two," Inspector Lee groused as she strolled back into Sharon's apartment. "You're gonna make me sorry I changed my mind about moving this all downtown."

"We don't want that," I said, pushing away from Derek. Usually I was no fan of public displays of affection, but lately I couldn't seem to help myself.

"Where's my girl?" Lee said, glancing around the apartment. "I've got some more questions."

I assumed she was looking for Robin. "She'll be right out."

At that moment, the bathroom door opened and Robin emerged, looking sheepish, hiding the plastic cup inside her jacket. She went into Sharon's kitchen and came out a moment later carrying a small brown bag that she handed to the assistant ME.

"Hey, Schultz, call me with the results

ASAP," Inspector Lee said.

The man waved without turning. "You got it." Then he disappeared out the front door.

"All right." Lee motioned for Robin, saying, "Let's do this." She escorted Robin halfway down the hall before turning back to me and Derek. "We'll probably be another half hour."

Then she led Robin into Sharon's small office and closed the door, leaving Derek and me with nothing to do but wait. And worry. Which I was really good at. At the moment, my mind was racing back and forth among every possible bad situation Robin might face.

"Why don't we go for a walk?" Derek suggested, interrupting my anxious thoughts. "I'll buy you something to eat."

"I could eat," I allowed, and he grinned. Derek was well aware of my capacity to eat anytime, night or day. I loved food. All kinds of food. I wasn't picky. You'd think I was starved as a child.

I grabbed my jacket, then tracked down Sharon in her bedroom and told her we'd be back in twenty minutes if anyone was interested.

Outside, the weather was sunny, cold, and breezy, but I didn't mind the chill after being cooped up inside Sharon's apartment for half the day.

Deciding on coffee and maybe a muffin, we headed over to a bakery I knew of on Twenty-fourth Street, a few blocks away. In deference to Robin, we decided to hold off eating lunch. But coffee and pastry didn't count as real food.

We held hands as we walked, and Derek talked about the morning he'd spent at his new offices. He'd recently opened a branch of Stone Security in San Francisco, which meant that from now on, he would be commuting between here and London, as well as flying all over the world wherever and whenever his services were required.

In his London, Berlin, and Rome offices, there was a combined staff of almost nine hundred, and forty of them had made the initial move with Derek to San Francisco. They were still bringing in furniture, arranging for services and vendors, and setting up all the myriad processes and functions and staffing it took to run a successful company in a strange new land.

I'd never asked and he'd never mentioned whether he'd relocated here to be closer to his clients in the Pacific Rim countries or to me. Maybe it would be presumptuous to ask, but I was hoping it was all about me. After all, he seemed happy to be living in my home with me. But I guessed it was also a smart business decision to have an office on the West Coast, since he had clients on both sides of the Pacific Ocean. I'd decided not to ask him. Not yet, anyway, because he would've told me the truth. I wasn't sure I was ready to hear it.

Sometimes I couldn't believe we had actually become so involved with each other. Derek resembled something out of a James Bond film, and by that I mean he truly resembled *James Bond.* Any Bond. Take your pick. Derek, of course, was better-looking, tougher, and classier than any of them. He was also loyal, bold, straightforward, and very, very hot. The first time I'd ever seen him, I was reminded of a sleek panther stalking its prey. At the time, I'd had the uneasy feeling that the prey just might be me.

Did I mention that he carried a gun? He did. He also made me laugh. I guessed I kept him laughing, too. I just had to trust he was laughing *with* me. He made me feel feminine and petite — not that I was Quasimodo or anything, but at five-foot-nine, I wasn't exactly elfin. Lucky for me he was six feet, two inches of blue twisted steel. Okay, the blue twisted steel was a bit of an exaggeration. But the part about being hot?

No exaggeration there.

And it sounds weird to say it, but he just plain *liked* me. And I liked him. A lot.

From his positive description of things in his new offices, it was clear that his partners and personnel were settling in nicely after more than a month of flux.

"You've been busy," I said, "but it sounds like your assistant may be the real hero."

"Corinne is invaluable," he said. "I would be lost without her. I wasn't even sure she would come with me, but she surprised me. Told me she and her husband decided they wanted an adventure."

"They sound like an interesting pair."

"They are. You'll meet them both next Saturday."

"I will?"

"I hope so. We're having a party to celebrate the official opening of the San Francisco offices. We wouldn't ordinarily schedule an office event on a Saturday night, but my partners are flying over from London, and a number of clients are coming in from out of town. We're inviting vendors, staff, friends, lovers." He raised one rakish eyebrow and flashed me a smile.

"Is that an invitation?" I asked.

"I'm not about to go without you."

"Sounds like fun," I said casually, while I

secretly felt all squishy and blissful because he'd invited me. Maybe I would slap myself later for being such a twit, but right now I smiled and reveled in the joy of it all. "I'd love to see your offices."

"Good. I'm looking forward to showing you around."

I knew I was wearing a big dopey smile, but I couldn't help it. Derek had revealed last month that he was moving here and I hadn't gotten over the thrill yet. I could still remember the moment he told me. I'd spent the entire day — well, at least those moments when I wasn't being threatened by a cold-blooded killer — preparing myself to say good-bye to him. Imagine my shock when he'd handed me his new business card showing a tony Nob Hill address as his new office location.

I'd been wearing this same silly grin ever since.

We turned on Twenty-fourth Street, the treelined heart of the Noe Valley community, and walked half a block down to the Noe Valley Bakery. As we entered, the intoxicating aroma of warm, sugary treats was the first thing that caught me. I stopped and stared in awe at the massive displays of fluffy cupcakes, airy croissants, and every type of gooey, yummy pastry known to man.

It wasn't easy, but I finally settled on a sensible blueberry muffin and a large coffee, while Derek ordered coffee and took a pass on the sweets. Since most of the morning crowd was gone, we were able to grab an empty table and sit for a few minutes.

After taking some sips of coffee and a bite of my muffin, I finally posed the question I'd been waiting all morning to ask. "Did you find anything important inside Robin's place?"

He eyed me for a moment, then said, "I assume you're referring to something other than the dead man."

"You can start with him if you want. What did he look like? What was in his pockets? Tell me everything."

He glanced at me askance. "You saw him."

"I know, but I've been working really hard to block out the vivid image, and now I'm no longer sure of what I saw. I just remember a bullet hole and a lot of blood." I shivered involuntarily.

"There was plenty of that. I'm afraid Robin managed to spread it throughout the house. Her bloody footsteps were everywhere."

I took a big gulp of coffee to soothe my suddenly dry throat. "Okay, we can step away from the subject of blood and dead bodies. I won't be happy if my appetite is so ruined that I can't eat this muffin, so let's keep it simple. Did he have a gun? Was there any information in his wallet? Please don't tell me he had photos of a wife and six children. Did you find any traces of whoever killed him? Did you see anything else that was weird?"

His smile was appraising. "Have you given any thought to going into law enforcement? You excel at interrogation."

"I've had some experience in that area, on the wrong end, unfortunately." I touched his arm. "I'm just curious, you know? And worried. Because it's Robin."

"I know, darling."

"I guess I just want to know whether you saw anything that would cause Inspector Lee to arrest her."

"Frankly, no." But a frown line marred his forehead. "I can't imagine they would think she ransacked her own apartment."

"Ransacked? What do you mean?"

"You didn't notice?"

"No. I must've been distracted by the body. You're telling me that someone searched her place?"

"It was a shambles, so if they were searching for something, they didn't do a neat job of it. Things were upturned and pulled off shelves, sofa cushions thrown every which way. Nothing truly damaged, just tossed about."

"Oh, hell, that stinks." Poor Robin, as if she didn't have enough to deal with.

"Yes, it does. However, what struck me as even more odd was that the victim had absolutely no identification on him. No papers, no passport, no driver's license, credit cards, cash. Nothing."

"No wallet?"

"No. I assume whoever killed him must've taken it."

"They must've," I said. "Nobody walks around without identification or money. Or a credit card. Hell, a Costco card. Something."

"True." Derek clutched his coffee cup. "But his pockets were cleaned out."

"Wow." I was stymied. "So the killer searched Robin's place and stole this guy's identification papers. I don't get it."

His eyes narrowed. "I don't either. And until Robin is strong enough to return to her home, there's no telling whether something was stolen or not."

"I doubt she'll want to go inside and find out anytime soon."

"No." He pondered the facts for a moment. "She was able to drive to your home, so she had her keys, at least."

"Right," I murmured. "And she had her purse. So I assume the guy didn't steal her wallet. Which kind of creeps me out even more. I mean, a burglary would make sense. But this." I rubbed my arms. "It's disturbing."

"Yes." He paused to take a sip of his coffee. "While looking through his clothing, I noticed his shirt label was in Russian."

"Russian? From a Russian shirt company? Printed in Russian letters?"

"Cyrillic lettering, to be precise."

"Right. Robin said he was from Ukraine. Do Ukrainians speak Russian?"

"It's a source of friction, but yes, Russian is spoken by many Ukrainians. The two countries were still united up until twenty some years ago." He finished off his coffee and tossed the cup in a nearby trash can. "Let's get back to the shirt, which I happen to know came from a well-known men's store in Russia."

"You know the store it came from?" I asked in amazement. But why was I surprised? The man had traveled all over the world. He'd worked with British intelligence, so he might've spent time in Russia. Or Ukraine. Or anywhere else, for that matter. He spoke, like, forty-three languages. Okay, seven or eight, but who was counting?

"Yes, I do," he said, sitting back in his chair. "Uomo Firenzi is a high-end men's store. There are several branches in Moscow and one in Saint Petersburg."

"Have you shopped there?"

"No. The clothes are of Italian design but they cater to . . . Russian tastes."

I smiled at the tone of distaste in his voice. "Not your style, I take it?"

"Beautiful craftsmanship, very expensive, but no, not my taste."

"Not Burberry enough for you?"

He pursed his lips to keep from smiling. "No. Not a bit of plaid or an elbow patch to be found anywhere."

"What a shame."

"Indeed," he said with a regal nod.

I sipped my coffee. "So he's Russian or Ukrainian. He's wealthy, with expensive taste in clothing."

"And exceptional taste in women," Derek added.

"Right, because he zoned right in on Robin. But he's got seriously questionable taste in friends."

"Or enemies."

"More likely." I chewed my last bite of muffin. "Which leaves us precisely nowhere.

Except wondering how or why in the world Robin got mixed up with this guy."

He patted my knee. "Let's go see how she's doing and perhaps find out more about this mysterious Ukrainian."

Before we left the bakery, I purchased four of their fluffy red velvet cupcakes, hoping they would cheer Robin up.

As we walked, my mind went back to wondering how Robin had dealt with the grizzly scene in her apartment earlier that morning. Had she realized her apartment was a mess? A shambles, as Derek said? And not just from blood and death. Someone had apparently torn her place apart.

She hadn't mentioned it earlier. Had she even noticed? Or had Alex's death eclipsed all else?

As we walked back on Noe Street and turned on Elizabeth, I asked Derek's opinion. "Do you think Robin simply didn't notice, or do you think someone came in later, after she was gone, to search for something?"

He gritted his teeth, indicating that he'd had those same questions. "My gut instinct tells me she simply didn't notice. She shut down, grabbed the essentials — her keys, purse, coat — and ran. That same instinct makes me think whoever killed Alex searched the place immediately afterward, before Robin awoke."

"Why do you think so?"

"The killer and the searcher are probably the same person. As long as Robin slept through the killing, why wouldn't they stay and search the place right then and there? Otherwise, they'd have to leave and take a chance on returning later, unobserved."

"True. And the thought of two different people breaking into her home in one night stretches the realm of probability pretty far."

"Yes, it does," he said, and took hold of my hand.

As we walked, I tried to imagine someone traipsing through Robin's apartment, throwing her things around, looking for God knew what. It was disturbing, to say the least, and I made a concerted effort to push it out of my mind. Instead, I focused my thoughts on those four sweet red velvet cupcakes inside the white box I was carrying. Ah, happy thoughts. Peace. Love. Food.

It was noon by the time we got back to Sharon's and found Robin slouched in the recliner again, looking exhausted. Inspectors Lee and Jaglom were sitting at Sharon's dining room table carrying on a quiet conversation. Sharon was in her kitchen, cutting something on her chopping-block table in the middle of the large, sunny room. She looked up and smiled, and I had the thought that despite her very real concern for Robin, she would be able to dine out on this story for a long time.

Inspector Jaglom focused his patient eyes on me. "We've told Ms. Tully that she's free to go for now, but she won't be able to go inside her place for a few days."

"She'll stay with me," I said.

He nodded, then caught Robin's gaze. "You won't leave town without contacting us first, will you, Ms. Tully?"

"I promise I won't."

Inspector Lee pushed away from the table and stood. "Commander Stone, can we have a word with you? It won't take long."

Derek handed me his keys and motioned for me to take Robin down to his car. "I'll only be a moment."

"Okay," I said, grabbing the key ring. Then I turned to the two detectives. "I guess I'll see you both later."

"No doubt," Lee said.

That's what I was afraid of.

While we waited for Derek in the Bentley, Robin rested in the backseat. An earlier request to pack up some of her clothes and essentials had been refused, so Robin would be stuck using my stuff for a day or so until we could get back into her apartment. I had extra toothbrushes and sundry items she could use, but beyond a sweatshirt and sweatpants, my clothes would be a problem for her. Robin was five feet, two inches tall with great curves, while I was seven inches taller and thinner by a size or two. I could see a shopping trip in our future.

"I bought you red velvet cupcakes," I said.

"You did?" she said meekly.

"Yeah, four of them." I held up the bakery box. "We can eat them all when we get home."

"That was really thoughtful."

"I know they're your favorite."

I heard her sniffle and turned around in time to see her dissolve into tears.

"They're not your favorite?" I asked.

She laughed through the waterworks. "Yes, they're my favorite. But I can't even think about eating. I'm just so sad, and worried, and I don't know what's going to happen next. But I'm so glad you're with me. I'm just so . . . thankful that you're hanging with me."

"Hey, you're my best bud," I said, reaching back to grab her hand. "That's what we do. Right?"

"That's right." She sat up, sniffed, and wiped away her tears with her sleeve. "I'm trying to stop crying, but hearing about those cupcakes put me right over the edge."

"I know. They do that to me, too."

Her smile was watery. "You're so easy when it comes to food."

"I'm sure that's a compliment."

"Of course." She squeezed my shoulder. "I love you, Brooklyn."

Now it was my turn to tear up. "Oh, honey, I love you, too. We'll get you through this. You won't be alone, I promise. I'm not going to leave you to deal with anything on your own."

Right then, Derek opened the driver's-side door and slid onto the smooth leather seat. His jaw was clenched so tightly that Robin and I exchanged worried looks.

"What's wrong?" she asked, her eyes growing wider.

As he started the engine, he gave me a somber glance meant to silence me, but we both knew that wasn't going to happen.

"Derek," I said, "what happened? What did Inspector Lee say?"

As he pulled away from the curb, he said, "She didn't get a chance to say much of anything. Before we could begin to talk, Inspector Jaglom received a phone call from police headquarters that caused them both to go ballistic."

Robin sat forward. "Why?"

He glanced at her in the rearview mirror. "They couldn't find any identification in Alex's clothing, but they saw the Russian labels. And from everything you told them about him, the cops are afraid this might become an international incident."

"That sounds ominous," I said.

"It is. Inspector Jaglom is afraid your Department of Homeland Security will be intrigued enough by your Ukrainian friend to take over the case."

"And that's a bad thing?" I asked.

"It could be. Nate told me the feds in this area have a tendency to shoot first and ask questions later."

"And what exactly does that mean?"

"It means that in an overabundance of caution, the feds might throw Robin in jail."

Chapter 5

Once we were back at my place, I started water boiling for tea. I didn't drink tea very often, but I found it comforting when I was feeling blue. Today qualified.

Derek walked into the kitchen, put his arms around me, and spoke quietly. "It might be a good idea if I checked into a hotel tonight. That way, you and Robin can spend time with each other without my interference."

"I heard that." Robin came rushing over to the bar that separated the kitchen from the living and dining areas. "Don't you dare leave on my account. I won't let you."

Derek turned. "I thought it would be preferable if —"

"No," she insisted, "it's not. I'd rather you stayed. I'll feel much safer if you're here. Oh, but . . ." She pressed her hand to her mouth as though she'd misspoken.

"What's wrong?" I asked.

She walked into the kitchen, ignored me, and glared at Derek. "Unless you'd rather stay at your hotel."

He shook his head. "That's not —"

"It's your decision, of course," Robin went on. "But why are you so anxious to leave? Do you know how lucky you are to have Brooklyn to curl up with every night?"

"I'm astonishingly lucky," he said, winking at me.

"Hey," I said, embarrassed now and reaching for the bag of double-fudge Milanos on the counter. "Let's have some cookies."

"That's right," Robin said, ignoring me as she shook her finger at Derek. "Why would you want to stay anywhere else?"

"Why, indeed?" Derek said nonchalantly.

"Exactly!"

"Um, Robin —"

"Sorry, Brooklyn," Robin cried, and grabbed me in a tight hug. "But I don't want to be the excuse he uses to leave you."

I looked at Derek. "Please stay."

"Don't beg," Robin whispered. "If he hasn't figured out you're the best thing that's ever happened to him, it's his problem."

I stared at the ceiling. "I wouldn't go that far."

Derek laughed. He seemed delighted with

the entire conversation. "I'll stay here tonight, if you don't mind."

Robin beamed. "Wonderful."

"Sounds good to me." Still slightly baffled by what had just transpired, I held out the bag. "Cookie, anyone?"

Robin grabbed hold of both our arms and pulled us closer, then looked back and forth from Derek to me. "I'm a little nutso right now, so thank you for tolerating me. I owe you both so much for coming to my rescue today. I'm not sure I can ever repay you, but I love you for it. Thank you."

"It's what friends do," Derek said.

"Well put," she said, and kissed him smack-dab on the lips. Then she turned and did the same to me.

I laughed and gave her a tight hug. "You really are crazy — you know that? But I love you, too."

She looked at Derek. "So it's settled."

"It's settled," he said with a nod.

"Guess we're having a sleepover," I said, still not sure what they'd settled, but glad about it.

"So what's for dinner?" she asked, grabbing the bag of cookies.

"I've recently developed quite a taste for pad thai noodles," Derek offered.

"My favorite." Robin clapped her hands,

then turned to me. "Do we have wine?"

"Oh, hell, yes." I quickly pulled a bottle out of the wine rack and grabbed the corkscrew. It was better than tea any day of the week.

Later that evening, as we watched reruns of *Nash Bridges* and nibbled on red velvet cupcakes, Derek's cell phone rang. I paused the show, because Derek had never seen it, and despite his best intentions, he was starting to get into it.

He mostly listened on his end, and the call was over in less than two minutes. Turning to Robin, he said, "That was Inspector Lee. They did find traces of Rohypnol in your system."

"I knew it," I said. "That bastard." I whipped around and grabbed Robin's hand. "Sorry. But really, what a jerk."

"Yeah, I guess so." She seemed a little dazed by the reality of what had been done to her.

"The inspector will call you tomorrow morning to set up a time to come by so she can discuss things in detail with you."

"Why did she call you?" Robin wondered aloud. "She could've called me and cut out the middleman."

"She probably thinks you took a Valium

and went to bed," I said.

She sank back into the couch. "Oh, what a good idea."

I looked at Derek. "Do you have to work tomorrow?"

"Yes, but I'll arrange to be here when she comes."

"Thank you, Derek," Robin said. "Again."

He waved away her thanks. "I'm just being meddlesome. I want to hear what the police are up to."

I chuckled. "Me, too."

"No," Robin said. "You're being heroic and protective, and I appreciate it."

I nudged her with my elbow. "You don't have to keep saying thank-you. You would do the same for us."

"I know, but . . . it's weird." She laid her head back on the couch.

"I know, sweetie."

A noise like hailstones pitter-pattered outside in the hall, and we all looked at one another. "What the hell is that?"

I jumped up and ran to the front door.

Three Asian children were running up and down the wide, well-lit outer hallway. As they raced toward my door, the lead child saw me and skidded to a stop, causing the other two to collide into each other. The last child tumbled to the floor, laughing.

"Children!" a dark-haired woman cried from the end of the hall. She had to be their mother.

They all stood at attention. The tallest child, a little boy, stared at me with wide eyes while the two girls looked at the floor. I estimated the boy was six or seven and his siblings a year or two younger.

"You're disturbing the peace of our neighbors," the mom said. "What did I tell you about making noise?"

I waved at the woman standing outside her door. "Hello. I'm Brooklyn. You must be our new neighbors."

"Yes. I am very sorry for the children's behavior." She approached my door slowly as she explained, "They have been cooped up all day, and I let them out to greet their father, who should be here any minute." She gazed severely at her children. "But that is no excuse for such rambunctious conduct."

"Sorry, Mama," they said in unison.

"Perhaps you should apologize to our new neighbor, so she won't think you are all little hooligans."

"Sorry, new neighbor," they said.

I bit back a laugh. "That's okay." I looked at the mom. "I heard them running and came out to investigate. Except for the elevator, this is a pretty quiet building." I cringed inwardly as I said it. I didn't want her feeling self-conscious and stifling her kids too much. On the other hand, did I really want to hear little kids racing up and down the hall all day? The answer was a big *no way.*

"I'm Lisa Chung," the woman said. She was beautiful and petite, with long black hair. She had a mild Chinese accent.

"I'm Brooklyn Wainwright." I shook her hand, then pointed toward my door. "These are my friends Derek Stone and Robin Tully."

She bowed slightly in our direction. "How do you do?"

"Did you just arrive today?" I asked. "We saw movers over the weekend but didn't see anyone actually moving in."

"Yes, the movers came ahead of us. We came in with the children this morning."

The Chungs had caused a stir a few months ago when they bought two loft units next door to each other, then tore down the shared walls to make one huge apartment to accommodate their family of five.

The boy gazed up at me. "Do you live here?"

"Yes, I'm Brooklyn. What's your name?"

"Tyler Chung and I'm six," he said. He was adorable, with straight black hair cut in a bowl shape around his face. All three kids wore jeans and T-shirts and looked red cheeked and out of breath from playing. "These are my cousins Jennifer and Jessica. They're five years old and they are twins. Their parents are dead. They live with us now."

"Tyler, that is more information than anyone needs to hear," Lisa said, but she had to smile at his lack of guile.

We all traded hellos back and forth.

"You're so pretty," Tyler said, still watching me.

"Why, thank you," I said, taken aback. It had been a long time since a six-year-old had flirted with me.

"He doesn't get to meet a lot of blondes," his mother said.

I laughed. "Well, it was nice meeting you all. And welcome to the building. I hope you'll enjoy it here."

"Thank you very much," she said with another short bow. "The children will not bother you."

"I'm not worried."

"We plan to have an open house sometime in the next few weeks. Perhaps you will all stop by."

"We would be honored," I said. "Thanks."

■ ■ ■ ■

The following morning, I woke up alone and a bit disoriented. Derek's side of the bed was still warm, and I ran my hand over his pillow. Then, feeling self-conscious, I pulled my hand back.

This whole new-relationship thing was crazy, I thought as I stared at the ceiling. I'd dated plenty of men. I'd even been engaged to a few of them. But I'd never before felt this baffling, thrilling, tingly craziness.

I liked it, but I didn't trust it. How could anything this intense stand a chance of surviving more than a few months at the most? I was essentially a positive person. I saw the glass as half-full, and I believed in miracles. Still, it was madness to think this blissful feeling could last much longer. Certainly not a lifetime.

And if that was the way my thoughts were moving, it was time to wrangle them back to reality. I vowed right then and there to take things with Derek one day at a time. No way in hell would I start making plans for the future. Okay, maybe we could schedule a dinner two weeks from now, but that was the outside limit.

The scent of robust coffee wafted into the bedroom, and mercifully, all my errant thoughts dissolved into the ether. Except for one: *Feed me.*

I stumbled out of bed and into the bathroom to wash my face and brush my teeth. I fiddled with my hair, then threw on a robe and walked into the kitchen, where Robin and Derek were sitting at the bar drinking coffee and talking quietly.

When Derek saw me, he smiled, stood, and kissed me. And here came those emotions again. Talk about feeling disoriented. The man blew my socks off. I gave myself ten seconds to simply enjoy the feel of his hard, rugged body pressed against me. Then he drew back and smoothed my hair away from my face. "Sit here, darling. I'll pour you some coffee."

"Okay, thanks."

"It's so nice to see you two together," Robin said, staring at Derek and me with a dreamy gaze.

I took a sip of coffee, then studied her with concern. But she seemed much better today. Her eyes were bright and she was already dressed and wearing makeup.

"You look great," I said. "Did you sleep okay?"

"I woke up early and couldn't go back to

sleep." She stretched her arms and yawned. "But the good thing is, I fell asleep right away last night, probably because of the wine."

"Wine always helps," I said. "Mm, coffee, too."

Derek walked into the kitchen to retrieve the third stool I kept there. He pulled it close and sat facing us.

After a few more sips of coffee, I started to wake up. "So what have you two been talking about?"

Robin turned. "Derek's agreed to talk to the police so I can get some things out of my apartment."

"You have?" I said. "That's nice."

"He's just a hero," Robin said, shaking her head. "That's all there is to it."

"You really are," I said, holding the warm mug with both hands. "Thank you."

He shook his head. "That's enough out of you two."

"It's cute the way he protests," Robin said.

Scowling, he pushed himself up from the stool. "I was going to make French toast, but now I'm not sure you deserve it."

"Oh, we do, we do," I crooned.

"We'll be good, I promise," Robin said, then giggled. Again, giggles weren't her style, but it was fun to see her able to tease and enjoy herself after her ordeal.

Over French toast, bacon, juice, and coffee at the dining room table, Robin compiled a list of items she wanted from her place. Most urgent, besides underwear and her favorite jeans, were her computer and the briefcase that held her calendar and tour and travel information.

As she spoke, I noticed that she really did seem better. Not so frightened of her own shadow, and not so muzzy as she'd been yesterday. Derek and I exchanged glances and I started to say something, then changed my mind. It was too soon.

Robin glanced from Derek to me and back to him. "Oh, go ahead and ask me the question. I know you're dying to."

"What question?" I asked.

"The one that's been hovering over the room with all the subtlety of Rodan for the past ten minutes."

"Hey, we were being sensitive to your needs," I insisted.

She smiled in acquiescence. "Well, you can stop it. I assume you want to ask me about Alex."

"Who's Rodan?" Derek asked.

Robin sat back and stared at him. "You've never heard of Rodan?"

"The flying monster?" I added. "Godzilla's buddy?"

"I know of Godzilla," Derek said, as he finished off a piece of bacon.

"*Rodan* is another old monster movie," I said. "My parents let us watch it when we were kids. It was very scary at the time. Prehistoric flying reptiles, killer bad breath."

Robin nodded. "Rodan blew deadly gaseous fumes out of his beaked mouth."

"Fascinating." Derek shook his head. "Clearly I've lived a life of deprivation."

"I'll say," Robin said, and turned to me. "Jeez, we can really go off on a tangent."

"You think?" I said, then shifted in my chair. "Okay, since you're feeling better, I'm hoping you'll tell Derek about Alex."

"Sure." She settled back and seemed to gather her thoughts. Her features tightened and I could see the flash of guilt and pain in her eyes. "I told you he was wonderful, right? He was. Handsome, funny, charming. He obviously had money, not that it mattered. He liked to do interesting things, or at least that was the impression he gave me."

"What kinds of things?" Derek asked.

"Oh, you know. He said he liked to go to art galleries, museums, the park, the beach. He talked about all kinds of music. Jazz and rock and bluegrass. He even mentioned the symphony. He loved food, all kinds. We first bonded over aloo jeera and kati rolls at Kasa. But he also raved about Giant dogs and garlic fries." She sighed again and her eyes sparkled with unshed tears. "I still can't believe this."

"So he liked baseball, too?" I asked.

"Yeah."

"A regular metrosexual," I said, then added, "I'm not judging."

"That's okay. I don't think they really exist."

"An urban legend?"

She paused to contemplate that one, then shrugged. "Anyway, he was adorable. And he liked me, Brooklyn. He liked women. You could tell, you know?"

"I know."

"Of course you do. He was a lot like Derek. Well, except he didn't carry a gun, of course. And he wasn't all . . . Well, I mean, he was normal."

"Excuse me?" I said.

Derek laughed.

Her eyes widened and she covered her mouth. "I didn't mean . . . sorry."

Waving away her apology, I said, "It's okay. He's really not normal."

"Yes, he is," Robin insisted.

I shook my head. "No, he's not."

"I beg your pardon?" Derek said.

"You're extraordinary." I smiled at him.

"Darling, you'll make me blush."

I laughed at that. "You've never blushed in your life."

"You could drive me to it."

Robin cleared her throat. "The point is that —"

"The point is that Derek is dangerous and carries a gun," I said. "He takes risks. He walks on the wild side."

"You're getting carried away again," Derek murmured.

"No, no," Robin said, leaning forward and planting one elbow on the table. "I get what she means. Okay, Alex wasn't so much like Derek. He was more laid-back. He reminded me of a . . . a fun-loving aristocrat. He wanted to show me a good time, take me places, spend money on me. That's what he said, anyway. He wanted to make me laugh. God, he was sexy. He made me feel sexy. I haven't felt that way in a while."

Not since my brother, Austin, broke things off with you, I thought, but didn't say aloud. "You said he was born in Ukraine."

"That's what he told me."

"Did he have an accent?" Derek asked.

"A very mild one. He said he came over here for college, and he was in his thirties, so he'd lost some of his accent."

"Did he say where he went to school?"
"Berkeley."
"Impressive."
"He is pretty smart," she said thoughtfully. "I mean, he *was* pretty smart. God."
Derek asked a few more basic questions, then moved to the crux of the matter. "You know he drugged you, Robin. Did you realize what was happening at the time?"
The question caught her off guard. She reached for her coffee and took a few nervous sips. "No. I remember feeling really tired, and then I guess I just fell asleep. But why would he drug me? We'd already had sex. Great sex, by the way. Amazing. Inventive. I mean, really great."
"Yeah," I said intently. "We heard you the first time."
"Sorry." But her teasing smile faded as her eyes clouded over. "Why would he drug me *after* we had sex? What would that accomplish?"
Derek sat forward. "It would allow him to search your place without interference."
"But why? I don't have much money lying around. I have artwork."
"Is it worth a lot of money?"
"Most of it's my own, plus a number of local artists. We're not talking Rembrandts.

Who would want to steal anything from me?"

"He must've thought you had something worth stealing," I said.

"Like what?"

I had no idea. "Maybe he was just a charming cat burglar who worked from the inside out."

"So I was a crime of opportunity?"

I winced. "I don't know. Maybe."

"So then who killed him?" she demanded. "A rival burglar? It doesn't make sense."

"No," I agreed. "That's definitely the sticking point. Why would anyone come into your place and kill this guy?"

"It wasn't random," she mused.

"No, of course not," Derek said.

She frowned. "I mean, if it was random, they probably would've killed me, too. And they didn't steal anything. Not that I know of, anyway. I have my purse, so they didn't rob me. So who were they and what were they after?"

I pondered the question. "A jealous wife?"

"Oh, God, no," Robin cried. "That's just too awful to consider. Maybe it was a business rival?"

"Or an old boyfriend of yours?"

"No guy is that hung up on me," she said drily.

"You never know," I countered. "Maybe Alex had a partner he double-crossed."

Derek finished off the last of his coffee. "Let's run a few scenarios. Perhaps Alex knew the other person. He expected the guy to come by later and help him rob your place, so he drugged you to keep you out of their way. He probably didn't expect his friend to kill him."

"That's quite a scenario," I said.

Robin shook her head. "But it still doesn't make sense."

"I know."

"I thought I'd met the man of my dreams," she said quietly, then rolled her eyes in disgust. "Obviously, I watched too much Disney as a child."

I squeezed her hand. "I'm sorry."

"If it's not too painful," Derek said, "I'd like you to take us through the entire evening."

"It might be a little painful," she said after a moment's consideration. "But if it can help clear up a few questions, let's go for it."

"Good. Let's take a quick minute to clean things up." Derek stood and cleared our plates, then filled our cups with more coffee. I got up and grabbed a notepad and pen from my utility drawer and we both sat down again.

Robin started at the beginning of her date with Alex, trying to remember the smallest details, such as what they both wore and what kind of car he drove.

Derek scowled at the mention of the car, and I knew he would've loved to comb through it. But it was probably in the police impound lot by now.

"Whose idea was it to wind up the evening at your place?" he asked.

"Mine." Robin paused. "Well, wait. Let me think about that. We were talking about San Francisco neighborhoods. He lives in the Richmond District and I mentioned living in Noe Valley. He said he'd heard about this fabulous new restaurant in Noe Valley. I laughed and said, 'That's like two blocks from my place,' and he was like, 'You're kidding. We have to go to this place.' Then he sort of changed the subject, told me he was having the best time ever, or words to that effect. I thought the same thing. I was having a wonderful time."

She took a slow sip of coffee before going on. "So then we were eating and talking, and a while later, he brought it up again. Said he wanted to take me to this new place, Serafina. It's Italian. On Castro. And somewhere in there, he said he'd heard a lot of great things about the Noe Valley neighborhood and wanted to check it out sometime. And by then we'd finished a bottle of wine, and so I said, 'How about checking out my neighborhood right now?' " She shook her head. "I thought I was being so alluring. What an idiot."

"You weren't an idiot," I said fiercely. "He used you."

"I guess," she said. "Anyway, essentially, I invited him over."

Derek's eyes were cold as steel as he qualified her statement. "The invitation was from you, but Alex manipulated you into extending it to him."

"Which means he'd already planned out the whole thing," she reflected.

"Probably so," Derek conceded.

"I can't believe it," she said, her lips tightening in anger. "That bastard set me up."

CHAPTER 6

Derek went off to get ready for work while Robin washed the breakfast dishes and I dried and put them away.

I kept an eye on her as she drained the soapy water and wiped off the counter. While we'd talked, Robin's eyes had sparkled with righteous anger, and I was happy to see it. I'd hated seeing her feeling so miserably guilty about Alex's death, as though she were somehow responsible for it.

No, it was much better for her to get pissed off and take action.

But now her shoulders drooped and she looked pale and worried.

"How are you feeling?" I asked carefully.

"I'm fine," she muttered.

"Yeah, right." I noticed she was staring at her fingers, avoiding my gaze. That couldn't be a good sign, either. "That must be why you look so perky."

"Perky. Good one." She wrung out the sponge more vigorously than necessary, then tossed it into its holder. Clutching the edge of the counter until her knuckles went white, she finally looked at me. "I'm afraid, Brooklyn."

"Of course you are," I said, clutching her arm. "You've been pushed through the wringer. But you're also mad as hell, remember? You're going to bounce back and be ready to kick some ass, right?"

"Oh, yeah, I'm a real ass kicker," she said sarcastically, and grabbed the dish cloth from me. She dried her hands off, then leaned against the sink. "The truth is, I'm totally freaked out. I don't want to see or talk to anyone. I just want to hide in my room and sleep."

"You can stay here as long as you want."

"What about my apartment?"

I thought about the glimpse I'd gotten of Robin's place and just managed to control a shudder. "You'll go back when you're ready."

"I'm not sure I want to live there anymore."

"Not right now you don't, and I totally get that. But it's your home. Eventually . . ."

She shook her head as she stared at the floor. "I'm too afraid to go back."

"So you'll stay here. But I guarantee, after a few days you'll be itching to get back there."

Robin didn't look convinced. If anything, she seemed to be shrinking into herself. "What if the killer returns? What if I can't get the blood out of the floorboards or the carpet? I close my eyes and all I see is the blood. I don't want to live there with all those bad vibes and memories."

"Okay, first of all, the killer won't be back, because we're going to hunt him down and make him wish he'd never been born." I'd never been more serious in my life. Robin had escaped the killer, thank God, but whoever had murdered Alex had killed something inside my friend, too. And that I couldn't stomach. Seeing Robin shaken, afraid, was tearing at my heart. "Your apartment can be cleaned. There are companies that come in and take care of that stuff. We can paint every room. We'll go shopping, buy new carpets, sheets, towels, pillows, new clothes, whatever you need to purge the place of any trace that something bad ever happened there."

Scowling, she threw the towel on the counter. "That's easy for you to say."

"Well, yeah, it is," I said, glancing around at my own apartment. I'd faced a cold-hearted killer, too, right here in my home. I'd managed to avoid spilling any blood, though, thank goodness. It had been hard enough to reclaim my sense of safety and security without having the memory of blood to color everything.

"How about this?" I said. "We'll have my mom do a purification ceremony. We can all prance around with clumps of burning sage and smudge the place clean."

She pressed her lips together to keep from smiling. Because, really, the image of my crazy mom dancing around, ponytail bouncing, waving sage, and chanting to ward off evil spirits? It was pretty funny.

Her smile was short-lived. "Look, I appreciate the attempt at humor, but you've never had to deal with . . ." She stopped talking as she noticed my eyes narrow down to slits. "Okay, um, I take that back."

"Damn straight you'll take that back." I leaned against the refrigerator door and folded my arms. "You know what I went through when that psycho killer showed up at my house."

She held up her hand. "I know, Brooklyn, but you have to admit this is different."

"Okay, you're right. I wasn't sleeping with the victim."

"Yes, that. And because . . . you know, the blood."

"Blood can be cleaned," I reiterated, trying to keep the exasperation from my voice. It's not that I was mad at her. I knew what she was feeling, and honestly, a part of me wanted to curl up in a ball and hide, just like she did. But another part knew that the only way to buck Robin up was to be tough. "Look, here's the deal. You can't allow some murdering creep to chase you out of your own home. You love that place. You've been there for years and you know all your neighbors and you've got all your favorite places to shop and eat."

"Yeah, I guess." She blew out a breath, but she was standing a little straighter. "Oh, hell, I don't know."

I grabbed her shoulders. "And think about it. Who in their right mind would give up a two-bedroom rent-controlled flat in the heart of Noe Valley?"

She smiled at that. "Now, that's the best reason you've come up with so far."

"There you go." I pushed away from the refrigerator and straightened the soap dish on the sink. "Look, I was scared to death to come back to this place after they carted the killer away in handcuffs. Intellectually, I knew there was nothing to worry about, but

I still had to beg my mom and dad to stay here with me for three nights. Finally I realized I was being silly. It was over. I was safe. And besides, Derek stopped by every day for a week."

"He's so nice," she said wistfully.

"Yes, he really is."

"You're so lucky."

"I know."

And with that, she burst into tears.

After we'd managed to calm Robin down, Derek left for his office and I convinced Robin to take a long, soothing bubble bath. Then I cleaned up around the house and took out the trash. We have a trash chute in the building, so I walked down the hall and around the corner to the small trapdoor in the wall. I tossed the bag through the opening and waited, listening for the satisfying thud as it fell into the garage Dumpster six floors below.

"Hello, Miss Brooklyn."

I turned and saw the little boy I'd met last night. "Hi, Tyler. How are you?"

"Fine, thank you."

"Tyler?" his mother called from the far end of the hall.

"I'm here, Mama," he bellowed.

"Whoa, who's doing all the yelling?" My

neighbor Suzie strolled up carrying a large white plastic trash bag. "Yo, Brooklyn, howzit?"

"Hi, Suzie," I said. "Have you met Tyler?"

"Hey, munchkin," Suzie said, grinning at the boy. "Are you our new neighbor?"

"Yes, sir," Tyler whispered. He stared in fascination at Suzie, whose fashion choice today was a sleeveless black leather shirt with matching bell bottoms and spike-toed boots. Her white blond hair was short and spiked, and she wore at least ten different earrings and studs in her ears. Happily, none of her other parts were pierced. At least, none that showed. She looked like a scary but sexy lesbian chain-saw artist, which was exactly what she was.

Tyler's mom came jogging around the bend. "Tyler, I called you to — Oh, hello."

"Hi, Mama," Tyler said. "This is our new neighbor."

"Good morning, Lisa," I said. "Have you met Suzie Stein? She has the place closest to the elevator on the east side of the building."

Lisa bowed. "How do you do?"

"I'm dandy," Suzie said. "I think you met my better half yesterday. Vinnie."

Lisa cocked her head. "I met Vinnie. She is half of you?"

Suzie chuckled. "No, she's my better half. That's a kind of silly way of saying we're a couple."

"Ah. She is your roommate."

"That's another way to say it."

"I am still have problems with some colloquialisms."

"You're doing great. Where in China are you from?"

"My mother is American. She moved to China and met my father. I was born and raised in Beijing. That's where I met my husband." She laughed. "My mother lives back here now and would love to rid me of my Chinese accent."

"It's charming," I assured her.

She went on to explain that her husband was a diplomat and they had moved here because of his new job with the Chinese consulate in San Francisco. His last assignment had been at the embassy in Khartoum for five years. The whole family had been taking English-immersion classes for the past three years in anticipation of her husband obtaining the San Francisco assignment.

"Sudan, huh?" Suzie said, chuckling. "Guess he earned this plum gig after all your time there."

"Naturally, we are happy with whatever

assignment he is given."

"Of course," Suzie said lightly, but one of her eyebrows shot up and she sneaked a glance at me.

Lisa looked down at Tyler. "You must go pick out a book to bring with you to the doctor's office."

"Okay, Mama," he said, and ran down the hall and disappeared around the corner.

"Hey, speaking of books," Suzie said, anxious to change the subject, "Brooklyn here is a bookbinder, so if you have any books that need mending, she's your gal."

"You mend books for fun?" Lisa said.

"Occasionally for fun, but mainly for money. It's my job. I repair and restore rare books. I also make new ones."

"She teaches classes — that's how good she is," Suzie said, sounding like a proud parent. "You should see her studio. It's amazing."

"Everyone on our floor is creative," I demurred. "Suzie and Vinnie are sculptors. Sergio is a chef. Jeremy is a hairdresser."

"My goodness, so much talent," Lisa said, then rolled her eyes as her children came laughing and running down the hall to find her. They gathered around her and Lisa pulled them closer. With a sigh, she said, "These little monsters are my works of art."

"Oh, that's sweet," Suzie said.

"I brought my book." Tyler held up a worn copy of *Where the Wild Things Are.*

"You have read that book over one hundred times," Lisa said.

"I like it." His grin faltered as the front cover separated and fell to the ground.

"It is falling apart," she said, then looked at me. "Do you repair these kinds of books?"

"I'll be glad to fix it for Tyler."

"Oh, dear, that was rude," Lisa said, waving away her comment. "It's not worth your time. I can buy another copy for ten or twelve dollars."

Tyler seemed not to have heard as he gazed up at me with a rapturous smile. "You can fix my book?"

I laughed. "Yes, I can fix it."

Lisa shook her head. "We can talk about it later. We are going to our new doctor for checkups." She urged the children toward the elevator. "Good-bye, Brooklyn. It was nice to meet you, Suzie."

"Have fun, y'all," Suzie said.

Tyler walked backward all the way to the elevator, his gaze trained on me the entire time. "Bye, Miss Brooklyn."

As the elevator door lumbered to a close and the family disappeared, Suzie chuckled. "Wow, kid's got a crush on you."

"I'm not sure why," I said.

"It's cute." Then she grimaced. "Guess I stuck my foot in it with the Sudan comment."

"Don't sweat it," I said, as we headed back toward her place. "She probably has to be discreet. Doesn't mean we have to be."

"Right on, *chiquita.*" She slapped my shoulder in solidarity. "Listen, I'm glad I ran into you. Splinters has been sick, so we've got him on some medication."

"I'm sorry. Is he going to be okay?"

"Yeah, no worries, but the vet says we should separate Pookie from him while he's on the medication. So we were wondering if you'd mind keeping Pookie for the next ten days or so. I know it's a lot to ask, but we know you love the cats as much as we do, and we'll come by every day and feed her and stuff."

"Are you kidding? I'd love to have Pookie stay with me." It was true, despite the fact that I was the world's worst pet sitter. But everyone deserved a second chance, right? And it wouldn't be for very long. I was pretty sure I could keep one cat alive for a week and a half, especially if Suzie and Vinnie came by to feed her every day.

"Thanks, pal," Suzie said, and pounded my arm. "I'll let Vinnie know it's a go. I'll bring Pookie and her stuff by in a little while. She'll be ecstatic."

My smile was tremulous. "Me, too."

It was two o'clock before inspectors Lee and Jaglom finally came by. Suzie had dropped off Pookie and her paraphernalia a while earlier, and the cat had already glommed onto Robin. When she lay down on the couch to take a nap, Pookie curled up next to her.

I was glad to see Robin drop off to sleep so easily despite being frightened out of her mind. She hadn't slept well the night before, and I would've offered to get up and keep her company, but once I fall asleep, I tend to sleep soundly. My dad always claimed I slept like a dead tree, which sounds appalling, but Dad is an outdoor kind of guy. To him, a dead tree is a thing of beauty. That's the story he fed me, anyway.

As he'd promised, Derek returned home a few minutes after the cops arrived and I breathed a silent sigh of relief. Despite my best intentions, I'd been anxious to have him be present while the police were here. I simply wasn't at the top of my game this time around, probably because it was Robin who was the chief suspect. The situation shook me, and I found myself depending on Derek to run interference. He didn't seem to mind at all, but my dependence on him was starting to annoy me. Damsels in distress could get boring really fast.

I offered the inspectors coffee and they both accepted, so everyone hung out around the kitchen bar while the coffee brewed.

"Derek thought you might be handing the case over to the Department of Homeland Security," I said.

"I may have spoken too soon," Lee admitted. "Our guy might not have been here illegally, like the feds first thought. According to Ms. Tully here, he attended school at Berkeley, so he might've been in the U.S. ever since. We're still checking records. Depending on his status, we may keep the case or we may have to pass it along."

"Does that happen a lot, where you trade off cases with the DHS?"

"Once in a while." She leaned a hip against the edge of the bar. "DHS covers a lot of ground. Lately, we've mostly been trading off immigration cases with ICE."

I nodded knowingly as I pulled five mugs from the cupboard. I watched *Law & Order,* so I knew that ICE was Immigration and Customs Enforcement. "Coffee's ready."

"Great," Inspector Lee said. "Should help me stay awake a while longer."

As I poured the coffee, Robin cleared her throat self-consciously. "So, Derek says they did find drugs in my system."

Lee turned to her. "Yes."

"So I'm . . . cleared? You're not going to arrest me?"

Inspector Lee looked at her for a long second or three. "That remains to be seen."

Robin blinked. "Do you need more information? Is there anything —"

"Yeah, what's that supposed to mean?" I asked.

Derek stepped into the kitchen and placed his arm casually around my shoulder. I knew why. He was getting ready to hold me back in case I tried to lunge over the bar and claw Inspector Lee's eyes out. There was no way in hell she was arresting Robin.

"Inspector, please explain," Derek said.

Lee shot Derek a defensive glare. "Just because she was on drugs doesn't mean she didn't kill the guy."

"And ransack her own apartment while she was at it?" he said. "Highly improbable."

Robin slid down onto the nearest barstool, gulping convulsively.

"This is crazy." I was livid. What the hell was wrong with Inspector Lee?

Derek shot me a warning glance.

"I'm sorry, but it is," I said.

Derek turned to Jaglom. "Nathan?"

"Come on, Jan," Jaglom cajoled his partner. "These are good people. Dial it down."

After a few tense seconds of a staring match between the two, Inspector Lee muttered, "Hell, I need a cigarette." We all watched as she walked across the living room to the wall of windows, where she stared out at my narrow view of the bay.

Jaglom leaned in. "She's been wearing the patch lately to help her quit smoking, so sometimes she goes a little . . ." He pointed to his head and circled his finger as if to say she was going nuts.

If this had been about only me, I might've been more sympathetic to her problems. After all, I liked Janice Lee. I really did. She was a good cop. Usually. But right now, she was screwing with Robin's emotions, and I was ready to beat her with a stick.

I banked my anger, poured coffee into the mugs, and passed them out. Then I walked over to Inspector Lee and handed a mug to her.

She took it and sipped silently. After a moment, she gritted her teeth and, still staring out the window, said, "Sorry. My mom's in the hospital, I've got an idiot for a brother, and all I want is a cigarette."

I nodded, acknowledging the apology.

"Sorry about your mom."

"They cut a few feet out of her colon yesterday and they're still running tests. There's an outside chance she'll be okay."

"Wow."

"Yeah." She shook her head in confusion or disbelief; I couldn't tell which. "They're hoping it's diverticulitis. We're afraid it's cancer. They're the experts, so maybe it'll turn out fine. But can I tell you the worst part of all this? It's seeing my mom in that hospital bed, looking so weak and sick. I mean, my mom is a tigress. I hate seeing her like that. It's rough, you know?"

"Sure. It's scary."

"It sucks, is what it is."

"Getting old ain't for sissies," I said.

"Tell me about it. Pisses me off."

I finally turned and looked at her. "Is there anything I can do?"

After a swift, searching glance at me, she said, "You're kidding, right? You were ready to tear the skin off my face a minute ago, and now you're offering help and consolation?"

"Hey, I have a soft spot for you." I patted the top of my head.

She chuckled.

"I shouldn't have gotten in your face," I said, "but it's my best friend you're screwing with."

"I get that." She nodded, took a sip of coffee, and stared out the window again. "She's lucky to have you in her corner."

"I tell her that all the time."

Lee snorted. "Bet you do."

She finished off her coffee and handed me the mug. "By the way. Your version of 'in my face,' Wainwright?"

"Yeah?"

"Lame. Really lame."

I laughed. "We're going to be sitting around drinking wine later. Why don't you come over after you clock out?"

She tried for a sneer but her eyes betrayed her interest. "You gonna be swilling that sissy white zinfandel crap?"

It was my turn to make a face. "Okay, now you're just trying to piss me off."

Chapter 7

As soon as Inspector Lee agreed to come by later for a glass of wine, she groaned and admitted she couldn't socialize while Robin was officially a suspect. But she took a rain check on the assumption that we wouldn't always be surrounded by dead bodies and suspicious circumstances. I considered it a good first step to friendship.

While I'd been doing what I could to schmooze Inspector Lee into a better mood so she wouldn't drag Robin off to jail, Derek and Robin were obtaining the real scoop from Inspector Jaglom. They gave me the whole story later as I loaded all the coffee mugs into the dishwasher.

The police had managed to track down Alex's apartment in the Richmond District, thanks to the information Robin had given them yesterday. Specifically, his name, Alexei Mikhail Pavlenko.

Jaglom reported that whoever had trashed

Robin's apartment and killed Alex had also trashed Alex's apartment.

"How can they tell it was the same guy?" I asked.

Derek handed me another mug. "The search was systematic and thorough. Nothing was destroyed, exactly, but things were upturned or tossed on the floor."

"Boy, first they kill the guy, then turn his place upside down. Seems rude, doesn't it?"

"To say the least," Robin agreed.

"But while the police were sifting through Alex's property," Derek said, "one of his neighbors showed up and inquired as to what had happened. When the fellow found out Alex had been killed, he jogged back to his apartment and came back with something Inspector Jaglom found rather interesting."

"What was it?"

"A small strongbox," he said. "Alex had given it to him and asked him to keep it in a safe place."

I halted in mid–dishwasher loading. "Oh, my God, do you know what that means?"

"Yes," Robin said. "He must've known he was in danger."

"Exactly," Derek remarked. "Which means he knowingly put you in danger."

I exchanged a meaningful glance with

Robin, who frowned. "I didn't think of it that way."

"Well, you should," I said, squeezing her shoulder in sympathy. "It'll keep you angry and alive."

If Alex weren't already dead, I'd have killed him myself. He could have gotten Robin murdered. The thought of that made me want to hug my best friend and kick a dead man.

"Did Jaglom tell you what they found in the box?" I asked.

Derek leaned against the post at the edge of the kitchen. "Various personal papers. And his passport."

"And?"

"He was indeed Ukrainian," Derek said.

Robin leaned against the sink. "And Inspector Lee was totally pissed off about it."

"Why?"

Derek explained that there was a turf war bubbling up among the Russian, Ukrainian, and Georgian neighborhoods of the Outer Richmond. This was the area of the city north of Golden Gate Park that included Lincoln Park and the beautiful Palace of the Legion of Honor. The Richmond extended all the way out to the Great Highway that ran along the beach. It was as well known for its influx of Eastern European immigrants as it was for the heavy blanket of fog that seemed to swallow it up most days around three o'clock.

Jaglom had confided that Inspector Lee had a low opinion of any kind of ethnic turf wars after living through a decade of Chinatown gang warfare in the eighties.

"Oh, come on." I looked at Derek skeptically. "They don't really think this was as simple as Robin being caught in a battle between rival gang members, do they?"

"It's absurd," Robin said. "He wasn't a gang member."

"Russian Mafia?" I suggested.

Her back straightened as she shot me a look of distaste. "No way."

"Sweetie, you knew him one night. For all you know he could have been the president of the Russian Mafia."

"I would have known," Robin insisted stubbornly. "Besides, he's Ukrainian, not Russian. And not Mafia."

"Oo-kay." I backed off. When Robin got that look in her eye, I knew she wouldn't be changing her mind anytime soon.

I glanced at Derek, who was tracking my movements as I pulled a bottle of Malbec from the shelf and found the wine opener in the drawer. Holding up the bottle, I said,

"It's not too early, is it?"

"Certainly not."

"Good. We need something to counteract all that caffeine we just ingested."

"I hope it helps," Robin muttered. "I'm stressed out."

"You and me both." I pulled glasses from the shelf while Derek took over the job of opening the wine bottle.

"What were we talking about?" I asked.

"Russian mobs," Robin groused, "and the fact that Alex was not involved with any of that."

Derek swirled the wine in his glass, sniffed the bouquet, and took a sip. "Despite rumors to the contrary, there is actually very little Russian mob activity in San Francisco."

"For real?" I asked.

"Yes."

Robin nodded in satisfaction. "So there. But even if there was, you know, *mob* activity here, Alex wouldn't have been involved. He wasn't that type. He was laid-back, social, fun. Not, you know, all . . . *mobby* and stuff."

I tried to bite my tongue, but it went against my nature. "Mobby?"

She rolled her eyes. "Whatever."

I gave her a pass. After all, she wasn't firing on all cylinders. And maybe it was time to change the subject. "How do you like the wine?"

She stared at the full glass in her hand and realized it hadn't touched her lips yet. "Guess I should drink some."

"Yes, you should. Never waste, never worry."

She took a healthy sip. "God, I love wine."

"Me, too," I said, smiling at her.

Derek swirled his wine again and sipped it. After a moment of what I figured was wine contemplation, he put his glass down on the counter. "This suspected turf war the inspector referred to may have more to do with the tensions occurring in the motherland than with anything happening here."

"Do you think that's why Alex was killed?" I said, then glanced at Robin. "I don't mean anything *mob*-related, but he might've gotten caught up in neighborhood politics. It wouldn't be the first time politics turned to violence."

Derek shook his head. "I have no idea, but I can look into it."

"I still don't believe it," Robin insisted.

"Okay. Well, how about pasta and a salad for dinner?"

"That's something I can believe in."

I smiled and Derek nodded agreeably. We left it at that impasse and began preparations for dinner.

The next morning, Derek left for work and Robin asked to borrow my computer to check out some tour itineraries. Vinnie stopped by to feed Pookie — thank goodness — and after she left, I decided to spend some quality time studying the Kama Sutra for the first time since Robin brought it over Friday night.

Let me be the first to say that, given all the implications of my growing up in a commune, you'd think I would know more about the erotic aspects of the Kama Sutra. But you'd be wrong. What can I say? It wasn't that kind of commune. Intellectually, I knew the book was an ancient primer on moral behavior and etiquette in marriage, as well as being something like a pictorial guide to sexual ecstasy, but beyond that, I didn't have a clue.

As I opened the book, I wondered if it might be a good idea to stop at a bookstore later that afternoon and pick up a copy of *The Kama Sutra for Idiots,* just for reference.

I decided to concentrate on the book itself first. I believed the restoration itself would be easy, but the evaluation process would be more difficult. The book had no copyright date, which was not unheard of in a rare, vintage book from another country. But because there was no date to work from, I would have to examine the bindings, the paper, the ink and paint used, the style of the gilding, even the age and origin of the language itself. All of this was essential when appraising a book like this. Which meant I would also need to pick up a good French dictionary with a detailed etymology.

Okay, enough dithering about appraisals and evaluations. I wanted to check out those pictures. I turned the pages carefully to the middle of the book and stared, captivated, at the incredibly detailed and realistic paintings. I couldn't help but ogle page after page of intricate illustrations of couples engaged in the most erotic sexual poses I'd ever seen. Some positions were so convoluted, I couldn't figure out how they managed to get into them. Pulleys, maybe?

"What are you doing?"

I jumped about three feet off my chair. "Nothing."

Robin laughed and circled my chair to see exactly what I was doing. "Oh, right. You were looking at dirty pictures."

"They're not dirty."

"So why did you jump like I caught you doing something bad?"

"You just startled me." I closed the book and wrapped it carefully in the cloth.

Robin continued chuckling. "Your face is red."

"Oh, shut up," I said, and laughed as I picked up the book and took it back to its safe nest in my steel-lined hall closet, under the false floor where I locked my most important documents and the rare books I worked on.

"I'm going stir-crazy," Robin said, following me down the hall.

"Did you get what you wanted off the Internet?"

"Yeah. Now I feel like walking or something."

"We could walk to South Park for coffee."

"Sounds great."

We threw on jackets and strolled two blocks over to the small city park that was my favorite discovery when I moved to the area. It was a green belt of trees, grass, and a playground one short block long, tucked away from the hustle and bustle of city traffic and surrounded by town houses, local businesses, shops, and restaurants. The coffeehouse stood at the far end of the block. There was one empty table outside, so we grabbed it and sat to enjoy lattes and scones.

"I'm sorry about last night and the whole mob thing," I said, once I'd taken a few sips of my double-shot latte.

"No, you were just trying to figure things out. I thought about it later, after I went to bed. Sorry. I should've been more open to the possibilities." She shook her head in regret. "I didn't even know this guy. I don't know why I was being so defensive."

I tore off a bit of scone and munched as I thought about it for a moment. "I'd say you were defending yourself as much as him. In your mind you're thinking that if Alex was a bad guy, then you made a bad decision. But you didn't. None of this is your fault."

"Oh, please." She laughed without humor. "For all I know, he could've been a serial killer. Those guys are supposed to be charming, right? Hello, Ted Bundy?"

"True enough."

"Alex was definitely charming," she admitted.

"Fine, but he wasn't a serial killer."

She sat back in her chair. "He was something."

"Still doesn't make it your fault. This isn't about you picking a bad guy. There's something bigger going on."

"Maybe he wasn't a bad guy, but he was

definitely the wrong guy. And, Brooklyn, I brought a guy I didn't even *know* into my home." Her laugh was short and desperate. "My home? I brought him into my bed! What the hell was I thinking?"

"You were thinking that he was cute and fun and sexy and charming and —"

"I should have been smarter about it."

"I'll agree with you there. Did you use protection?"

"Of course! I'm not that stupid."

"Then what else are we supposed to do? Should we have guys fill out questionnaires before we go out with them? Once in a while we meet a nice guy and we take a chance, that's all."

She nodded, gripped her latte with both hands, and sipped. "I . . . I was tired. Jet-lagged. I'd just spent three days with my mother. She makes me crazy, makes me feel . . . you know, inferior, somehow. She fills a room until there's no air left for me to breathe. So I guess when some good-looking guy expressed some interest in me, I just . . . grabbed that attention with both hands, you know?"

I touched her arm. "I know. You can't keep dwelling on this or you really will go crazy. So please stop beating yourself up over it."

She rolled her eyes, then smiled tightly.

"Okay, I'll stop."

"Promise."

"I promise."

"Good."

She sighed. "Thank you."

"I'm not sure why, but you're welcome."

"Just for hanging in there with me." She stared down at her latte as if looking into the past. At that night. She shivered.

"Come on, let's go back," I said. "It's cold out here."

She stood and zipped up her jacket. "It's springtime in San Francisco. Of course it's cold."

As we strolled up Brannan, I pointed out the new and elegant tower of condos being constructed one block south of us. I wasn't happy with the high-rise aspect, but any construction was a good sign that the neighborhood was once again vibrant after a year or two of economic uncertainty.

"This is a great area," Robin said, gazing around.

"Yeah, I was so lucky to find my loft. I really love it around here."

I lived on the south edge of SoMa, or South of Market, close to Giants Stadium (which my dad loved), with a view of the bay. Yes, you could turn a corner and see the random blighted, burned-out factory or deserted housing project, but that was true of most neighborhoods in the country these days. I tended to avoid those dodgy blocks and stuck close to the fun parts. Overall, this was a lively, happening area. And it was freeway-close to everything else in the Bay Area.

"Maybe I should think about moving over here," Robin said.

"That would be great," I said, excited at the thought of her living even closer to me. "We could have so much fun. But, Robin, that's not something you need to think about right now."

"I know." She shivered from the breeze that seemed to be blowing straight off the bay and right up Brannan. "Especially if this street is always a wind tunnel like it is today."

"Not always, but it's definitely cold today. Let's run."

We scurried up the block, wrapping our arms around ourselves to keep warm.

"Hey," I said as we slowed down, passing one of my favorite neighborhood Thai restaurants. "We should take you shopping later."

She eyed me. "You hate shopping."

"But you need clothes to wear."

"True. We'll go someplace cheap and get

some sweats. It's not like I have anything to dress up for."

"That works for me."

She made a face. "I guess I should try to find out when I can move back to my place." She didn't sound happy at the idea, and who could blame her? On the other hand, she did have to reclaim her home or she'd never feel safe anywhere again. Not that I would ever push her to leave.

"We can call the police when we get home," I said. "But you know you can stay with me as long as you want."

"Thanks, but I'm starting to feel like a third wheel."

"No, you're not."

She smiled. "It would be different if you and Derek were an old married couple, but you've just begun a new relationship. My being there has got to be cutting into your personal romance time."

"Not so much," I said, grinning. "You don't need to worry about us. We're doing just fine."

She glanced at me sideways and wiggled her eyebrows. "Really? Care to share the details?"

I refused to blush. "No. But much to my surprise, everything's going really well with us."

"Good. You deserve a wonderful man in your life."

"Yes, I do," I said, laughing.

"But still, I shouldn't stay there much longer."

"You're going to make me mad if you keep saying that."

"Okay, I'll shut up."

"If you really don't want to stay with me, we could drive you up to Dharma for a few days."

She looked puzzled at the suggestion. "If I want to go to Dharma, I can jump in my car and go."

"Yeah, but this way, we could keep you company. It might be hard to drive all that way alone." Truthfully, I was afraid a long drive like that would give Robin too much time to focus on the nightmare of what had happened and to start punishing herself again. "We can drive you up, stay for dinner, then drive back. You can give us a call anytime and we'll come pick you up."

"Listen to you, saying 'us' and 'we.' It's very cute."

Now I was blushing, but I ignored the sensation. "So, what do you say?"

"I wouldn't have my car," she argued. "It would be weird."

"You know you can borrow anyone's car

up there." I waved the thought away, realizing that Robin would never go for it. She liked to be in charge of her comings and goings, hated borrowing anything. It was a matter of control, and I could totally relate. Being stranded in Dharma at the whim of whoever was in charge of picking her up would make her nuts.

"Never mind," I said. "It was a silly idea. You're too independent to want to be anywhere without your own car. I'd feel the same way."

"Thanks for the offer, though."

"You're welcome." We stopped at the light at Third Street and an idea occurred to me. "But if you did go up there for a few days, I could take care of getting your apartment cleaned up for you. You could relax, get a massage, hang out with friends, then come back to a sparkling clean apartment. What do you think?"

She didn't say anything, but her lips were twisted in thought. Finally she looked at me. "I would hate to leave that up to you."

"You'd really hate it, or you'd just feel bad about it?"

"I'd feel really bad about it."

"Okay, then it's settled." I nodded. "I'll take care of it."

"That's crazy. You don't have time to do

that for me."

I met her gaze. "Do you trust me?"

Scowling, she muttered, "I guess."

I laughed. "And would you do it for me?"

"Of course." She didn't have to think about it.

"There you go."

The light changed and we crossed Third just as a woman on the other side of the street began screaming in some foreign language I couldn't name. I didn't think much of it, as I'd become inured to the occasional deranged rantings of homeless people as they walked down the street. But curiosity won out, and Robin and I turned to see what the problem was.

The dark-haired woman was young and fairly attractive in jeans and a camel jacket. She didn't appear to be hurt, just livid. She pointed with urgency in our direction as she continued screeching. Looking both ways up and down Brannan, she caught a break in traffic and started running across the street.

"Jeez," Robin muttered, glancing around. "She's ready to kill someone."

I looked around for the target of her wrath and noticed a heavyset woman dressed in black pants, black trench coat, head scarf, and dark glasses, standing in front of my building. Was the other woman yelling at her?

As the screaming woman from across the street got closer, the trench-coated woman took off running up the block and disappeared around the corner.

What was that all about? She looked vaguely familiar, but I didn't have time to worry, because at that moment, the screaming woman rushed onto the sidewalk, stormed right up to Robin, and punched her in the face.

I gasped and tried to grab hold of the woman, but she knocked Robin down to the sidewalk, then jumped on top of her. It was surreal. She was pummeling Robin, slapping and beating her in the head and face as she babbled and cried in some foreign language.

Robin yelled back as she swatted at her attacker, trying to push her away while also trying to protect her face. I managed to grab the woman by one shoulder and arm and yank her back, so she turned and slapped me. Robin got to her knees and grabbed hold of the crazed woman by both arms so she couldn't swing out and hit either of us. Robin struggled to a standing position, yanking the woman up with her and away from striking distance.

"You keel him, you beech!" the woman screamed in English as she wiggled and squirmed to get away. "You keeller! You keel Alexei!"

"What the hell?" Robin cried, struggling to keep a grip on both her arms. "I didn't kill him!"

The woman slammed her foot down on Robin's, causing Robin to release the wildcat and swear loudly as she hopped around.

Crazy Lady was stretching her arm back to slug Robin again when I grabbed hold of that arm and clutched it tightly in mine. Robin snatched her other arm, and between the two of us we got her under control for the moment.

She kept repeating something in her language. It sounded like, *"Date-eh it-eh om you! Date-eh it-eh om you!"* Something like that. It was hard to understand, since she was belting it out at the top of her lungs.

"Can you hold her?" I yelled, and reached one-handed into my purse for my phone. "I'm calling the police."

"Hurry."

"Nooo!" the woman screeched, and ripped one arm away from Robin's grip. "Keeller!"

"Jesus, shut up!" Robin shouted.

True to California life, people were staring at us, but not stopping. Heck, in this neighborhood they probably thought we were doing a street performance.

She whipped her arm away from my grasp and turned to slug Robin again. I came from behind and shoved my knees into the backs of her legs, causing her knees to buckle. Robin pushed her down to the ground and sat on her back, straddling her so she couldn't escape. But she bucked and rolled, making it look like Robin was riding one of those mechanical bulls.

"Call the police!" Robin shouted.

"Already got them," I said, and rattled off my address to the 911 dispatcher.

The crazy cow kept trying to buck Robin off her. She tried swinging her arms around to smack Robin, but it was useless.

I noticed Robin's eye was beginning to swell badly. Her strength was ebbing.

I heard sirens. "Police are on their way."

That news caused the woman to bellow and rear up again, so I sank down and sat on her legs to keep her from kicking. Together Robin and I managed to hold her down.

But the woman wasn't finished. She swung her elbow back and connected with Robin's thigh. Robin howled in pain but didn't give an inch.

Robin was usually the nicest human being

on the face of the planet, but she'd had a hard week and wasn't willing to be pushed anymore. She grabbed a thick clump of the woman's hair and yanked at it. "Chill out or die, bitch."

Over an hour later, Robin lay on my living room couch, her left eye swollen closed and most of her cheek dark red and bruised. She was holding a bag of frozen peas to her face and whimpering only a little. I knew I had bruises, too, but nothing compared to Robin's. Her face would turn black and blue and purple over the next twenty-four hours, and it wasn't going to be pretty for a week or so.

I walked to the kitchen sink and filled a plastic bag with ice and wrapped it in a soft cloth. When I laid it on the other side of her poor face she grimaced, then whispered, "It's too cold."

"That's why we call it ice."

"Funny," Robin murmured.

"We want the swelling to go down, sweetie," I said softly. "I'm so sorry it hurts."

"Me, too."

"We'll only leave it on for about ten minutes at a time."

She gave a determined nod. "I can take it for ten minutes."

"We shouldn't have gone outside," I lamented. "You wouldn't be hurt if I hadn't insisted on getting out of here for a while."

"Who knew she was watching the place? Freakazoid." She groaned. "Hurts to talk."

"Then stop talking."

"You wish," she murmured, but then settled into the couch and let the ice pack do its healing.

The first thing I'd done once we got inside was call my mother to ask for the best remedies for Robin's wounds. After getting a full list of items from Mom, along with lots of woo-woo advice to purge Robin's karma of bad juju, I quickly called Derek to tell him what had happened. He offered to stop at the health food store on his way home to pick up everything Mom recommended.

I read off the list. Sage tea, good for both drinking and soaking with a compress to reduce swelling and heal bruising; vitamin K cream to accelerate healing; arnica to banish bruises; and chunks of fresh whole pineapple, which contained an enzyme that also helped reduce bruising.

Mom also recommended grinding up parsley for its anti-inflammatory properties, but I blew that one off and slipped Robin a couple of ibuprofen instead. And as a bonus, I still had some Vicodin in the medicine cabinet to help knock her out later.

Personally, I'd popped a Xanax as soon as we got inside. I was a nervous wreck.

I expected the whack job who attacked Robin to be behind bars very soon. Earlier, two policemen had arrived on the scene to find Robin and me still squatting on top of her. After taking our statements and the statements of several brave people who'd stepped forward as witnesses, they'd arrested and handcuffed her. She might've revealed her full name to the police, but she kept glancing at us, noticing we were listening to her every word, so she would give them only her first name, Galina. All we were able to glean in the short but really fun time we spent with her was that she was a friend — lover? — of Alex's and clearly blamed Robin for his death.

An ambulance arrived and two paramedics rushed over to check out our battle wounds. Despite her ever-swelling eye and bruised cheek, Robin refused to go to the hospital and had to sign a waiver to that effect.

As the EMTs packed up their gear, a black Lincoln Town Car cruised by slowly, then stopped on the opposite side of the street. The windows were blacked out, so I couldn't see inside the car, but I knew instinctively that whoever was sitting there was watching us. It gave me the willies.

Robin noticed the car, too, and so did Galina, who began screaming like a banshee at them. The driver drove off slowly, and Galina, despite being handcuffed, turned around to flash her middle finger at it. I had to give her points for her passion.

The car was too far away for me to make out the license plate number. The driver might've been an innocent lookie-loo, but I doubted it, given Galina's reaction.

I asked the policeman to contact Lee or Jaglom and let them know that they would want to interview Lunatic Galina in connection with Alex's murder. The one officer got Inspector Lee on the phone right then, and I could hear her barking orders through the officer's earpiece.

Galina fought the officer who tried to push her gently into the back of the patrol car. So it wasn't just us; she was angry at everyone. Her anger and passion reminded me of someone else in my life, but my head was so full of strange puzzles and weird facts at the moment, I couldn't remember who it was.

As I watched both police officers struggle with her, it occurred to me that maybe she was the one who had killed Alex. Maybe she was a jealous lover who'd seen him going out on a date, followed them back to Robin's place, where she killed him in a rage, and trashed the apartment. Now she was stalking Robin. She might've even trashed Alex's apartment.

Of course, if Galina had killed Alex in a jealous rage, surely she would have killed Robin, too. She didn't seem like the type to rein in her emotions at a time like that.

So she probably wasn't Alex's killer, but she might've been the one to ransack Alex's apartment. Now she was stalking Robin because . . . she thought Robin killed Alex? Or she thought Robin knew something? Or she thought Robin had something of hers? Or Alex's? Why?

The jealous-lover scenario worked for me. I just wished I knew what she was yelling in Russian or Ukrainian or whatever language she'd been spewing.

But the more I thought about it, the more I realized the jealousy angle worked only until I got to the part where Alex had drugged Robin. Why? I played it out a few more times but couldn't get Galina to fit into the bigger picture, and I wound up back at the beginning of the puzzle.

Really, nothing made sense when combined with the fact that Robin had been drugged by Alex. Maybe I was trying too hard or overlooking something obvious. I couldn't figure it out, and I found myself rubbing my temple to rid myself of the headache that was cropping up. It was a minor ache compared to Robin's, though, and as I watched her struggle to find relief in sleep, I vowed to track down the bastard who'd killed Alex and ruined Robin's life. And I would make him pay.

CHAPTER 8

That night, after I'd made sure Robin was asleep, I walked into my bedroom and stumbled into Derek's arms. I didn't know I was so close to the breaking point until my eyes blurred with tears and I felt myself shaking.

"God. She could've been killed," I said. "The first strike was such a shock, and then she was hitting Robin in the head, punching her hard. There was blood."

Derek shushed me, rocked me, whispered nonsensical endearments in my ear as if I were a child who needed consoling. And in that moment, that was exactly how I felt. Still shaken from the murder in Robin's home, now I was worried about her safety. Derek walked me over to the small love seat under the window, sat down, and pulled me onto his lap. And held me.

I couldn't remember any man ever holding me in his lap, not since I was five years old, and the man was my dad. It was a strange moment for me. Sweet, but strange.

When I was finally able to speak without whimpering, I said, "It took a while, but between us, we managed to kick her ass."

Derek chuckled. "I always said you two were tough. Did the woman give you any idea why she came after Robin? Did she say anything?"

"Just what I told you earlier," I said, and sighed. "She kept shouting at Robin in a foreign language. The only English she used was when she called her a 'keeller,' accused her of killing Alexei."

"She had an accent, obviously," Derek said.

"Yes. A thick one. Russian, Eastern European, something like that. It was classic Boris and Natasha."

"Boris and Natasha?"

I blinked at him. "Come on. Rocky and Bullwinkle? That had to make it to England at some point."

He frowned. "Rocky the flying squirrel and Bullwinkle the moose?"

I laughed softly. "Exactly. So there were these two silly spies, Boris and Natasha. Anyway, never mind. But Galina sounded like Natasha. Right out of a spy movie, like *From Russia with Love*. You know?"

"Ah, yes, of course." He smiled. "Darling, can you remember any of the words or sounds she spoke in her language?"

At that moment I realized his mood had shifted subtly from consoling lover to interrogator. And I was okay with it. Interesting.

"Yes, she kept repeating this one phrase, and now I can't get it out of my head. It went something like, *'date-eh it-eh om you.'* I'm probably saying it wrong."

" *'Date-eh it-eh om-you'?"* he repeated.

"Yes."

" 'Give it to me.' "

I glanced around. "What?"

"That's what she was saying. It's Ukrainian. 'Give it to me.' "

" 'Give it to me'?" I said, puzzled. "Give *what* to me? What does she want?"

"I have no idea."

"Me neither." I stretched my muscles, felt the ache in my back from grappling with Galina. "God, she was insane."

"You're in pain."

"I'm in better shape than Robin."

"Did you take something to help you sleep?"

"I took a Xanax a few hours ago, but that wore off. Just a few minutes ago I took some over-the-counter pain stuff. I didn't want anything too strong."

He frowned, kissed my cheek and my temple, then brushed his lips over mine. "I'll make sure you sleep."

"Will you?" I smiled.

"Yes." He stood, lifting me as he rose, and carried me to the bed. It delighted me, flustered me. I buried my face in the smooth skin of his shoulder.

I'd never been much of a girlie girl, never gone in for sugary sweet bedroom accessories like my sisters had. There were no frills in here, no lace, no froufrou brass bed with ornate curlicues. Instead, my room was furnished in pale woods, crisp whites, a light green love seat with green and white pillows. The effect was cool, clean, appealing. To me, anyway. But now I felt outrageously feminine as I lay next to Derek on cool white sheets. He was so big, so masculine, so intense.

"You'll sleep now," he said.

"I'll try."

He shifted to hold me, fitting me against him, my back to his front, until we were aligned perfectly together.

"You'll sleep," he murmured in my ear, and I no longer doubted whether he was right.

But before I drifted off, I remembered something I'd forgotten to ask him. "Do you mind that Robin is staying here with us?"

"Of course not." One of his hands rested on my stomach and the other smoothed a path down my side until it rested lightly on my hip. "I offered to move back to my hotel because I thought she might be more comfortable if I weren't here."

"No, it makes her feel safe to have you near." I rested my hand over his. "I like your being here, too."

"It's settled then," he said, his breath ruffling my hair. "I'm not going anywhere."

Early the next morning, Robin emerged from her bedroom and walked slowly to the couch just as Derek was about to leave for a run around the neighborhood. I winced when I saw her face.

"I know I look like hell," she muttered. "And oh, joy, I feel like it, too." It took her a few seconds of careful maneuvering to sit comfortably on the couch.

"I think the swelling has gone down," I said, studying her.

"Maybe a little. But my face still looks like a punching bag."

"Let me see it." Derek sat on the coffee table in front of Robin and gently touched her cheek and temple around her swollen eye. Yesterday, that whole area was dark pink, but today it was mottled black and blue and purple.

While Derek examined the bruising, I filled a small Ziploc bag with ice and wrapped it in a clean dish cloth.

"The swelling is better today," he said. "And the blood has clotted where the capillaries broke, so it's already healing quite well."

"And yet it's hideous," Robin murmured, and took the ice bag from me. "Go ahead. You can say it out loud."

"Never," he said, smiling as he ran his knuckles along her undamaged jaw. "You've been heroic through it all. Yes, you're a bit battle scarred now, but within a week you'll be healed and back to your beautiful self."

She shifted her gaze to me. "He's good at this."

I smiled and nodded, so grateful he was there. Nothing like a gorgeous man telling a woman she's beautiful to make her feel better about life in general.

"I'll be back with bagels and cream cheese in short order," Derek promised before enveloping me in his arms and kissing me soundly.

Just for a second or two, I melted right into him. Then I walked with him down the hall to the front door and kissed him once more before sending him off on his run.

"You're domesticating him," Robin said when I returned to the living room.

"Domesticating?" I said, and laughed at the very idea. Derek was way too dangerous to ever be called domesticated. Shaking my head, I said, "Not likely. He still seems wild and untamed to me."

"Don't worry. He's still got that 'don't mess with me' vibe going for him, but he's turned into a pussycat around you."

Good to know, I thought, but said, "Don't ever say that to him, I beg of you."

"I won't. But he's still a pussycat."

I smiled. "To be honest, ever since I first saw him, I've thought of him as a big jungle cat. A panther. Or a jaguar. Always on guard, always on the hunt."

"Panther works for me. Very sexy." She sighed and laid her head back against the cushion. "It's just nice to see what a real man is like around the house."

"Now, that I totally agree with. But just so you know, he's not completely perfect — he sometimes forgets to take out the trash."

"What a beast."

"Isn't he?" I said. "And you would never know it, but he reads car magazines obsessively. You know, with articles about tires and steering wheels? Can you imagine?"

"That's unexpected. But it's kind of manly."

"I suppose," I said with a laugh.

Pookie jumped on the couch and meowed at Robin. "Hey, speaking of big jungle cats," she said, pulling the cat into her lap and stroking her back.

I walked into the kitchen to start the coffee and a pot of tea, trying to keep an eye on Robin as I worked.

She wore the black sweatpants I'd bought her yesterday afternoon. Our official shopping expedition had been canceled, naturally, but she still needed clothes, so shortly after Derek had arrived with the items my mother had recommended, I'd raced out to the local Old Navy store.

Typically, Robin never would have stepped foot inside a discount store, but these were not normal times. She wasn't going anywhere special, and sweatpants were the most comfortable thing in the world to wear. I bought her three pairs — black, navy, and red — plus three cute hoodies in contrasting shades, along with socks, undies, and three cotton turtlenecks in black, white, and beige. That was the extent of my flair for fashion.

"Will you be able to chew a bagel?" I

asked, as I pulled coffee mugs out of the cupboard.

"If I can't eat a bagel, I'll slit my wrists."

"We could pulverize it in the blender, add a little milk, and you could drink it through a straw. A bagel smoothie."

"That's disgusting."

"I know." I grinned as I walked over to the couch and took the ice bag from her. "Ten minutes on, ten minutes off."

"It's bad enough that I look like shit," she said, and gingerly touched her damaged eyelid. "I really don't want to think about having to eat through a straw for the next week."

"You're able to talk okay, so I imagine you can move your jaw well enough to eat something. We'll heat up the bagel just enough to soften it, and it should be fine."

"I'll make it work."

The water began to boil and I ran back to the kitchen, where I poured hot water into the teapot with the sage tea bags. "I think the sage compress worked really well with the ice to bring down the swelling. You really don't look as bad as I thought you would."

"That's a bald-faced lie," Robin said. "I look like I was run over by a truck."

"A very small truck, maybe. But you're less puffy, and it looks like you can actually open your eye now."

"It still hurts a lot."

I walked over, handed her another bag filled with ice, and sat on the couch. "I'm sure it does, but I'm so proud of you for kicking that bitch's ass."

She chuckled. "Your mother would have a cow if she heard you talking like that."

I shook my head. "If Mom had been there, she'd have helped us kick her ass. Of course, afterward, she would have helped the woman cleanse her aura and dust off her dosha, then suggested ways to reach enlightenment. . . ."

"Don't make me laugh," Robin said.

"Sorry." But I was glad to see Robin's sense of humor returning.

"Hell." Robin splayed her hands on the cushions. "I really know how to pick them, don't I?"

I patted her knee in sympathy. "Don't go there again. Remember? None of this was your fault."

"Oh, come on. It's not bad enough that Alex had enemies who wanted him dead. Now I have to find out he had a girlfriend?" She shifted on the couch to get comfortable. Pookie shifted with her. "It's a little humiliating to realize how thoroughly he used me."

All true, but this probably wasn't the time to say so. "We don't know if Galina was his girlfriend."

She stretched her shoulders bit by bit and I could tell she still ached all over. "I hope not. I hate knowing Alex might've been involved with someone as psychotic as her."

"I hope not, too," I said. "But if it's true and he was cheating on her with you, that's one more reason to bring him back from the dead, just to smack him upside the head a few dozen times."

She sat up abruptly. Pookie jumped off the couch as the bag of ice slid down her cheek. "Oh, my God, Brooklyn. What if she was his sister?"

I reached over and grabbed the bag. "Put your head back." I smoothed her hair away from her face, then repositioned the bag and rubbed her arms until the tension loosened in her shoulders. "Look," I said, "we'll just have to wait and find out what the police say about her."

"All right," she muttered. "Where's Pookie?"

At the sound of her name, the cat jumped up on the couch and kneaded her claws in the thick material. Robin pulled the cat close and Pookie went boneless in her arms, then curled up on her lap and purred loudly. I tried to stifle my hurt feelings, but the fact was, she rarely did that for me. Pookie, I mean. She didn't pay much attention to me at all.

I sighed. "Until we have more information, you should just close your eyes and try to relax. Don't think about Galina anymore."

"Okay."

I was glad she couldn't see me cringing at the idea that Galina might've been Alex's sister. I really didn't want to feel sorry for that vicious woman. But I had to admit that if someone had killed my brother, I could picture myself doing exactly what Galina had done, namely, tracking down the person I thought was responsible and smashing her face in.

After munching her bagel and cream cheese, Robin took a nap with Pookie, and Derek went off to work. I decided to take an hour or two and drive over to the Covington Library to show the Kama Sutra to Ian McCullough. As president and head curator of the highly respected Covington, Ian would be able to help me appraise the book and might even want to buy it for the library, if Shiva's friend Rajiv were planning to sell it.

Ian was also in a position to throw bookbinding work my way, so it was always a good idea to keep in touch. Besides, I'd known him forever. He was my brother Austin's college roommate as well as my ex-fiancé. That hadn't worked out, obviously, but we were still great friends.

I bypassed the ubiquitous morning traffic hassles by skirting the Civic Center and zigzagging my way through SoMa over to Divisadero. From there, it was straight on up to Pacific Heights. On the way, I called Ian's secretary on my cell to make sure he was in and available. Should've thought of that first, but I was a little distracted lately. Luckily, he had no meetings and planned to be in the office all day.

My luck held out as I snagged a parking space on the street. I took in the graceful Italianate building with its famously lush gardens and walked up the wide central marble stairway. The stately iron doors were open, and I entered the hushed foyer, then walked into the grand hall, a massive room three stories high that held many of the most sacred and rarest of all the books of the world.

I'd been coming to the Covington since my early teens and had never grown tired of it. I loved this place. It defined me.

I edged my way past the exhibits because

I didn't have time to peruse anything today and didn't want to be tempted. But I promised myself I would come back very soon. I'd missed the Covington and its magnificent collections.

Minutes later, I was knocking on Ian's door. His secretary gestured for me to go right in, so I cracked the door open.

"Knock, knock," I said, peeking inside.

"Brooklyn!" he cried. "Come in."

"Sure you're not busy?"

"Not when it's you." He pushed back from his desk and strolled across the wide, stylishly appointed space with open arms. After a rousing hug, he led me over to one of the elegant wing-back chairs in front of his mahogany desk. "Sit. What's going on? What a treat. Do you want to have lunch?"

"I can't stay for lunch, but thanks. I just wanted to say hello and see how you're doing. How's Jake?"

"I'm fine, he's fine, and we're fine. So what's in the bag?"

I laughed. "Okay, enough niceties. I wanted to show you a book I'm working on."

"Let's see it," he said, leaning his hip against the edge of his desk.

I looked around the room. "Let's use your conference table."

"Perfect." He waved his hand for me to precede him to the dark wood table set along a wall of windows that presented an incomparable view of the Golden Gate Bridge and Marin County beyond the blue waters of the bay.

I carried the book across the room and placed it on the table's smooth surface. "Check it out."

"Wow," he said, sitting down and running his hand along the joint of the front cover. "Awesome."

"Is that your professional opinion?" I asked, teasing him.

He opened the book and studied the frontispiece. "No. Professionally, I would say this book totally rocks."

I laughed again. We were both such book geeks, it was scary. This was another reason marriage to Ian had been such an absurd idea. I mean, other than the fact that he was gay, our temperament and our likes and dislikes were so identical, we would've bored each other to death.

I watched his examination of the Kama Sutra. It was fun to listen to his oohs and ahhs, along with the occasional moan or gasp.

While he enjoyed himself, I took a moment to glance around and check out his office, and noticed a new painting on the wall behind his desk. I knew for a fact that the painting hid a wall safe, so size mattered. Even though this painting wasn't particularly large, maybe four or five feet in both directions, it was impressive. It was modern and stark, yet intriguing in its simplicity, showing a woman wearing a navy sweater and skirt, sitting in a red chair, drinking coffee. On the wall behind her was a window. Splashes of white, black, and blue filled the background.

"You have a new painting," I remarked.

He dragged his attention away from the book and followed my gaze. "My Diebenkorn lady. Do you like her?"

"A lot, and I'm not even sure why, because it's not really my style. But I'm also jealous that you can snap your fingers and get a fabulous work of art installed in your office."

"One of the many perks." He returned his attention to the Kama Sutra, turning pages, studying the endpapers, the inner joints and spine. Finally he looked up at me. "You shouldn't be jealous of me when you get to work with something like this every day."

"It really is amazing, isn't it?"

"Yeah. I'd love to display it. Is it for sale or available for loan?"

"I don't know, but I could find out." I explained the situation. My work would take a few weeks; then I would be glad to contact Rajiv and find out his plans for the book.

"Great," Ian said. "Let me know, because this would be an excellent addition to our exhibit of sacred texts."

"I'll definitely let you know. Oh, and this should make you laugh. Thanks to Robin, I'm now involved in a bizarre murder investigation involving a Ukrainian or Russian connection to something or other that —"

His office door swung open without warning — and the air around me chilled to freezing.

"Ian, Bill won't let me use his tools." The voice sounded like the bleating whine of a bloated sheep. "I want you to — What the hell is she doing here?"

Minka LaBoeuf.

My worst nightmare. My back stiffened, my throat tightened, and my ears plugged up. My whole body went into lockdown mode. It was the only way I could survive her repugnant presence, the only way I could deal with my intense aversion to her voice, her negativity, her existence. Her pleather wardrobe.

"What are you looking at?" she demanded

as she pushed past me and reached for the Kama Sutra. "Hey, that's French! I know French! My father's half French! Why didn't you ask me to work on this book?"

I pulled the book away firmly and glared at Ian. "You hired her again, didn't you?"

He gave me an abashed scowl. "Bill thought she could help out with the new arrivals from the Merced collection."

"Only if you want to declare the whole thing a loss," I declared, and briskly wrapped up the Kama Sutra, mainly to protect it from Minka's bad vibes.

Hadn't Ian learned that Minka was an anathema to books everywhere? And to me, too. If I'd known she was working here, I might've rethought this visit with Ian. She could ruin my day just by walking into the room. And why hadn't she knocked on Ian's door? Talk about freaking rude. Honestly, she needed to wear a bell around her neck to warn people she was coming.

"She was injured at BABA last month, so Bill took pity on her," he explained quietly.

I knew about her injury. I'd been there. Still, that was no excuse. "He should've taken more pity on the poor books."

"I know," he murmured.

"Hello, I'm standing right here," Minka griped. "I can hear what you're saying." She turned her back on me and faced Ian. "I should be working on that book, Ian. I heard her say there's a Russian connection. My grandmother was born in Estonia, so I'm practically Russian. And I saw the text. It's French and so am I."

I rolled my eyes. "You don't know what you're talking about, as usual."

Ian stood and worked up a gracious smile. "Sorry, Minka, but I'll talk to Bill in a few minutes. Why don't you use your own tools until then?"

"If I use my own tools you're going to have to pay me more."

"You're paying her?" I said, outraged.

"Shut up," Ian hissed, trying not to laugh.

Minka stomped her foot and let out a little shriek. "God! You're both a couple of superficial jerks!" And she flounced out the door.

I started to breathe again.

"Damn it, Brooklyn," he said. "Now I'm going to have to be nice to her."

"Why? She's so close to worthless it's ridiculous."

"Exactly. She's cheap. That's her best quality." He put his hands on his hips. "Do you want to come in and do the work instead?"

"Cleaning books? Are you kidding? No way."

"You superficial jerk," he grumbled.

"Hey, you're one, too."

He laughed out loud. "Can't you just see that on a T-shirt?"

Twenty minutes later, I walked to my car. I felt a sudden chill, and that was when I noticed Minka standing across the street, glaring at me. She held up two fingers, pointed them at her eyes, then pointed them at me, as if to let me know she would be watching me. It gave me the spookiest feeling and reminded me that she was more dangerous than she looked — although she looked pretty lethal. Those fake-leather plastic pants she wore could kill anyone.

I checked my tires before I got into my car. It wouldn't have been the first time she'd slashed my tires, even though I was never able to prove it was her dirty work. As I drove away, it hit me. Now I remembered who the vicious Galina reminded me of. Minka LaBoeuf.

"That was my mom," I announced to Robin later that afternoon after hanging up the kitchen telephone. "She insists that I take you up to stay at her place for a few days."

Robin wandered over and sat on a barstool. The look she flashed me was skeptical, to say the least. "I'm supposed to believe your mom came up with that idea all by herself?"

"Why not? You know she loves you." I smiled brightly as I continued chopping garlic for a steak marinade recipe I'd stolen from my dad. "Okay, fine. I might've suggested that you needed a quiet place to rest and recuperate. Preferably outside of the city. After that, it was all her idea."

Robin groaned. "I don't want to burden your poor mom with my problems."

"My *poor mom?* You're kidding, right? She thrives on this kind of stuff. She did such a great job nursing Gabriel back to health that he still shows up for lunch and dinner almost every day."

"She must love that."

"You know it." Scooping up the garlic bits, I tossed them with grated ginger into a heavy-duty plastic bag that held three rib eyes. After pouring healthy doses of olive oil and organic tamari into the bag, I zipped it closed, mushed everything around, and placed it in the fridge to do its thing.

Robin closed her eyes and breathed in the pungent fragrances. "That smells so good."

"You can't go wrong with garlic and ginger."

"You've been cooking a lot. You don't have to, you know. We could do takeout."

"It's nice to have people to cook for." I met her gaze. "And Mom feels the same way. She'd love to have you stay there. It's just her and Dad in that huge house."

"I'm not really good company right now, Brooklyn. In this mood I could even depress your mom."

I shook my head. "Impossible. You know she's itching to slather her latest concoctions all over your face. Probably whipping them up right now."

She winced and lifted one hand to her face. "That's what I'm afraid of."

"Can't blame you for that." I found the bag of lettuce in the fridge and emptied it into the salad bowl, then grabbed a tomato from the vegetable basket. "She said she's been practicing enchantment spells and wants to try them out on you."

Robin's good eye widened. "Oh, God."

"You know she chanted away my sister Savannah's acne. Just think what she can do for your lovely bruises."

"I do long to have skin as clear as your sister's."

I chuckled as I chopped the tomato. "Dad

says she did a rain dance the other day."

"Did it rain?"

"Of course." I sifted through the vegetable bin and pulled out half a cucumber. Before chopping it, I pulled three glasses from the cupboard. "I thought we'd have sparkling water tonight instead of wine. Okay?"

"Good idea," she said. "I already have a headache, so alcohol would only make it worse." Leaning forward, she rested her elbows on the bar's smooth wood surface. "I really hate this. I hate being dependent on you. Or your mom, or Derek, or anybody."

"I know, but you need to get over that." I walked around the bar and sat on the stool next to her. "Look, you were just brutally attacked by some nut job with a stellar right hook. The fact is, you may still be in danger."

"I doubt it." Her lips tightened. "What the hell did I do to piss off that bitch?"

"You didn't do anything." I grabbed hold of her hand. "She's just nuts. But look, they could release her from jail at any time, and even if they don't, she might have cohorts watching the place. Remember the black Town Car?"

"I'd forgotten about it." She grimaced. "Thanks for replanting that scary seed."

"I'm sorry. But that's why it can't hurt to leave the city for a few days. At least while you're in Dharma, you can get out of the house, take walks, enjoy nature. If you stay here, there's no way I'll let you leave the confines of these four walls."

Her shoulders slumped as she accepted the reality of her situation. "Fine, I'll go to Dharma. But I'll drive myself."

"Not a good idea."

"I don't want to be there without my car."

"I know, and I have the perfect solution."

"Why am I not surprised that you've already got this whole thing planned out?"

"Because I'm a genius. We all recognize that, right?"

She laughed. "Okay, genius. What's the plan?"

"I drive your car and Derek will follow us there."

"He won't want to do that. He'd rather drive up there with you."

"He's already offered to follow us. I asked him this morning." I patted her hand and stood. "Besides, it's only an hour's drive. We can survive without breathing each other's air for sixty minutes."

She sat back and considered the plan. "Okay, I guess it's a good idea. Except for the part where you drive my car." Robin owned a vintage Porsche Speedster. She never allowed anyone but herself to drive it.

I rubbed my hands together. "See, that's the best part of the plan."

"No way."

"No offense, but you're a little too jumpy to drive. And there's the small detail of your eye being swollen shut. That's going to make it hard to focus on the road."

She harrumphed and flounced for a minute, then gave me a grudging nod. "Fine."

"Great." I moved back into the kitchen to start on the cucumber. "It's settled."

The doorbell rang and Robin flinched. "Who's that?"

"I don't know." I headed for the front. "Probably Vinnie or Suzie."

She followed me into the workshop. "Look through the peephole first."

"I will."

She moved to my desk and grabbed the phone. "I'm ready to dial nine-one-one."

"Stop worrying. We would've heard the elevator if it was someone from outside the building." I stared through the peephole but didn't see anyone. That was weird. Maybe they took off.

"Who's there?" she whispered.

"I don't know, but I'm going to find out."

I swung the door open.

Robin let out a tiny shriek and brandished the phone receiver above her head.

Six-year-old Tyler blinked in surprise. "Miss Brooklyn, I brought you my book."

"Hi, Tyler. Please come in." With a smile, I waved him inside. "Do you remember my friend Robin?"

"Hello," he said, and nodded solemnly. "Did you hurt yourself?"

Robin's hand went to her cheek as she remembered her swollen face. "Um, yes, I did."

He continued to stare at her. "Are you playing a telephone game?"

"A telephone — Oh." She waved the receiver, then placed it in its cradle. "Yes. But we're finished playing."

"Tyler, does your mother know you're here?" I asked.

He nodded again. "She'll be here in a minute, but I didn't want to wait." He thrust the book at me. "See? Because the pages are falling out now."

There was another knock at the door. Robin's shoulders jerked.

"Easy," I whispered.

"You know what?" Robin said, shaking her head. "I'll be in the other room."

"Do you want me to fix another ice pack

for you?"

"I can do it."

I let her go, then opened the door for Tyler's mom. After a brief tour of my workshop, Lisa was satisfied that I knew what I was doing when it came to books.

"Can you fix it right now?" Tyler asked.

"It's going to take me a few days, because I want to do the best job possible for you. Can you wait until Saturday to get it back?"

He looked up at his mother with a serious expression on his face. "What day is today?"

"Today is Wednesday," she told him.

He stared at his hand and counted the days off on his fingers. "Wednesday, Thursday, Friday, Saturday." He gazed at me. "That's four days."

"That's right."

"Okay."

"Okay."

"How much do I have to pay you?" Tyler asked.

I smiled at Lisa, then looked at Tyler. I picked up the book and weighed it in my hands, thought for a moment. Then I knelt down to talk on his level. "I'll have to take the book apart here, glue new endpapers here, then sew these pages together. See?"

"Uh-huh."

"So I'm going to have to charge you . . .

five dollars."

He nodded once, firmly. "You have a deal."

We shook hands, and Lisa smiled proudly. Leaning close, she confided, "I told him it might cost one hundred dollars, so now he thinks he's a smart negotiator."

With a quick grin for Tyler, I said, "I was thinking of charging you fifty dollars."

He shook his head. "It's too late to change your price. We shook hands and everything."

Giving Lisa and Tyler the quick tour of my workshop had made me anxious to get back to work on the Kama Sutra. But that work would have to wait until Robin was out of the city and safely delivered into my mother's care.

So first thing the next morning, I called Inspector Lee to make sure it was acceptable for Robin to go to Sonoma. She gave her approval, of course, since it was pretty obvious from Galina's attack that Robin had become a target. I gave Lee my mother's phone number, just in case.

After I packed Robin's three sweat suits, various accessories, and meager supply of toiletries, the three of us hit the highway.

Driving Robin's vintage Porsche Speedster was a total blast for me, though not so much for Robin. I could actually hear her teeth grinding as I revved the engine on the straightaway out on Highway 37. I might've ground the gears once or twice, but it wasn't my fault. The car was old. Yes, it was a classic, but let's face it: The old thing wasn't as fluid as it once might've been. But Robin acted as if I'd taken an ax to the engine just by shifting gears. I knew she was a little sensitive, so I didn't take her swearing and cringing personally.

At one point along the highway, Derek flew by in his Bentley Continental GT. He passed on Robin's side and she gazed over at him. When I glanced over, I saw Derek laughing uproariously. Was Robin making a face? Was I being mocked? I ignored them both. This was the sort of thing a true friend like myself had to endure once in a while.

An hour later we parked in my parents' driveway, and I couldn't stop smiling as Mom and Dad came out to greet us.

Mom wore a long-sleeved, full-length rainbow tie-dyed dress that floated and swung around her boots as she jogged down the stairs of the front porch. She'd dyed and sewn the dress herself from thick cotton knit that accentuated her tall, still-youthful figure.

Dad was dressed in the familiar faded

Levi's he'd always worn whenever he worked with the grapes in the fields. Today he wore another Mom original, a sage-colored tie-dyed henley shirt that looked almost new.

They were still in love, still adorable, and if you squinted just a little, you could picture them as two young Grateful Dead fans who first met at a Dead concert in Ventura County almost forty years ago.

After many hugs and outraged cries over Robin's injuries, Mom touched Robin's forehead, her third eye, where higher consciousness was centered, and chanted quietly, *"Om shanti . . . shanti . . . shanti."*

My mother used this chant whenever anyone around her was distressed. *Shanti* is the Sanskrit word for "peace." Repeating the word three times brought peace and protection from the three disturbances. The first of these disturbances was said to come from God, things like floods and earthquakes and hurricanes. The next came from the world around us, such as noisy neighbors, barking dogs, telephones ringing incessantly. The third came from within and was the one disturbance we could actually control. This included the negative emotions we tended to bring upon ourselves, such as jealousy, fear, anger, and sorrow.

All the pent-up tension seemed to melt from Robin's shoulders and she smiled. "Thanks, Becky. I'm so glad I'm here."

"Me, too, sweetie," Mom said. She wrapped her arm about Robin, Dad grabbed her small suitcase, and Derek and I followed them into the sprawling ranch house in which I'd grown up.

"I've made sandwiches and potato salad for lunch," Mom said, then turned to Derek. "You'll stay for the day, won't you?"

Clearly, Derek was the authority as far as Mom was concerned. She was probably right to consult him instead of me. I would've been happy spending a night or two, but Derek had an actual office to run back in the city.

Dad poured everyone a glass of the new sparkling wine he'd been experimenting with at the winery. Robin took one sip, then set her glass down. I could tell she was still in pain and was glad to see Mom come over and rub Robin's shoulders. She relaxed instantly.

We ate lunch under a huge oak tree on my parents' terraced patio overlooking the vineyards Dharma was famous for. Off to the left of the house and rambling up the hill was the apple orchard Mom had started the first year we moved into the house. In honor of Robin's arrival, Mom had made her fabulous Crazy Delicious Apple Crisp for dessert.

Many Thanksgiving moons ago, when, as usual, I'd insisted on pumpkin pie after the huge meal, Mom also brought out her fledgling attempt at apple crisp. Not impressed with the presentation at first — it wasn't pumpkin pie, after all, and I was so devoted to pumpkin pie that my family and friends had taken to calling me Punkin — I forced myself to take one small taste. I didn't want to hurt Mom's feelings, after all. Then I took another bite. Then another. In the end, I declared it my new most favorite dessert ever. Especially the way Mom made it, with spicy, lightly sweetened apples and the crunchiest, most crumbly, crispy layers of yumminess on top. Her secret ingredient was a luscious caramel sauce she added at the end. And ice cream on the side of the dish didn't hurt, either.

Whenever I visited my parents now, I always went home with a bag of apples. Everyone in town did. Mom was known as the Apple Lady at the local grammar school. I guess that was better than being known as the Murder Scene Queen. Just saying.

After lunch, Mom helped Robin move to the chaise longue and tucked a blanket around her. With great care, she daubed some cream on Robin's swollen face and set a glass of bright green parsley water on the nearby table for her to drink.

I hoped Robin knew better than to touch that stuff. I still had nightmares about parsley juice, Mom's cure-all for most ailments.

Then Mom turned to another of her cure-alls. She pulled a disposable lighter from her pocket, lit a small bundle of sage incense, and blew on it until it was smoky, filling the air with its pungent aroma.

"I'll now recite an original healing love chant," she announced. She bowed to Robin, then bowed to the four directions and hummed loudly. Waving her arms and shaking the bundle of smoking sage above Robin's head, she began her chant.

Father Sun, Sister Moon,
Sweep out darkness, sweep out doom.
Mother Earth and all the clouds,
Dance the dance and sing out loud.
Free our Robin from this pain,
Take the hurt but leave the flame.
The flame of passion burns anew
And love is found when hearts are true.
Your eyes will meet, your hands will
touch,

You'll get the one you want so much.
You'll do the funky Twist and Shout
That's what I'm-a talkin' 'bout!
Everybody sing! Hey, nonny, nonny,
  nonny!
Hey, hey, hey!

I started to applaud but Mom stopped me. "Not yet, there's more." Then she swayed and hummed and continued in an even deeper yet louder tone.

Sacred stones, circle of magic,
Here is the Dance, here is desire.
Circle of magic, do your thing,
Dance of desire, light my fire!
Everybody sing! Hey, nonny, nonny,
  nonny!
Hey, hey, hey!

There was a moment of silence, followed by a burst of applause.

"Wow, Mom, that was really something," I said.

"Beautiful, honey," Dad said, his eyes moist with emotion. "I think that was your best one yet."

"I feel the fire," Robin said, and I didn't dare meet her gaze.

Mom laughed breathlessly. "That was

crazy!" Her cheeks were flushed pink as she fell back into her chair. "Now, Robin, that spell was created especially for you. It's meant to cleanse your aura, lift your spirit, and allow your heart to find joy again."

"Sounds like you threw in a little dose of the wild thing, too," Dad said, dancing in his chair as he wiggled his eyebrows.

"Oh, jeez," I muttered.

"I do what I can," Mom said modestly. She bounced up and kissed Robin's cheek. "We'll take good care of you here, sweetie."

"Thank you, Becky," Robin whispered.

Derek squeezed my hand as he said to Mom, "It was lovely, Rebecca."

"Why, thank you, Derek," she said, beaming. "I've been trying out a few new chants. I don't know if you could tell, but I improvised some of the words."

I raised my hand. "I could tell."

"I'm feeling better already," Robin said, nodding in encouragement. She coughed as Mom blew more sage smoke over her head.

Then Mom stopped abruptly and listened to something only she could hear. "I believe it's working."

At that moment, the sliding glass door opened and my brother Austin walked out to the patio. He'd come straight from the vineyards and was still wearing his dusty cowboy hat, faded jeans, scruffy boots, and a white T-shirt covered in dirt.

Sometimes I forgot how beautiful he was. His skin was tanned from the sun and his dark blond hair was streaked with gold.

Austin had traveled all over the world but had finally returned to Dharma a few years ago to live and work the land with his family and friends in the commune. He wasn't some kind of weirdo hippie freak, I swear. On the contrary, he loved football and beer and cars and girls. He liked to shoot and hunt and fish. He also loved good books and fine wine. And he loved this place, the hills, the trees, the grapes, the earth. He was basically an all-American guy, if you didn't count the fact that he was raised in a commune with two Deadheads for parents. You know, the kind of parents who would name their firstborn son after the Texas town in which little Austin was conceived after a wild night watching the Grateful Dead perform with Willie Nelson and Bob Dylan. Apparently it had been quite a show.

I gave a little cry of joy, jumped up from the table, and ran to hug him. His blue eyes danced with pleasure when he saw me.

"Hey, farmer," I said. "Gosh, you're filthy, but it's still great to see you."

He ruffled my hair. "Hey, book girl, you

look fantastic."

I brushed some residual dirt off my sweater as Derek stood. Austin greeted him jovially as they shook hands. They'd always liked each other, which was a relief. I'd tried dating guys my brothers hated, and those relationships were always doomed from the start.

"Hello, Austin," Robin said after the greetings died down.

At the sound of her voice, he smiled at the rest of us. "There she is." Then he turned and got his first look at Robin. "Holy shit, what happened to you?"

I smacked his shoulder. "Knucklehead."

Robin tilted her head to meet my gaze. "What every girl longs to hear."

He whipped around and faced Mom. "Why didn't you tell me she was hurt?"

Mom frowned and shook her head. "Why would I tell you anything, sweetie? It's not as if you care about Robin one way or another, is it?"

"Care about —" He shook his head in disgust, then walked straight over to Robin's chaise and crouched down beside her. "Of course I care about you."

"Really? Who knew?"

He touched her chin gently with his fingers. "I hope I'm not hurting you."

She sniffed. "You're not."

Stroking her hair, he whispered, "It's really good to see you."

"It's good to see you, too, Austin."

I edged a few feet closer so I could hear everything they were saying.

Austin said, "I understand you'll be staying here for a few days."

"That's the plan."

Austin glanced over his shoulder at Mom and Dad. He was frowning. If I didn't know him better, I would've said he looked confused. But Austin was never confused. He'd always professed to know exactly what he was doing.

Returning his gaze to Robin, he murmured, "I've got to do this, babe."

"Do what?" Robin asked in a tentative voice.

"Trust me?"

She stared deep into his eyes as if mesmerized. "I guess so."

In one sweeping motion, he lifted Robin out of the chair and into his arms. "You're coming home with me."

"Put me down," Robin insisted.

Dad jumped to his feet. "Austin, no."

"Austin Wainwright," Mom declared, "you put that girl down right this minute. She's in pain and needs her rest."

He turned patiently and said, "She'll get plenty of rest, Mom. But . . ." He shook his head again, looked around as though he were seeing us all for the first time. Then he gazed at Robin. "I need her with me."

"I'm not sure that's a good idea," Mom said, clutching her hands nervously.

Robin shoved her hand against his chest. "I won't sleep with you."

"Yes, you will."

"In your dreams."

He whispered something to Robin that made her laugh — despite her best intentions, it seemed. Then Austin stalked toward the wide walkway at the side of the house and disappeared with my best friend in his arms.

Chapter 9

"I guess I don't know my own strength," Mom muttered, as she crushed the still-smoking sage into a small bowl.

"You've got strong magic in you, Becks," Dad said, and gave her a quick hug. "Especially when it comes to the wild thing."

"I'm not listening to this." I pressed my hands to my ears and stared at them in complete bewilderment. Did Mom and Dad really think it was her chanting that brought Austin here? Was that what caused him to go temporarily insane? To fall into lust? To kidnap my BFF?

I glanced at Derek, who was watching me thoughtfully. "What do you think?"

"Not to discount your mother's skills," he said, sitting back in his chair, "but I think Austin and Robin appear to be two consenting adults who've known each other a long time."

He was right, of course, but it didn't make

me feel any better. I supposed stranger things had happened up here in Dharma land. I just couldn't think of anything right off the bat. Robin and Austin had always been hot for each other, but the timing had never been right for one or the other. Now . . .

Was that what had happened? Was the timing suddenly right? Was it all about Austin and Robin? Or was Mom's power increasing? Was she starting to chant love spells that actually worked? And if it was only an enchanted love spell that got them together, wouldn't it wear off eventually? Wouldn't one of the interested parties complain that they'd been coerced into something that wasn't of their own free will?

Whoa, what was I smoking?

There was no such thing as a love spell, enchanted or otherwise. Clearly, Austin and Robin had just experienced a simultaneous moment of supreme lust. I could dig that.

My only concern now was that I didn't want Robin to get hurt again. But there was nothing I could do about it except follow Derek's lead and keep it simple and positive.

After all, Robin had looked so happy and Austin so downright determined when they left. Who was I to worry or judge or interfere? All I'd wanted to accomplish in bringing Robin to Dharma was for her to be safe, away from bad people and out of the city. I'd achieved that goal.

I turned to Dad, who still looked shell-shocked. Feeling about the same, I held out my wineglass. "More, please?"

"Good idea, Punkin," he said, and filled everyone's glasses with golden, bubbly liquid.

As we all recovered from the shock, Mom filled us in on what was happening around Dharma. We talked and laughed and enjoyed the view of the rolling green hills covered in vineyards, broken by picturesque thickets of gnarled oak trees.

Mom was particularly proud that Annie's kitchenware store, Anandalla, had been written up in several cooking magazines. Annie Karastovsky was relatively new to Dharma. She was the long-lost daughter of my former bookbinding mentor, Abraham. The whole town, and especially Mom, had adopted her as their own.

Gabriel's recuperation was another of Mom's triumphs. The formerly mysterious stranger who had saved my life in a noodle shop on Fillmore Street in the city, Gabriel was still in Dharma after almost dying last month, when he was struck in the head by a killer's bullet. That attack had led to a daring sting operation and the arrest of a murderer. Gabriel had recently moved into a bungalow a mile away from Mom and Dad. I was surprised to hear that he seemed to be enjoying the slower pace of life up here. In his spare time, he was helping out Guru Bob with his massive library project.

Guru Bob, by the way, was more properly known as Avatar Robson Benedict, the leader of the Fellowship for Spiritual Enlightenment and Higher Artistic Consciousness, the artsy Sonoma County commune my parents had joined years ago, back before the commune got rich from the grapevines they grew and the winery they built. Back before the commune property was incorporated and morphed into the charming town of Dharma. Back when we all lived in Airstream campers. Those were the good old days.

Mom regaled us with the antics of the Wiccans who lived in the next glen over and how they'd finally accepted her into their coven.

"Wait'll they hear about the power of my love spell," she said.

"Do you think they'll elect you chief witch?" I asked.

She laughed. "Oh, sweetie, you make it

sound like the PTA." But her eyes glittered with intent as she added, "No, they'll install me as grand raven mistress of the most high druidic pentangle, if they know what's good for them."

"Okay, now you're scaring me."

Finally, after securing Mom's promise to call me with any news of Austin and Robin, Derek and I took off for the city, crossing the Golden Gate Bridge just before sunset.

As we wound our way through the Presidio, then onto Lombard until we reached Van Ness, my thoughts focused on Austin and Robin again. Were their paths about to merge for real? Or was it just that Mom's ability to bust a love spell was more potent than we'd thought? Nope, I reminded myself. It wasn't a love spell. Just some heavy-duty lust. Nothing wrong with that.

"Never a dull moment with your family," Derek remarked as he parked the car in my building's garage. We laughed about the afternoon as we stepped inside the old-fashioned, industrial-size elevator and rode it all the way up until it shuddered to a halt on the top floor. The ancient elevator was one of my favorite features left over from the corset factory that had inhabited this building once upon a time.

In contrast to the clunky old elevator, the

corridors leading to the lofts were modern and elegant, with pale blue walls, contemporary white sconces, and wide sisal runners laid over the original dark wood flooring. Since mine was the top floor, there were skylights in the halls to further lighten the space.

Derek and I held hands as we walked to my door. It felt comfortable and *right* somehow to be coming home with him. But maybe that was just me, still reeling from my mother's enchantment spell.

"Thanks for taking the time to drive up there with us," I said.

"I was glad to do it. I would've hated to miss your mother's stories of Wiccans and covens. Although," he teased, "the 'hey, nonny, nonny' chant was my favorite."

I laughed as I reached into my bag for my keys. "I'll give Robin a call tomorrow and see how she's doing."

Without warning, Derek shoved me against the wall and grabbed hold of my chin to force eye contact with him.

"Stay right here," he whispered, and drew a gun from his waistband.

Wow. He had gone from indulgent lover to warrior man in a heartbeat. "What're you —"

"Do as I say."

That was when I noticed that my front door had been smashed to splinters and was dangling drunkenly from one hinge. "Oh, no."

He pressed his finger to my mouth to quiet me.

With his foot, Derek nudged open what was left of the door and proceeded to slip inside, holding his gun out in front of him. He checked one way, then the other.

His gun. Where the hell had that come from? I was pretty sure he hadn't been carrying it in Dharma, but now? Didn't matter. I was glad he had it with him.

I ventured a few steps closer and managed to catch a look at my studio. A gasp escaped from my throat. It was a shambles. Derek whipped around and dropped his hand so his gun was aimed at the floor. With his other hand, he pointed toward the hall.

"Back. Move. Now," he said with deadly emphasis.

I nodded slowly and stepped into the hall. He edged back inside to continue his search.

Normally I would've bristled at Derek's commands, but now all I could do was hold my hand over my mouth. I felt sick and scared to death. My home had been trashed. Again. The last time it happened, during the investigation into Abraham Karastovsky's death, I'd known what the intruder had been looking for. This time, I didn't have a clue.

Robin.

"Oh, God." I slid down the wall until I was sitting on the floor.

We'd gotten Robin out of the city just in time. I released the breath I'd been holding, so relieved to know my friend was miles away from here and safe.

There was no way this stupid act of vandalism was an isolated incident. It had to be connected to Alex. And Robin. And that lunatic Galina.

What the hell kind of shit storm had Robin stepped into?

And yes, my mother would have washed my mouth out with soap if she'd heard me using that language, but I didn't care right now. Whoever had killed Alex and trashed Robin's place, and then gone on to tear apart Alex's apartment, had to be the same jerk who'd just wrecked mine.

And I still had no idea what they were looking for.

Last time this happened, I'd been devastated. This time I was just plain mad as hell.

I felt useless and stupid sitting out in the hall. Derek was inside risking his life and I was twiddling my thumbs.

"Well, I can call the cops. Duh." I grabbed my cell phone and dialed 911 to report the break-in. After a few moments, the dispatcher confirmed that a patrol car was in the area and would arrive shortly. I thanked her and hung up, then punched my speed-dial code for Inspector Lee, refusing to dwell on the fact that I actually had her private number. On speed dial.

Derek walked out of my place and returned the gun to his waistband. "There's no one inside. Whoever did this is long gone. Are you calling the police?"

"They're on their way," I said, pushing myself up to a standing position. "Now I'm waiting for Inspector Lee to answer."

"Good." He peered up and down the hall, his eyes shadowed and wary. He looked every inch the tall, dark, and dangerous security expert I knew him to be.

"Derek, where did that gun come from? I didn't even see you —"

"Wait. Now, what's this?" he said.

I let out a terrifying scream as something wrapped itself around my legs. The cell phone flew out of my hand. Derek grabbed it, put it to his ear, and walked away, shaking his head — in amusement, it appeared.

I looked down. "Tyler! Jeez, you scared the . . . Never mind. Are you all right?" He looked a little dazed as I knelt down and hugged him tightly, then held him at arm's length to check that he wasn't injured.

"The bad man broke your door," he said in a tense whisper.

"What bad man, honey?"

"Did you catch him?" he demanded. "Did he take my book?"

"No, no," I said. "I'm sure your book is fine."

"But I saw him. He was a mean giant and he threw your stuff around. Did he break my book?"

I would decipher his ramblings later. Right now, only one thing concerned me. "Tyler, where were you when you saw the bad man?"

His smile was cunning. "I was hiding."

"Hiding where?"

He pointed to the stairwell door a few yards down the hall. The stairs led down to the ground floor. "In there."

"Did the man see you?"

"No," he said patiently. "I was hiding, but I could see through the crack."

"Right. Did you see what he looked like?"

"He was big!" To demonstrate, he stretched his arms out as far as they would go. "And he was ugly and mean. He kicked your door. He kicked and kicked and didn't stop until he got inside. Did he take my book?"

The thought of the big man discovering Tyler made me dizzy and sick.

"Did he? Miss Brooklyn?"

I shook myself back to the moment. "What, honey?"

"My book," Tyler said, tilting his head to stare at me as though I'd gone off my rocker. "You were supposed to fix it."

"Right. Your . . . book . . . Oh, shit, my book." The Kama Sutra! I headed for my studio.

"That's a bad word," Tyler said, folding his arms across his chest.

I turned. "Tyler, I want you to go home right now."

His lower lip wobbled. "But I want my book."

"I'll get it in a minute."

"I want it now."

Oh, for God's sake. Was he going to cry? I would start crying, too, and then we'd all be a mess. There was a reason I didn't have kids. I took a calming breath. "I'll make sure it's okay, honey. I know the bad man didn't take it."

He looked doubtful, but then he nodded, turned, and walked to his front door. Where he stopped and waited, watching me.

And that was when two things hit me. First, where were his parents? Why hadn't they heard someone smashing my door down?

Second, and probably more important, this little six-year-old was the only witness to the break-in. That wasn't good. But on the positive side, Tyler might be able to identify the man who killed Alex — if it was the same person.

The police would want to talk to Tyler, might even bring a sketch artist over to get a detailed description. His parents were not going to be happy about this. I hated to be the ones to tell them, but I looked around and didn't see anyone else stepping forward to do the job.

"Wait, Tyler. I'll go with you."

I figured the Kama Sutra was either still where I'd hidden it or it was gone. I would find out soon enough. Right this minute, Tyler was the priority. I ran back to Derek, who was still on the phone with Inspector Lee, quickly explained the situation, then jogged back to face the wrath of Tyler's parents.

The good news was, the Kama Sutra was right where I'd left it, in the safe box under the floor of my hall closet.

The bad news was, Tyler was grounded for life.

To say that his parents were upset with him for hiding in the stairwell was putting it nicely. Now he was the only witness to a crime and could possibly identify a murderer.

Tyler's father had been in his office in the back of their apartment on a conference call. His mom had been giving her two little girls a bath, during which they'd screamed and laughed nonstop. Neither parent had heard the door-bashing racket going on in the hall.

I tried to calm them both down, but I wasn't doing a very good job. Inspector Lee showed up shortly after that and I was off the hook. She took young Tyler under her wing, impressing me with her charm when it came to kids as well as with her ability to deal with Mr. and Mrs. Chung respectfully and authoritatively. Maybe it was due to our own casual, bantering relationship style, but I'd never realized that Inspector Lee could communicate so intelligently or maturely on almost any topic. My mistake.

In this case, Lee had one big point in her favor. Despite growing up in San Francisco's Chinatown, where many of the immigrants spoke only Cantonese, Lee also spoke Mandarin, thanks to one of her aunts. Henry Chung, Tyler's father, spoke Mandarin, too. He also spoke perfect English, but Mr. Chung, very angry that his little boy had been drawn into the investigation, had drawn some sort of psychological line in the sand and decided that he would speak to the police only in Mandarin. It was satisfying to see the shock of surprise in his eyes when Inspector Lee answered him in perfect Mandarin.

The fear that Tyler had been traumatized for life faded as Mr. Chung watched his little boy jump up and down at the chance to work with the police artist. Tyler was also anxious to reenact the scene for the police, so both parents stood in the hall, each holding the hand of one of their little girls, as Inspector Lee led Tyler over to the doorway leading to the stairs.

Before she had him scoot behind the door, Inspector Lee asked, "Do you know how to tell time, Tyler?"

"Yes, I have a watch." He thrust his arm out for her to see his red plastic wristwatch.

"Can you tell me how long you think the man stayed here breaking the door down?"

Tyler frowned. "Not very long."

"Five minutes?"

"Oh, no. Maybe . . . ten minutes?"

Lee glanced at her partner and Jaglom shrugged. Who knew what ten minutes translated to in little-boy time? Lee thought of another question. "Did you see the man go inside?"

"Yes," he said spiritedly, excited to know the right answer. "He was inside; then the elevator made that loud noise and the man ran out of there."

"How did he leave the building?"

"Down these stairs." Tyler pointed down the stairs he was on.

His father grimaced at the realization that the man had been within inches of his son.

"Now, Tyler," Lee said, pointing at Derek, "do you think the bad man was taller than our friend Derek?"

The stairwell door was partially open, and Tyler stared at Derek, who stood in front of my doorway pretending to kick it. His studious gaze moved from Derek's feet up to his face. "I think so. Bad man was fatter. But his hair was that color." He pointed at Derek.

"So he had dark hair?"

"Yes."

"Did you see his face?"

"Yes."

"Can you describe it?"

Tyler held his breath and blew out his cheeks.

Lee glanced at Jaglom, who was taking notes, then back at the boy. "Okay, you've made it pretty clear he was heavyset."

"Fat," Tyler said firmly. "And ugly."

"Okay, thank you, Tyler," Lee said with a tight smile, then checked her watch. "Now I think it's way past your bedtime, isn't it?"

"That's okay," he said, folding his arms across his chest. "I can keep working."

Lee chuckled as she walked with him over to his mom and dad. "He did a great job. I'll bring the artist by your place tomorrow morning."

His parents nodded.

Lee looked down at Tyler. "And if I have more questions for you, I'll ask them at that time, okay?"

Tyler glanced up at his parents. "Okay?"

"Yes, it's okay," Lisa said, resigned to the fact that, rather than being distressed, Tyler was having the time of his life.

Lee thanked them all; then Mr. Chung hefted Tyler up in his arms and they returned to their home down the hall.

"Bet they're happy they moved in here," I muttered.

"I'm not saying a word," Lee said, holding up both hands.

"I appreciate that."

One of the crime scene guys walked out my door and I was reminded that my place was a complete mess. I was too tired to fume over the injustice of it all.

"I don't suppose you'll have Tyler look through mug shots," I said.

Lee shook her head. "And give him nightmares for a year? Probably not."

"I know. But I hate that we have only Tyler's word that the guy who broke in was fat and ugly."

Lee closed her notepad. "The way I see it, the guy could look like Keanu Reeves and Tyler would call him ugly because he was scared of him."

I gave her a reluctant nod. "That's probably true."

"Huh," Lee said, clearly thinking about it. "Actually, I wouldn't mind finding Keanu Reeves breaking down my door."

It was well after midnight when the police hammered a beat-up slab of plywood over my door and draped it in yellow crime scene tape. Suzie had taken Pookie home for one night, so Derek and I left to spend the night in his suite at the Ritz-Carlton. I made sure Tyler's book was safe on the shelf, but I wrapped up the Kama Sutra and packed it in my overnight bag. I wasn't willing to risk it behind a flimsy wall of plywood.

Walking through Derek's sumptuous hotel suite, I was reminded of the incriminating evidence we'd found here during the last murder investigation. Would all our best memories revolve around murder? Or I supposed I could dwell instead on the fact that Derek still kept this suite available to use while he transitioned his business from London to San Francisco. Was this his escape hatch for when he grew tired of our relationship?

As I hung up my clothes in his closet, I resolved to ignore those neurotic thoughts and dwell instead on the fact that he chose to stay with me at my house.

But I knew one of his assistants was working with a local real estate broker to find a suitable home for him in the city. Eventually, when he found the perfect residence, he would move out of my place and into his own. And that was probably for the best. Frankly, I was surprised we were still enjoying each other's company after a full month of living together. It couldn't last much longer, could it? We were so different from each other. He was traditional upper-crust English; I was laid-back California commune. He was dangerous, secretive, and carried a gun. I was peace, love, and free speech. We were completely wrong for each other, and yet we had fun. We loved to eat good food and drink good wine and we argued and laughed and fought — and made up, of course. He liked my family. He laughed at my jokes. But beyond the fun stuff, Derek had more integrity than anyone I knew, and that coincided with my desire for justice and good to prevail. I thought that was a pretty important quality in a guy. And I couldn't ignore the fact that he was so gorgeous. I wasn't sure if it was his face or his body or his accent that made him so hot, but . . .

"I know it's late, but I've ordered hamburgers from room service," he said, coming up behind me and slipping his arms around my waist.

"With French fries?" I asked.

He kissed my neck. "Of course, darling."

"Sweet." Resting my head against his bare skin, I savored the solid, muscular feel of his chest.

Okay, in this moment, it was definitely his body. Call me shallow. The guy was hotness personified.

The following morning, Derek dropped me off at my place and I began cleaning up the mess. I arranged to meet the guy from the door company and a locksmith who'd been recommended by our homeowners association.

Looking at all the disorder in the light of day, I could see that there wasn't that much actual destruction. Drawers had been pulled out of my desk and the contents dumped on the floor; materials and supplies had been swept off the countertops. There were a few broken jars, but for the most part, everything could be straightened up easily.

Much worse would be the job of cleaning fingerprint dust off every flat surface in my house. I'd found out the hard way the last time my place was broken into that this stuff was a pain in the butt to clean up. The powder was made of graphite and seemed lighter than actual dust. The minute the crime guys fluttered those dainty little dusters over anything, particles flew all over. I learned that even water wouldn't soak up those darn particles, so it was useless using a sponge to clean things up. The black powder had settled into one of my small area rugs and some cloths I used for cleaning books, and they had to be replaced.

One of the previous crime scene guys had recommended a product, and I was relieved to find a small amount left under my sink.

It was a thick gel that broke down the bonds between the graphite ions. Don't ask me how. That bit of information exhausted my vast knowledge of the science of bonding.

Three hours later, my studio was back to normal and I had a new door with a stronger dead bolt. The rest of the house took only another hour or so to straighten up, because the intruder hadn't done as much damage there. Based on little Tyler's story, Inspector Lee theorized that the rest of the house was barely touched because the guy had run out of time.

Maybe, as Tyler had suggested, he'd heard the elevator stirring to life and had rushed out while he could. That was one more reason I loved that old creaky elevator. You always knew when someone was coming home.

As if on cue, I could feel the light vibration that signaled the elevator was being summoned. Two minutes later, Derek walked in. After changing from suit and tie to jeans and a light sweater, he joined me in the kitchen, where he whipped up a pitcher of martinis.

"This is a treat," I said, sipping my drink. "Do you want to listen to music while we cook?"

"No, I had something else in mind for us

to do before dinner."

I smiled, watching him as he took a quick first sip of his drink, then set his glass down. Extracting a notepad and two pens from the telephone drawer, he led me over to the dining room table and gestured for me to sit.

Okay, this was not what I thought he meant.

As Derek took the chair on the other side of the table facing me, he ripped off a few pieces of paper and handed them to me with a pen.

"What are we doing?" I asked.

His lips twisted into a wry grin. "We're going to play your favorite game."

Puzzled, I shook my head. "I'm no longer sure what you think that might be."

"We'll call it Find the Killer," he said, setting the pad down and clicking the top of the pen. "You go first. Tell me everything you know about the night Robin first met Alex."

CHAPTER 10

"You know I love to play the Killer game," I began, taking a moment to register just how much my life had changed in the last few months. Brooklyn Wainwright, bookbinder-cum–murder solver extraordinaire. "But do you really think it matters how she met him?"

"I'm beginning to think it matters very much."

"She told us what happened that night."

"But we're missing something. I want to start at the beginning and make notes."

"Good idea." I doodled ever-expanding circles on my paper. "But the way I see it, Alex is — or *was* — a key player, but Robin was just an innocent bystander. So why does it matter how they met?"

"Why was he killed inside her home?"

"Because someone was after him and followed them to her place, and found a way inside and . . . Heck, I don't know. It was convenient?" But it wasn't, of course. And there was the whole drugging-of-Robin issue. Nothing made sense about this.

"I've come to the conclusion," Derek said, "that Robin is connected to the mystery behind Alex's death."

I thought about it and sat forward with my theory. "Maybe Alex stole something from someone else and Robin got in the way."

Derek leaned in. "Did Alex steal it? Or did Robin steal it?"

Frowning, I inched back. "Robin didn't steal anything. If Robin had stolen something, wouldn't the killer have killed *her* instead of Alex?"

"Very good point," Derek said, encouraging me along. "So you think Alex stole something? Maybe he stole it from Robin."

"Robin doesn't have anything worth stealing," I argued. "And who knows if Alex stole anything or not? None of it makes sense."

"You're right," he said firmly. "None of it makes sense until we fill in the blanks."

"How do we do that?" I sipped my drink and stared at him. "Wait. You have information."

"I do."

"Well, spill it."

With a smile, Derek pulled out his smart

phone and slid his finger across the surface until he found what he was looking for. He showed me a picture of a tiny metal box held in someone's hand.

"What is that?"

"It's a photograph of a mini flash drive. The smallest one they make, currently. It plugs into a plastic port and fits into the USB slot of any computer. It's an effective and innocuous way to transport information from one computer to another."

"Okay. Is that what Alex stole?"

"We think that was his intention." Derek leaned forward again and spoke softly. "What we know for sure is that a highly placed Ukrainian operative working in deep cover in Toronto was activated recently."

"Activated?"

"Yes," he said, making me nervous as he watched my reactions closely. "He was sent to San Francisco to retrieve an item of crucial importance to the government."

"The Ukrainian government?"

"Yes."

"I'm assuming that you got this information from your people at Interpol?"

He said nothing, just continued to look at me with the barest hint of a smile. I suppose he thought it best not to say out loud exactly where he'd obtained this information, but Interpol was a safe bet. Still, a part of me was irked. Was he trying to keep me safe from culpability? Or did he simply not trust me? Or did he not trust Robin? Wait. Did he think my house was bugged? Okay, that was ridiculous. I took a deep breath and tried to reel in my overactive imagination.

"So I'll assume the highly placed guy is Alex, right?"

"Yes."

"And the crucial item?" I waved my hand at his phone and the picture of the flash drive.

"Exactly," he said, holding the phone up again to show the photo. "A flash drive. A tiny one." He put the phone down and held up his thumb and forefinger to indicate how small the metal flash drive was. "This big."

"Tiny. I get it." What I was really getting was a bad feeling in my stomach. "And who was he retrieving it from?"

"A soft target."

"Okay." Apparently, we were playing Twenty Questions. That was fine; I liked to play games. "What's a soft target?"

"Robin is a soft target."

I sat back in my chair and stared at him. I wasn't so crazy about this game anymore. "You know that makes no sense, right? But let's continue for the sake of argument. How long ago was this guy sent from Toronto?"

"Six days ago."

With a heavy sigh, I got up and pulled the small calendar from the wall above the kitchen telephone and counted off the days. "So he came to San Francisco almost a week ago and found the flash drive or whatever he was looking for. Then he just happened to stop at Kasa for dinner and met Robin there." I pointed at last Thursday, the night Robin returned from India.

"Did he find the flash drive, *then* meet Robin?" Derek asked. "Or did he meet Robin in order to *find* the flash drive?"

"Are you trying to make me mad?"

"No, darling," he said in a soothing voice, and reached out to touch my hand. "I'm trying to find a killer."

I clutched his hand in mine. He was being objective and I was getting emotional, and that wouldn't help solve anything. I took a moment to breathe and realign my thoughts. "Okay, we both know Robin is innocent, right?"

"Of course, but she's also at the center of something thorny. We need to unravel each individual thread in order to help her out of it."

"Agreed." I looked at the calendar again. "So, I'll go with the theory that Alex found the flash drive Thursday, then met Robin that night. So maybe someone else was after the flash drive, too, and they tracked down Alex Saturday night at Robin's place. Where they killed him late that night, or rather, early Sunday morning."

"Perhaps. Continue."

"Okay. I'm thinking of that perfect bullet hole in Alex's forehead." I gulped back a shiver of dread and continued. "So whoever killed him was probably another so-called professional operative, right?"

Derek nodded, but said nothing.

"So how professional is it," I continued, "to kill another operative in the home of some innocent civilian who has no connection to anything? Wouldn't they wait and whack him on his own turf?"

He smiled at my use of the lingo. "That's a good point, and there are two different ways to proceed from there. The first is to assume that the killer wasn't a professional, but the expert bullet placement belies that theory."

"Right. What's the second?"

"The second is to assume that Robin was not the innocent civilian we thought she was."

"And that's impossible," I insisted, "so we've hit a dead end."

"No, we'll just continue to work through it until we arrive at our original theory."

"What's that?" I asked, sounding crabby.

"That Robin is innocent, naturally."

"Oh." Somewhat mollified, I nodded. "Okay, let's keep talking."

"Let me introduce one more tangle," Derek said. "Perhaps I should've mentioned this before, but another agent was apparently dispatched to do the brush, but once Alex was killed, she was told to track down the drive."

"She?" I echoed. "Would that be Galina?"

He lifted a shoulder. "My source didn't have a name to give me. I was only told it's a woman."

"But Galina seemed more like a spurned lover than a highly trained operative," I grumbled.

"She also worked out of Toronto, so perhaps you're right. Perhaps they were lovers."

I thought about that for a moment. "The fact that they were lovers probably saved our lives."

"How so?" he asked.

"Galina was as strong as a bull. I have no doubt she could've killed us both with two well-placed karate chops. But she was emotional. She was on a wild rant, out of control, so Robin and I were able to get some punches in and distract her enough to push her down to the sidewalk."

"Excellent theorizing, darling," he said with a proud smile.

"Thanks," I said, grinning, then remembered something else he'd said a moment ago. "I'm afraid to ask, but what's a brush?"

"Brush pass. One agent passes off the item to another."

"Good to know." I leaned forward on my elbows. "So Alex was supposed to get the flash drive and pass it on to Galina. But Alex obviously didn't find it and neither did Galina, because she kept yelling at us to give it to her, right?"

"That's right."

"So we're kind of back to square one."

"Not at all. A day later, your home was broken into."

I shook my head. "Wow, I almost forgot. Broken into by some big ugly guy, according to Tyler. So who's that guy? And why break in here?"

"Because they all think Robin has the flash drive."

That shiver of dread grew more pronounced and I rubbed my arms to make it go away. "They broke in to find Robin."

"They want the flash drive, not Robin."

He said that to make me feel better, but it didn't work. Alarmed, I stood and flexed my hands nervously. "Do you think someone followed us to Dharma? Is Robin in danger there?"

He jumped up and grabbed hold of my arms. "It's all right. She's with Austin, and I have Gabriel watching the perimeter."

"Oh." I blinked in surprise, then wrapped him in a tight hug. "Thank you for thinking of that."

"Shall we call it quits for the night? Are you tired?"

I stayed tucked close to his solid body for another moment. He was like my own private security blanket, and I savored every inch of him.

Finally, though, I lifted my head and looked at him. "I'm not tired. I want to keep going. But I'm starving, so let's cook while we talk."

"Perfect." He kissed me, then let me go, following me into the kitchen to help.

We whipped up a big salad with chunks of veggies and shredded chicken. I'd forgotten all about my martini, so Derek poured me another very weak one. Back at the dining room table, we resumed our theorizing game.

"What do you think is on this flash drive?" I asked.

"I've got my people working on that. All we know so far is that it contains information that is critically important to the government."

"Why do they think Robin has it? Alex could've left it in a safe-deposit box. Or somewhere in his apartment." I stopped and held up my hand. "Wait. He had an apartment here and he went to college here, supposedly. But he was deep cover in Toronto? How did that work?"

"He worked in San Francisco for a Toronto-based company and traveled back and forth regularly. It was a good cover."

I was still frowning. "Show me again how big this flash drive is."

Derek finished a bite of salad, then said, "Give me your hand."

I reached out and he took hold of my hand. Wrapping his thumb and finger around the first knuckle of my pinkie, he said, "It's smaller and thinner than the tip of your little finger."

"Huh." I tried not to obsess over the feel of his hand touching mine. I ask you, how could scarred knuckles and a callused palm be such a thorough turn-on? "How in the world are we supposed to find something so small?"

"It's probably hidden in something bigger. It might even be hidden in plain sight. Affixed to a small makeup mirror in Robin's purse or slipped inside a checkbook or cigarette case. Or a key ring."

"So we're back to thinking that Robin had it?" I popped a tomato chunk into my mouth.

"Just theorizing." He pushed away from the table and disappeared down the hall, then returned with my purse. "May I?"

"Sure."

Reaching into my bag, he first pulled out my small bottle of aspirin. "You could tape the flash drive to the bottom of the inside of this container and fill it with aspirin. Or you could cover it in plastic wrap and shove it into a jar of face cream, then smooth out the surface. Something like that won't show up on an airport security screen."

"You know too much about this stuff."

"It's a job."

I put down my fork, feeling defeated. "We'll never find it."

"That doesn't sound like my daring sleuth." He grabbed my hand and shook it playfully. "This is why we need to go through Robin's movements that night, step by step."

"You really think Robin was a soft target?"

"It's the only way to explain why Alex drugged her."

My shoulders slumped. "Another detail I forgot about. So you're thinking Alex drugged her so that while she was sleeping, he could hide the flash drive somewhere in her house."

He waved his fork. "That's one possibility, of course."

"But you clearly don't think so." I pondered as I sipped my martini. I'd never been crazy about the taste of martinis, but I did like the feeling of sophistication that drinking them gave me. Sort of like playing dress-up when I was young.

"It would make more sense if he thought Robin had it," I conceded. "Then he drugged her and searched for it."

"It would make more sense," he restated, probably for my benefit.

I took a quick bite of crunchy romaine, then shook my head. "But that would mean that Robin had the flash drive. And why in the world would she have a flash drive with Ukrainian government secrets on it?"

He stared at me steadily as he chewed.

"What?" Then it hit me and I choked on a

laugh. "You can't be serious. You think Robin is some kind of . . . what? A secret agent? A spy? You're way offtrack."

"All right," he said with a casualness I didn't trust for a second. "You tell me. Why did Robin have something so critical to the Ukrainian government that they would send one of their top operatives to steal it?"

"Who says she had it?"

"We're just tossing around scenarios right now. Examining things from all angles. Every possibility is on the table until it's eliminated."

"Then let's eliminate this one first."

"Yes, let's," he said mildly. "Tell me how Robin met Alex."

"Okay, she walked into a take-out restaurant. Alex was already in line and they struck up a conversation. There was no preset meeting, no weird intrigue, no brush pass." I used air quotes to indicate my contempt for the whole idea that Robin could be involved in some idiotic spy game.

"All right," he said. "Then what?"

I started to go on, then stopped. I searched my memory banks and played back my original conversation with Robin. Something was off about my starting point. And it bugged the heck out of me to admit it. "I was wrong. Robin was in line at the restaurant when Alex came in after her."

He reached for my hand in a show of sympathy. "Go on, love."

"While they were waiting for their food, they struck up a conversation."

"Did Robin tell you who spoke first?"

I thought back to the night we talked about her encounter with Alex. "She didn't say. She just said that they were having a fascinating conversation and when their orders were called, Alex said he didn't want to be like ships passing in the night and never see her again, so they got a table and ate together."

"Do you remember Robin telling you anything about him that I haven't heard yet? Anything at all?"

All right, Derek was getting to me. I rubbed my cold hands together because I was starting to worry now. Still, there was no chance in hell that Robin was a spy. "We should probably get her on the phone for more details, but I do remember her saying that he was an engineer born in the Ukraine. He came over here to go to Berkeley and never left. He was cute and funny and sexy, blah, blah, blah."

"Blah, blah, blah?" he said.

I chewed on my lip. "I shouldn't belittle her feelings for him. She was so happy. She blushed when she talked about him. Robin never blushes. And she called him Mr. Wonderful."

"She cared for him," he mused. "I saw that, as well."

"That's right. You were here when she talked about how he liked museums and ball games and all that stuff."

"Yes, and you called him a metrosexual."

"Exactly."

"I still have no idea if that's a good thing or a bad thing."

"I'm not sure, either," I said, laughing. My smile faded slowly. "She really seemed to like this guy Alex, and I was worried, somewhat selfishly, I guess. Because I know she's been in love with Austin forever, and I've always wanted them to get together. Of course, now it seems they have, so we'll see what happens."

"Did you share your concerns with her at the time?"

"Yes. She blamed Austin for not making a move in her direction. Said she wasn't going to sit by the phone waiting for his call."

"No, she doesn't seem the sort who would sit around waiting for a man."

"She's definitely not." I sipped my cocktail. "And you were here when she told us about Alex manipulating her into inviting him back to her place."

His lip curled in derision. "Yes, I remember that part. So now where are we?" He consulted his notepad. "Let's go on. Tell me again what the name of the restaurant was?"

"Kasa. It's an Indian restaurant. There're a few of them around the city. We laughed about that, because she'd just returned from India. But she still had a taste for Indian food."

"Just a moment." He dropped the pen on the notepad, glanced around the room as though he'd lost something, then turned to look at me. "She'd just returned from India?"

"Yes, she took a tour group there. I told you."

"No, you didn't. You left out that rather interesting detail." His forehead was creased in thought. "How recently did she return from her trip?"

I gave him an odd look. "Are you sure I didn't tell you this already?"

"No, you absolutely did not."

"I'm sorry. I guess I've been distracted."

"Yes, well." He scribbled something on his notepad. "Plenty of distractions lately."

"I'll say." Most of the distractions had been caused by Derek and his sudden constant presence in my life. Not that I was complaining. I gathered up our empty plates and took them into the kitchen. Derek beat me to the sink and took over, washing the dishes as we talked. I got the funniest little twinge around my heart as I watched him work in my kitchen. Talk about distractions.

"Anyway," I continued after forcing my gaze away from his wet, soapy arms, "Robin was on her way home from the airport when she stopped at Kasa to get dinner to go."

He ran hot water over each dish and utensil and placed them in the drainer. "And she was in India for what? Two, three weeks?"

"Three weeks."

"Any idea where she went?"

"I know she landed in New Delhi and the trip centered around that area of the country. She took them to Agra to see the Taj Mahal. I think they rode elephants in Jaipur and camels somewhere else. You know, the usual. Then the group flew home and she flew to Varanasi to see her mother."

"Her mother lives in Varanasi?" He tilted his head to look at me. "Why didn't I know this?"

Frowning, I considered the question. "I'm really not sure. Anyway, she stayed with her mom for three days, then flew home."

"And then she flew home," he mused. "I

assume she gathered her baggage, obtained her car from long-term parking, and headed for home. Unless someone picked her up. Did you?"

"No," I interjected. "She drove her neighbor Sharon's car to the airport and left her Porsche at home in the garage."

"Why didn't she just call a cab?"

I shrugged. "She did, but it didn't show up and it was getting late, so Sharon gave her the keys to one of their cars. They have, like, four old cars."

"Why didn't Sharon just drive her?"

I smiled at his logical questions. Sometimes circumstances just weren't logical. "Sharon was sick, and Robin didn't mind paying the parking lot fee. It's a tax writeoff for her."

"Okay," he muttered. "Okay. So she's driving home. It was a long flight. She was hungry, so she stopped to pick up takeaway at this Indian restaurant."

"That's exactly how she described it."

He nodded as he dried his hands on the dish towel. "So she was waiting for her food when a good-looking fellow walked in and struck up a conversation with her."

I leaned back against the counter. "You're making it sound like he was following her."

"Am I?"

"You are. And that answering-a-question-with-a-question thing that you do? It drives me a little cuckoo."

"Does it?"

I made a face and he grinned. "Sorry, love."

I didn't believe him for a second. "Where were we? Oh, yeah, that creep had to have been following her. That's where you're going, right?"

"Yes, that would be my guess."

"Your guesses are usually accurate," I said with grudging admiration.

"Thank you, love." He held my face in his hands and kissed my forehead. "I know this is tough for you. Do you want to stop?"

"No, I'll be better once we figure this out," I said, and began to pace the short length of the kitchen. "So he asked her out to dinner, where he manipulated her into inviting him to her home. And then he . . . what? Drugged her in order to search her house for a tiny flash drive?"

"Go on."

"What I can't understand is, why do these people think Robin has the flash drive?"

"Because someone alerted them to the fact that she was bringing it back from India."

"But who? And why? And how?" I looked

at him with suspicion. "I don't believe for a minute that Robin had anything to do with this, but I'm willing to admit that Alex might've been under the *illusion* that Robin brought the flash drive back from India."

Derek smiled his approval. "All right, let's continue on that track."

"Okay, but I had another thought. There must've been a lot of planes coming in around the same time as Robin's."

"Yes?"

"So maybe someone on Robin's plane or in the terminal dropped the flash drive into her carry-on bag, then followed her out and signaled someone like Alex to keep following."

"It's a possibility."

"A lame one, right?"

He held up both hands. "I didn't say that."

"I appreciate it." I stared at the floor as I started pacing again, this time moving out to the living room, where there was more room to roam. "Here's another possibility. Maybe Alex was told to look for a certain woman and he mistook Robin for that person."

"Mistaken identity?" He moved his head back and forth as if weighing the possibilities. "It could happen."

I sighed. "It's far-fetched, I know."

"Darling." He stepped into my path and put his hands on my shoulders. "How much do you know about Robin's tour guide business?"

Confused, I looked at him, then did a double take. "No, no, no. Don't go there."

"It's a simple question."

I jerked back from him. "You honestly believe her tour guide company is a cover for espionage activities?"

"Is it?" he asked mildly.

"Stop that." I jabbed my finger at his chest. "Stop doing that question thing and stop thinking Robin is a spy." I was seriously cranky now.

He wrapped his arms around me and rubbed my back. He caught me off guard or I would've sidled away from him.

"I have no doubt that Robin is completely innocent," he said, and kissed the top of my head.

I clutched his waist as I glared at him. "You're damn straight she is."

"Of course she is." He met my gaze. "Another theory you haven't mentioned is that Robin did have the flash drive and simply didn't know it. Perhaps someone slipped it into her luggage, as you suggested. Or she might've brought it back from India as part of something completely innocuous.

A souvenir or a trinket. She's obviously American, and there might've been people scoping the terminals, looking for someone like her. A random choice. Someone friendly, innocent, trusting. Who better to use as a mule to smuggle something into the country? Once she was safely inside the U.S., they sent someone to collect it."

"I like the random theory, but I can tell you don't believe it."

"Not really, but it's important to consider every possibility."

"Okay, we've considered it and discarded it. So you actually think Robin knowingly carried this thing all the way from India to the U.S."

"Not knowingly, perhaps. She might've been unaware of it. It was hidden in something, perhaps. But I definitely believe she brought it back with her."

"In the book," I muttered. My spine began to tingle, and it wasn't from Derek's enthralling touch. I inched away from him so I could think more carefully. "Derek, Robin brought back the book."

"The book?" he repeated slowly. "What book? From India? Have I seen it?"

I felt my cheeks getting warm at the thought of showing Derek the Kama Sutra. "You haven't seen it yet. It's a rare book a friend of Robin's mother sent. They want me to restore it."

"May I see it?"

"Of course." I dashed down the hall to the closet. Derek followed me and watched as I unlocked the panel that revealed the false floor. "This is the book I was worried about when the big ugly guy broke into my place."

"Why were you worried about it?"

"You'll understand when you see it." I lifted the shopping bag out of its hiding place and handed it to Derek, then closed and locked the panel.

"You've aroused my curiosity."

"Let's go to my workroom," I said, leading the way. "The light's better in there."

Once we were seated at the worktable, I pulled the old leather satchel from the shopping bag and unbuckled it, then slipped the book out.

"That's an interesting old saddlebag," he said.

"It's cool, isn't it? But wait till you see this." I unwrapped the white cotton cloth and pushed the book toward Derek.

"Well, that is certainly no souvenir," he said. His tone was light, but his jaw flexed with tension.

"It's in decent condition, so go ahead and

look through it. You won't do any damage."

He stared at the red leather cover and inspected the jewels. "Magnificent."

"It really is."

He turned it so that the spine faced him. "What is . . . Ah, the Kama Sutra. Another detail you neglected to share."

"Did I?" I smiled. "There goes my brain again."

With a half grin, he said, "Is that why you didn't show it to me?"

"Of course not."

It was clear by his sardonic expression that he didn't believe me. "Has anyone else seen it?"

"Just Ian."

"You showed Ian the Kama Sutra and not me?" He laughed. "What am I to think of that?"

"Oh, no. I just knew he would appreciate it — you know, intellectually. Because it's a book. Not because . . ." Oh, God, was my face red?

"I do love seeing you flustered," he said, his smile broadening.

I frowned. "Then you must be in heaven right now."

He bent over, kissed me, then murmured, "Close to it." Then he took hold of the book. "Well, let's have a look."

"Yes, good idea."

After a moment of studying the cover, he said, "I'm going to assume these jewels are the real thing."

"That's my understanding." I pointed out the obvious gems. "Sapphires, rubies, emeralds. I think these small clear gems are diamonds, but I'll have to verify that."

"And Robin's mother sent this to you?"

"Yes. It belongs to her mother's friend." I gave him an abbreviated history of Shiva Quinn and her friend Rajiv Mizra. "Anyway, Shiva is a bit of a collector and Rajiv is, too. Abraham once recommended me to Shiva, so it was nice of Shiva to pass my name on to Rajiv."

"It certainly was. Does Rajiv plan to sell it?"

"He's not sure. He wants to know how much it's worth before he decides."

"So you're to estimate its cost on the open market? Is that why you showed it to Ian?"

I nodded. "Yes, and because I knew he'd go ape over it."

"I'm sure he did." He continued to study the book, turning it this way and that. "What does the restoration entail?"

"Basically, I'll separate the leather from the boards, take it apart, reinforce the ties and the boards and the spine, repair some light tears, clean it up, and put it back together, stronger than ever. I probably won't remove the gems. It would be too difficult and I would hate to lose one. I'll use an air gun to get rid of the dust and I'll wipe away as much grime as I can."

He rubbed his fingers over several of the colorful gems embedded in the peacock's feathers on the front cover. "Delicate work."

"Yes. There are several torn pages, and fixing them will be the most challenging part." And despite the situation and my fears for Robin's safety and the ludicrous idea that she might be a spy, I was dying to get my hands on the book again. Just staring at it made me want to reach for my knives and get busy. So I curled my hands into fists and dropped them in my lap. "For the most part, it's in excellent condition. Very strong. It should repair easily. I'm dying to get started."

"Why haven't you started yet?"

I laughed. "Distractions, remember?"

He picked up the book and stared down the edge of the front cover, then pressed it carefully. "It's padded."

"Yes."

"You'll remove it?"

"Right. I've got to check the batting,

strengthen the spine, and reglue the endpapers."

"Can you do it tomorrow?"

I regarded him warily. "You think there's a miniature flash drive hiding in there?"

"Stranger things have happened."

With a nod, I said, "I'll start on it tomorrow morning."

"Good. The sooner you do that, the sooner we might have some answers to our questions. And it just might save Robin's life."

"That's good enough for me."

He studied the book for another few minutes. Opened the pages, ran his hands over the calligraphy, examined the paintings and brushstrokes, inspected the positions. "It's quite extraordinary."

"Yes." I sounded breathless. I'd been just as fascinated watching him as he was with exploring the book.

"And it's written in French," he murmured. "That's unexpected, isn't it?"

"It is."

He looked up at me. "Have you studied the Kama Sutra?"

"Only a bit," I said, as I ran my fingers over the corded spine. "I suppose everyone has a vague knowledge of it. You know, positions and such. But wasn't it written as a social primer of sorts? Marital etiquette or something like that?"

"Yes, that's exactly what it is." He turned a page and stared at the French script. Was he translating the words? "An Englishman, Richard Burton, is said to have written the definitive English translation. I was compelled to study it extensively for an assignment once upon a time."

I laughed. "Oh, don't stop there. I want to hear about this assignment."

"I can't say too much — only that one of our own government operatives had been co-opted by a sex therapist working at a spa somewhere on the coast of Sardinia, who planned to extort certain secrets."

"Sounds like fun."

He chuckled. "Elucidating, yes. Fun? Not really."

"Well, that's a shame."

He lifted the book again and perused the ornate red leather cover. "This is really outstanding."

"I think so, too." I gave up, took a deep breath, reached over, and stroked the spine. "What does *Vatsyayana* mean?"

He looked amused as our hands touched. "He's the author."

"Oh." Warmth spread up my neck. My cheeks would be turning pink any second now. Again. "I guess I should've known that.

And I should probably know what the words *Kama Sutra* mean, but I don't."

"It's Sanskrit," he said, moving closer. "*Kama* is 'love.' *Sutra,* loosely translated, means 'a lesson' or 'a rule.' So essentially, the Kama Sutra contains the rules of love."

"Ah, I see."

He turned to a page in the middle of the book. "Here's a rule you might be interested in. It refers to pressure points." He read the text in perfect French, an experience I found insanely erotic.

"Um . . ."

"In the corresponding illustration" — he pointed to the facing page — "you can see how the woman's anxiety has been eased."

"Oh . . . yes."

"Let's try that." He took my hand and rubbed a spot between my thumb and first finger. At the same time, he pressed his leg against my thigh.

I couldn't breathe.

"Do you feel that?" he murmured.

"I feel . . . Oh . . ."

"Yes, you do." He moved in and covered my mouth with his. His lips were firm and his intention was clear. My heart thrummed against my ribs as he softened the kiss; then his lips moved along the ridge of my jaw to my ear. It was pure instinct that made me stretch to accommodate his every move. I felt a twisting and turning in the pit of my stomach and I heard myself moan with need. The sound and its unfamiliarity brought me back to reality, if slowly.

Derek stood and pulled my chair back and I slid off it. His mouth hovered within reach of mine and I didn't hesitate. I stretched up and pressed my lips to his. He enclosed his arms around me and deepened the kiss, just as someone battered their fists against my front door.

The door flew open and a man burst into my house, waving a gun.

I screamed.

"What the —" Derek shouted, then shoved me behind him. "Get back."

I watched as Derek boldly slapped the man's gun hand, then grabbed and shook it. The gun went flying as the man fell to his knees.

He was big with a pockmarked face. Big and ugly. Was this Tyler's bad guy?

"Who do you work for?" Derek yelled as he grabbed the man's shirt and tie and shook him.

From where I was crouched, I could see blood dripping onto the floor. "Derek, he's bleeding."

Derek took hold of the man's jacket lapels

and whipped them apart. A large splotch of blood was seeping through his white shirt.

"Who did this to you?" Derek asked in concern. "Who are you?"

The man blinked up at him. He was heavyset, and his eyes were red rimmed.

"Who sent you?" Derek asked again, then spurted out a flurry of words in a foreign language. Russian? Ukrainian? I didn't know, but the man nodded quickly and replied in the same language.

Derek barked out one more sentence.

The man sighed deeply, muttered something else, then crumpled to the floor.

CHAPTER 11

"Call nine-one-one," Derek said brusquely as he slammed the front door. "Get an ambulance here."

I scrambled for the phone on the desk as he checked the man's neck for a pulse, but within seconds, he swore under his breath.

"Never mind the ambulance," he murmured in resignation. "He's dead."

I continued holding for the operator. "We still need to get the police here."

After reporting the break-in and telling them about the dead guy in my house, I called Inspector Lee. She answered the phone on the first ring.

"Why am I not surprised to hear from you?" she said.

I gave her a brief rundown of what had just happened and she assured me she'd be there shortly.

As I spoke on the phone to Inspector Lee, I watched Derek check the dead man's pockets and clothing labels. I assumed he was looking for identification and any telltale clues as to what Mr. Big had been doing here and why.

In an inside pocket, he found the man's passport. Taking out his phone, Derek snapped a picture of the open passport, flipped the page, took another picture, then slipped the passport back in the man's pocket. I figured he would be sending those photos to his pals at Interpol.

In another pocket, he found the passkey to my building as well as a key to my loft. He held them up for me to see, then raised a brow in amusement as I bared my teeth at them. Damn, I was willing to accept that a shady locksmith had been paid to make a copy of my new key, but how had the guy obtained a key to the building? It was aggravating in the extreme.

Derek slipped on a thin rubber glove — where in the world that came from, I had no idea — and picked up the man's gun, examined it, smelled it, held it at arm's length, and aimed it at the wall, then lowered his arm. He extracted the thing that held the bullets, then counted the bullets. Placing the gun on the worktable, he snapped another picture. It was as fascinating a routine as anything I'd ever seen him do, and that was saying plenty.

After I ended the call with Inspector Lee, I wrapped the Kama Sutra in its layers of protection and stuck it back in its hiding place at the bottom of the hall closet.

As I walked into my workroom, I noticed that Derek was slipping the man's shoes off to study the brand.

"What in the world just happened here?" I muttered, rubbing my scalp with both hands. My life just kept getting more and more bizarre. Strangely enough, that wasn't really a complaint.

I brushed my hair back from my face and went to check my front door, just to make sure there was no damage. I hadn't locked the dead bolt because I always liked to do it just before I went to bed. But from now on I planned to keep the door bolted at all times.

There was a sudden pounding at the door and I jolted.

Derek grabbed me from behind and held me, calming me as though I were a scared kitten. "It's okay. It's someone at the door. Probably a neighbor. You're fine."

I breathed in and out, then shook my head in self-disgust. "Thank you. You're right; I'm fine. I'll just get the door now."

I opened the door and saw Suzie. With

one strong hand, she clutched the arm of — Minka LaBoeuf? Wearing a black trench coat and a beret? What in the world was going on?

Minka squirmed and tried to pull away, but Suzie was much more powerful. It took some heavy-duty muscles to operate a chain saw every day.

"Suzie?" I said in a daze. "Why . . . What . . . Huh?"

"This one was skulking around your door," Suzie said, jerking her chin toward Minka. "I asked her what she wanted and she said she knew you. I said, 'So what're you doing out in the hall?' and she tells me to go fuck myself."

"Minka, what the hell are you doing here? And how did you get inside the building?"

"I followed that big guy in," she said in a huff. "Then this bitch grabbed me."

Suzie winked at me. "Just watching out for you."

"Thanks, Suzie."

"You know why I'm here, Brooklyn!" Minka cried. "I'm sick of you stealing my jobs. I want that book."

"And you thought breaking into my building . . . Wait a minute. Were you standing outside the other day when that crazy screaming woman attacked Robin?"

Minka's eyes widened. "Uh, that wasn't me."

"You're such a liar. Why do you think I would ever hand the book over to you?"

"I have powers of persuasion," she said with a toss of her overprocessed hair. "I'm Russian, you know."

If I thought my life was bizarre before, it had just become seismically weirder. "Okay, first of all, Minka, the book isn't Russian. There's nothing Russian about it. You overheard something completely unrelated to the book."

"Well, the book is French and I'm French, too."

"It doesn't matter." I closed my eyes and prayed for strength, then said, "Look, I got the book from a client of mine. Ian didn't give me the book. That day you saw me at the Covington, I was just showing it to him. So there was no way he was going to let you work on this book, because it wasn't a Covington project. If you'd bothered to ask a question or two instead of assuming the worst, you wouldn't have wasted your time and mine. And Suzie's."

"Well, why didn't you just say so in the first place?" she said with a sneer, as though this were all my fault. I'd once likened her curly-lipped sneer to that of a snarling dingo, and the description still fit her.

She wasn't finished. "You've got to be the biggest pain in the — Oh, my God! Is he dead?"

She pushed me out of the way and pulled Suzie along as she charged into my house, then stopped and stared at the big Russian sprawled on my floor.

"Okay, time to go," I said. I grabbed Minka's other arm and turned. Suzie helped me yank her out the door. We didn't bother waiting for the elevator but pulled her down six flights of stairs and out the front door of the building.

She screamed the entire way down, the general theme being that I was either a serial killer or a magnet for murder or just plain cursed.

"Bye-bye," Suzie said as she pushed her out the door. "Nice meeting you. Not."

We watched Minka stomp down the sidewalk and get into her funky old rattletrap of a car. As soon as she drove away, I hugged Suzie. "Thank you. I couldn't have handled that alone."

"No problemo. Let's take the elevator up," she said.

"Good idea," I said with a laugh.

She left me at my door and ambled back to her place.

I walked inside and stared at Derek, who was holding a bullet up to the light and examining its surface.

"She seems to be back to her old feisty self," Derek said mildly. "I would've stepped in to help, but Suzie appeared to have the situation well in hand."

"Yeah, she was a rock," I muttered, then frowned at the man on the floor. "Minka said she followed this guy inside. So how do you think he got a key to my place?"

"Bribed the locksmith?" Derek suggested.

"That's unacceptable. Aren't they supposed to be bonded or something? What is wrong with people? I'm going to report him to the police."

"Good idea." He put the bullet back in the clip thing and looked at me. "At least your door wasn't shattered again."

"You're right. I'm really happy about that." Then to prove it, I burst into tears. I wasn't thrilled to be crying in front of Derek, but I guessed it was better than fainting from the blood that was smeared on my floor.

He hugged me tightly and rubbed my back and said all the right things. I could've stayed there in his arms for another few hours or so. Silly, I know. But he was strong and sure of himself and I was so glad he was there. Besides, he smelled so damn good and his cashmere sweater was soft against my cheek. It was as close to nirvana as I was going to get anytime soon.

"I'm just tired," I explained once my eyes were dry.

"Of course you are," he said, leading me through the short hall to my living room. "We'll sit in here and wait for the police."

I curled up next to him and rested my head on his shoulder. "Thanks."

"For what?"

"Everything. I'm starting a list."

He chuckled and squeezed me closer.

"What did the guy say?" I asked finally. "What language were you speaking?"

"Russian. He wanted the flash drive. I said we didn't have it, and even if we did, we wouldn't hand it over to a murderer."

"Oh, good one." Sitting up, I tucked my legs up on the couch. "What'd he say to that?"

"He insisted he didn't kill anyone who didn't deserve it."

"Whatever that means."

"My thoughts exactly." Derek rubbed his knuckles along his clenched jaw. "He told me he was Russian, working for his government. He knows about the Ukrainian woman, Galina. He thinks she killed Alex."

I pursed my lips in thought. "I'm not sure I'd agree with that one."

"No, I have my doubts that she killed him," Derek said. "From the way you've described her, she seems too unbalanced to have pulled off an execution of that precision."

I grimaced at the unforgettable image of that perfect round bullet hole in Alex's forehead. What truly concerned me was the audacity of someone who would kill a man right next to a living, sleeping woman. "Did you believe anything he said?"

Derek thought about it. "I believe he was Russian. Other than that, his answers were feeble and confusing. But he did say something odd that makes me wonder what we're dealing with."

"What did he say?"

"He said, 'It's not what you think. I'm one of the good guys.' "

" 'One of the good guys'?" I didn't know what to think of that, so I just shut up and let it sink in for a few minutes.

"Darling." Derek rubbed my cheek gently. "We must drive back to Dharma tomorrow and talk to Robin."

My shoulders sagged a bit, but I'd already reached the same conclusion. "I'm afraid you're right. She's in this up to her hip bones."

"It appears she is." He touched my leg in a comforting gesture. "Now, that doesn't mean she's guilty of anything, but I'm convinced she has more knowledge of this affair than she may even realize."

"I agree," I said. "I'd like to know more about Shiva's friend Rajiv, too."

Derek tapped his fingers on the arm of the couch. "I hate to suggest it, but this Rajiv might've cultivated Shiva's friendship precisely to use her daughter as an unwitting courier."

The thought made me angry all over again. "If that's true, I hope your Interpol friends can track him down and make him pay."

"If it's true, I'll be happy to arrange it."

"Good." I sighed and leaned back into the pillows of the couch. "The sooner we can resolve all this, the sooner I can go back to a life free of Ukrainians and Russians knocking down my door every other day."

"The American dream."

"Yeah." I laughed dolefully. "I guess I should call Robin and let her know we're coming."

Derek jumped up, found my cell on the table, and brought it back to me. With a smile for him, I pressed Robin's number and waited. There was no answer, so I left a message, then called Austin's house. His voice mail picked up and I left another message.

"I guess they're out tonight." Or maybe they weren't picking up the phone. After all, they were still under the dubious influence of Mom's enchantment spell. "I should call my mom, too," I mused. "Let her know we're coming."

There was no answer at my parents' house either.

"What's going on in Dharma tonight?" I wondered aloud. "Why isn't everyone home and in their jammies?"

"Perhaps there's a community event."

"Probably so." But I had to rub my arms against a sudden chill. "Are you sure Gabriel's healed enough to keep watch on Robin?"

He hesitated. "Yes."

"You're not convincing me."

"I'm not convincing myself," he grumbled, and pulled out his cell to check in with Gabriel. Pushing himself up from the couch, he said, "I'll let him know the latest and make sure he stays alert to any unusual activity."

I smiled and mentally added one more

item to my list of reasons to thank Derek Stone.

It was another late night of police procedure. Happily, no fingerprint dust was involved. However, our two intrepid inspectors, Lee and Jaglom, were unable to shed much light on who the dead man was, beyond what Derek had gleaned from his own search of the man's passport and belongings.

Derek had already sent the information off to his contacts at Interpol.

Meanwhile, Inspector Lee warned that the FBI or some obscure Homeland Security agency still might step in, now that it seemed even more likely that the threatened turf war between the Russians and the Ukrainians was heating up. Apparently, it was all heating up inside my apartment.

Derek said nothing to contradict the police take on the situation, but I knew he didn't agree with the cops' assessment. At least, not as it pertained to Robin and her problems, which had nothing to do with a turf war and everything to do with a missing flash drive that some people were willing to kill for.

But unfortunately, Derek was not in a position to divulge the full story to the inspectors. It was turning into a highly sensitive international situation, and something Derek was not at liberty to turn over to the local police. I assumed that officials at the highest levels of government would eventually step in and take over. Meanwhile, my two main concerns were that Robin was safe in Dharma and that she'd told me everything she knew about Alex and Rajiv and the Kama Sutra.

It was a relief when the investigator got all the blood he needed from those few drops spilled by the Russian and gave me the okay to clean and sanitize my workroom floor right then and there. The thought of having to put off cleaning for days while the blood was analyzed was too depressing to think about.

The police traced my intruder's bloody footprints from the curb outside my building, across the sidewalk, up the interior stairwell, and down the hall to my place. The same way he'd escaped the night Tyler had seen him.

Currently, there was a car parked where the footprints began out by the curb, but as the police inspected it, the owner ran over from the Thai restaurant across the street. So it was not the dead man's car.

So he'd been shot, then dropped off in

front of my building? It didn't make sense. But then, nothing about this chilling situation made much sense at all.

The following morning, I called Robin one more time, and again there was no answer. I assumed no foul play was afoot, because Gabriel had reported to Derek that everything was fine in Dharma. I had to conclude that Robin was simply too enthralled with Austin to answer the damn phone. Fine. I guessed we would show up and surprise her.

Before leaving for Sonoma, I packed the Kama Sutra carefully into my briefcase, more unwilling than ever to leave it here while we were gone. Then I called the head of my homeowners association, who lived on the third floor, and let him know that the hall rugs on the sixth floor needed cleaning. I didn't mention bloody footprints. They would have to figure that out for themselves.

Before Derek pushed the elevator button, I jogged down to Vinnie and Suzie's place to let them know we would be gone for the day. They promised to look in on Pookie and keep their eyes and ears open for weirdos. Then we headed off to Dharma.

Derek maneuvered the Bentley through the tollgate plaza and onto the Golden Gate

Bridge. The sun came out from behind a cloud, and the view of Marin was beautiful. I pulled sunglasses out of my purse and put them on as we left the bridge for land and continued driving through the winding hills above Sausalito.

"The Kama Sutra must hold the key," Derek remarked as we descended into the flatlands. "Everything happened after Robin returned from India with the book."

"I think you're right," I said. "I'll start taking it apart as soon as we get home this afternoon."

He leaned over and squeezed my knee. "We've got my office party this evening."

I winced. I'd completely forgotten! Earlier in the week, I'd been so thrilled that Derek had invited me to the party, but now it was the last thing I wanted to do.

"Oh, I knew that," I said lightly. "I'm really looking forward to it."

He laughed. "Of course you are, darling."

"I am," I said, trying to sound both sincere and insulted that he would doubt me.

"Yes, I am, too," he said genially, letting me off the hook. "Unfortunately, the timing couldn't be worse. We have more important matters to deal with."

"If we get home early enough, I still might

have time to work on the book."

He nodded. "We'll see how the day goes."

As the freeway widened near San Rafael, Derek increased his speed. "If the Ukrainians were aware that the flash drive was hidden somewhere inside the book, why didn't they just break into Robin's car and take it while she was dining at the Indian restaurant with Alex? That way, they would've had what they wanted that first night."

"And Robin would never have been involved."

"Exactly," he said.

"And chances are Alex would be alive. Nobody would be hurt. Except the book." I turned in my seat to face him. "I'd hate to imagine what damage they would've done to the book."

He smiled indulgently. "Yes, God help them if they'd destroyed the book. The wrath of Brooklyn would be unleashed."

"That's right," I said, chuckling. "I would've tracked them down and made them pay."

Derek tapped his thumb on the steering wheel in contemplation. "So Robin went home with the book that night. It doesn't make sense that Alex or one of his people didn't simply go through Robin's house and find the damn thing."

"I'm glad they didn't," I said firmly. "Robin stayed home and slept all day. If she'd awakened and found them, they might've . . ." I shivered.

His eyes narrowed to black slits. "If they were any good at all, she never would've known they were in her house."

I shook my head. When he said stuff like that, I was reminded that he could be as dangerous as he looked.

"And that night," he went on, "she brought the book to your house. Alex didn't know it, but his window of opportunity closed at that moment. I must say, I'm not impressed with his operative skills."

"I have this picture of him as a ladies' man. You know, a smooth-operator type." I shook my head in disgust. "Maybe he thought he could pull off the job by cozying up to Robin instead of just taking care of business. And that got him killed. I know it's mean to say this, but I'm not all that sorry he's dead."

"Darling, I love it when you're vindictive."

"Don't laugh. I already feel bad for saying it." I bunched up my fists. "But he just makes me so angry that he endangered Robin. I never even met him, but I want to punch him."

He grabbed my hand and kissed it. "You

mustn't feel bad. You're being protective of your friend, and that makes you fierce and sexy. It's quite a turn-on."

"Oh, please." I couldn't help but laugh while heat rose up my neck. "Now you're making fun of me."

"Your cheeks are pink," he said in amazement, and his dark eyes gleamed with laughter. "How charming." Turning my hand over, he kissed my palm, all the while keeping his eyes on the road.

"You're going to miss the off-ramp," I murmured, when I could breathe normally again.

"Never," he said with a grin. "I'm a highly trained professional."

We drove to my brother's house along a road that meandered through the vineyards, rising slowly until we reached the top of the highest hill overlooking Dharma.

"The view is spectacular up here," Derek said.

"But he's so isolated."

"Yes, that's certainly part of the appeal."

Austin's house was relatively small and shaped like an alpine cabin, with a back deck that extended out over a small canyon. I hadn't been inside in a few years, but I knew it was one large high-ceilinged room with an open kitchen and a sleeping loft reached by climbing up a ship's ladder. It was cozy and wonderful for one person or a very intimate twosome.

It took them almost five minutes to answer the door when I knocked. They both wore bathrobes and satisfied smiles. I couldn't help but thank all the gods in the heavens that we hadn't arrived ten minutes earlier.

"Hey, Derek," Austin said pleasantly, then looked at me. "Brooklyn, what are you doing here?"

"Where have you guys been?" I demanded.

"We went camping for a few days," he said with an easy grin. "Just got back a while ago." He swung the door open and waved us inside.

"Do you want coffee?" Robin said on her way to the kitchen. The swelling on her face had almost disappeared, but the skin around her eye was still bruised. All in all, she looked much better. Rested and relaxed. I guessed Austin was treating her well.

"No, thank you," Derek said.

I followed Robin into the kitchen. "Camping? You?"

"I know." Her smile stretched a bit wider. "But it was fun. Did you know there are hot springs up here? I never even knew about them."

"I've heard my brothers talk about them for years, but I've never seen them."

"You should," Robin said with a serene smile. "It's so beautiful. But it's a hike."

"Yeah, that's the part where I'm having trouble picturing you."

Robin laughed, poured herself a cup of coffee, then walked over and sat on the wide, tan leather sofa that faced the rustic fireplace. "So what's going on?"

Austin stood and leaned one elbow on the sturdy log mantel. The pose was casual but his eyes were watchful.

Derek sat on the brick hearth directly across from Robin and rested his elbows on his knees. "We won't take up much of your time, but we had some questions to ask you."

"Yeah, we didn't want to disturb you," I said, settling into the bentwood rocking chair Austin had made by hand years ago. "But you people really should answer your phones."

"Brooklyn, don't be angry," Robin said softly. "Austin took me out to get my mind off of things. We didn't take our phones."

I left the chair and knelt in front of her. "Honey, I'm not angry. We were just worried. See, after we dropped you off up here the other day, we got back to find my door bashed in and my place trashed. Then yesterday, another guy broke in again and it turns out someone had shot him, so he died right there in my workroom. And the police think it's a turf war, but then Derek got some information from Interpol that there's a missing flash drive, and the Ukrainians . . ."

I stopped talking when I noticed the two of them staring at me in varying degrees of horror.

Robin sat forward, gripped my shoulders, and peered at me. "What is it with you and trouble? I've barely been here two days. How could that much happen in two days?"

I shook my head. "I don't know. But I've got to say, I'm really glad you were here instead of at my place. These guys are playing hardball. We think whoever killed Alex is looking for this flash drive that you might've brought back from India. Derek and I are pretty sure it's connected to the Kama Sutra."

"The Kama Sutra?" Austin frowned and glanced from Robin to me to Derek. "I'm not following any of this."

"It's a long story," I muttered.

Robin shook her head. "But how could the book have anything to do with Alex? I got it from my mother's friend Rajiv. I don't understand."

I lifted both shoulders in bewilderment. "We don't know yet, but that's why we came here. We're hoping you can shed some light on a few things."

Robin's eyes clouded and she sighed heavily. "It's never going to go away."

"Yes, it is," I insisted, hating to see Robin feeling so down. Just a few minutes ago, she'd been all smiles and now . . . "But look. The sooner we find out where this flash drive is, the sooner —"

"That's enough." Austin brushed past me to sit next to Robin on the couch. He enveloped her in his arms and whispered, "Come on, babe. No more worries, remember?"

Then he gave me a fulminating stare and I mentally shrank a few inches. If he weren't my big brother, the look wouldn't have bothered me so much, but Austin had always been able to nonverbally smack me down with little effort.

"Look, I'm sorry," I said, meaning it. "We just really need some answers. But maybe we can come back later and . . . I don't know." Feeling helpless and frustrated, I gazed at Derek.

He patted the brick next to him, and I retreated to the hearth to sit, putting some distance between me and my brother.

Derek spoke directly to Austin. "It's of the utmost urgency that we talk to Robin. We can give you some time to get dressed; then we can either come back here or meet you in town. Is there a restaurant or café you can suggest as a meeting place?"

"I've got a good idea," Austin said, more amenable now that Derek had spoken. My brother could be exasperating and old-fashioned when the mood hit him. "Let us get ourselves together, get dressed, and we'll meet you at Mom and Dad's in an hour. She's expecting us for lunch."

"And we'll talk?" I asked.

Robin lifted her head and looked from Austin to us. Her eyes were clear as she nodded at me. "We'll talk."

Chapter 12

I knew I shouldn't have been annoyed at Robin, but I was. She was acting like a twit, trying to pretend nothing had happened. I understood that she'd been through hell, but now wasn't the time to hide. I needed her to be proactive.

She was my best friend and always would be, so I couldn't be mad at her forever. But at the moment, having just watched her ignore me while clinging to Austin, I couldn't help but think she was milking the situation.

Yeah, yeah, she woke up to a bloody dead body in her bed. And yeah, she'd had sex with him the night before, so yes, absolutely, that was a total bummer. But hey, I'd been a witness to murder, too. More than once, but who was counting? It's not like I was making it a little kids' competition between us. *Neener, neener, I've seen more dead bodies than you have!* It wasn't like that, I swear.

I was just disappointed that instead of soldiering up and answering a few critical questions, she'd pulled the girlie-girl card and used Austin as a shield.

So yeah, I guess I was a little pissed off. But like I said, I'd get over it. No worries.

Derek parked the Bentley in front of my parents' house. "Shake that off," he said calmly.

I looked down at my shirt, then brushed my jeans. "Shake what off?"

"The chip you're carrying on your shoulder. It won't do you any good to walk into your parents' house carrying all that anger."

I shrugged. "I'm okay."

"No, you're not." He cupped and turned my chin until we were eye-to-eye. "You're upset. I don't blame you, but I know your lovely mother. She'll pick up on that vibe in two seconds flat and proceed to harangue you until you've willingly revealed every naughty thing you've ever done in your life."

I didn't want to let go of this warm and righteous anger bubbling inside me, and I definitely didn't want to smile. But hearing Derek utter the word *naughty* tossed my best intentions right over the edge.

"All right," I said, and sighed. Why couldn't I have a poker face like normal people? It wasn't fair. Every little emotion I experienced showed up as clear as day on my face.

Derek waited patiently until I was no longer twitching in irritation.

"All right, I'm good. See?" I flashed him a supersize grin.

"That's my happy girl," he said drily. "Your mother will never guess it's not real."

"I'm counting on that."

He climbed out of the car and jogged around to meet me. "I promise you can yell at Robin later."

"I'm holding you to that."

"Hello, sweeties!" Mom cried a minute later when we announced ourselves through the front door screen.

I walked into the family home I grew up in and felt myself turning into an eight-year-old. All I wanted was lots of hugs and love from my mom and dad. They complied, then acted properly overjoyed when I begged for an invitation to join them for lunch.

"Wonderful!" Mom said. "Austin and Robin will be here, too. And I left a message for Gabriel, but I haven't heard back."

"He hasn't missed a meal so far," Dad said jovially.

"It'll be good to see him," Derek said, and sounded like he meant it.

Then Dad lured Derek away with an offer to taste his latest barrel experiment, a melding of cabernet franc, merlot and petit verdot that he was downright giddy over.

Mom led the way to the kitchen to put the finishing touches on lunch. But as soon as we entered the sunny room, she turned and patted my cheek. "What's wrong, sweetie?"

Damn, she was good. What would be the point of having a poker face anyway? Mom would always be able to see past it.

As if I were Pavlov's dog, I started talking the minute Mom gave me that look. "Nothing's wrong. Oh, well, except I just had a silly little run-in with Austin. But seriously, it's no big deal. In fact, they should be here any minute and I'm as happy as pie about it."

"So you've already stopped off at Austin's?"

"Yes, Derek wanted to ask Robin a few questions about that guy she was dating recently."

"The one she found murdered in her bed."

I grimaced. "That's the one."

"What about him?" She whipped an apron out of a drawer and wrapped it around her waist. As we talked, she grabbed two pot holders, opened the oven door, and removed a huge casserole dish of lasagna. I didn't want to give Mom too much information about big guys knocking down my door and dying in my house, because she would worry about me. But she turned and looked at me with those clear blue eyes and I couldn't seem to stop myself.

"There are more questions than answers. Someone's still out there causing trouble, and we need Robin to fill in some blanks."

"So let me guess what happened," Mom said. "Austin became the ferocious knight in shining armor, protecting his lady fair, Robin, from your impertinent questions."

I chuckled. "*Impertinent?* You've been watching reruns of *Pride and Prejudice* again, haven't you?"

"Busted." She let out a trill of laughter. "I can't get enough of that Colin Firth."

I followed her into the dining room, where she'd already set out serving dishes filled with potato salad, Japanese cole slaw, marinated green beans, and a green salad, along with flatware, plates, and napkins on the wide Mission-style table we'd used forever. I placed a trivet in the middle of the table and Mom settled the lasagna on top of it.

"I blame you for Austin's behavior," I said, nudging her as we returned to the kitchen.

"Me?"

"Yes. Your enchantment spell has turned them both upside down and inside out. Robin's perfectly happy with her head stuck in the sand, and Austin's gone into total protective mode. It's freakish."

Mom made a *tsk*ing sound as she pulled a bowl of fresh corn-and-blueberry pasta salad from the refrigerator. "I'd love to take credit for that, sweetie, but honestly. Enchantment spells?" She rolled her eyes at me. "You know it's all a bunch of hooey, right?"

"Hooey?" My eyes goggled. "Mom, are you feeling okay?"

She laughed again. "Oh, sweetie, you're so gullible."

"Moi?" I said, my voice squeaking in outrage. "Come on, Mom. Hooey is your raison d'être."

She bopped me with a pot holder. "Silly. Help me get the rest of the food on the table."

It was a beautiful day, so we filled up our plates and took them outside on the terrace. Dad had made lemonade, and there was plenty of wine and beer. Gabriel showed up a bit late with apologies, then eagerly filled his plate with Mom's food. He'd recovered from his injuries and looked amazingly healthy and handsomer than ever, if that was possible. I secretly wondered how long it would be until he grew tired of the quiet life in rural Sonoma County.

Despite Austin glowering at me occasionally, I was happy to be here for so many reasons, but especially because there was so much food. I didn't remember starving myself lately, but I was scarfing down food like I hadn't had a meal in weeks.

Mom insisted on clearing the dishes by herself, so the rest of us pretended to relax on the terrace, enjoying the sunshine and the views.

It was Dad who finally got the ball rolling. "Don't you kids have some things to talk about?"

"Yes, we do," I said.

Dad nodded and pushed himself out of his chair. "I'll go help Becky in the kitchen."

Robin met my gaze. "Do we?"

Austin scowled again.

"What is up with you two?" I said irately. "We just have a few questions. It's no big deal."

Robin swallowed a sip of wine. "Right."

"You don't have to do this," Austin said when she reached out and clutched his hand.

"Austin, enough," I said. "She *does* have to talk about it and she knows it." I turned to Robin. "What is wrong with you?"

She straightened her back and said in a quiet voice, "I just don't want to think about Alex anymore. I was hoping I could use this time away from the city to try to put the entire ugly experience behind me. I need to do that if I ever want to be whole again."

I grabbed her free hand. "Please believe me: I want you to be whole, too. I want that for you more than anything in the world."

Stiffly, she nodded her gratitude.

"But unfortunately," I said, trying to keep my tone even, "you left town, and the ghost of your dear Alex is now haunting *me.* And I'm sorry, but that's partly your responsibility, Robin. If you truly want closure, the least you can do is answer a few questions."

She pulled her hand away. "Well, aren't you the queen of compassion?"

"No," I countered, "I'm the queen of big messes dumped in my lap by other people."

"Now, just a minute," Robin said, her old fire rearing its head.

"No, you wait a minute," I snapped. "I love you, but there's a huge crap storm raining down on me, and I need your help to make it go away."

Robin frowned, but she didn't argue.

"Hell, Brooklyn," Austin began.

I held up my hand to stop him. "I don't need this from you, Austin."

"Leave him out of this," Robin said.

"Jeez Louise, will you two give me a break?" I jumped up from my chair and paced back and forth in front of her. "Austin, you can just butt out."

He looked astonished but said nothing, so I kept going. "All of a sudden you're Robin's white knight? Where was this devotion a month ago?"

"Hold on there," he argued, while Robin looked at him thoughtfully.

"No," I said, then reconsidered. "Sorry. I apologize. That has nothing to do with why we came here. We're here because we need to figure out what's going on if we ever want it to stop."

He didn't look happy, but at least he was quiet, so I turned to my friend. "Now, please, for God's sake, Robin, all we want to know is, where did you park your damn car the night you stopped at Kasa?"

She was taken aback at that. Frowning, she said, "That's all?"

I didn't meet her gaze. "There might be another question or two, but let's start with that one."

She stared out at the hills, thinking, then

looked back at me. "I parked on the street, directly in front of the restaurant. On Eighteenth. What does that have to do with anything?"

"Could you see the car while you were inside Kasa dining with Alex?"

"Yes." She glared at me. "You've been to Kasa. The whole front wall is windows. So, yeah, I could see my car the whole time. Why?"

Derek took over seamlessly. "We believe the people who killed Alex are looking for something that was planted in the book your mother gave you to bring to Brooklyn."

"The Kama Sutra?"

"Yes."

She looked from Derek to me. "Is that the flash drive you were talking about?"

"Yes," Derek said. "It's not a regular flash drive, but a very tiny one, the latest technology. And it's said to have highly sensitive information on it."

She tipped her head to one side and gave him a skeptical smile. "Sounds like a spy novel."

"Doesn't it?" Derek said lightly. "I assume you left the book in your car when you stopped at Kasa."

"I did."

"And it's obvious that no one broke into

your car or tampered with it, because you would've seen them."

"Right."

"Okay. Very good." Derek changed the subject. "Now, when you were visiting your mother in Varanasi, did you meet the friend who owns the book?"

"Rajiv?" She sat back in her chair and folded her hands. "He wasn't there on this trip, but I've met him a few times before. My mother said he'd gone to New Delhi to visit one of his daughters."

"Can you tell me about him?" Derek asked.

"What do you want to know?"

"Let's start with his name."

"Rajiv Mizra. Shiva's known him for years." Her lips thinned stubbornly. "He's a perfectly nice, normal guy. Not a spy, okay?"

Derek waved his hand nonchalantly. "Of course not."

But a subtle look passed between him and Gabriel, who'd been sitting on the periphery, gazing at the view, looking like he didn't have a care in the world. After a moment, though, Gabriel pulled out his phone and checked the screen, then texted something. Was he checking out Rajiv Mizra as we spoke?

"Rajiv is Indian?" Derek asked.

Robin nodded. "Yes. I think he said he was from Mumbai originally. I guess it was Bombay back then."

"Tell me about him," Derek said, then spelled out what he meant. "Is he young? Old? Conservative? Religious? Is he a wealthy man? Smart? What were your impressions of him?"

Robin seemed to relax a little. "He's middle-aged, I guess. Probably around fifty, like Shiva. He's smart, politically involved. I have a feeling he's been in love with her for years."

"And when you say 'politically involved,' do you mean he's part of the government?"

"No, no," she said, shaking her head. "He's just a big talker, likes to rant about the politicians and government waste, like we all do, I guess. He loves movies and drags Shiva off to the cinema all the time. She acts like it's such a chore, but I think she enjoys it, too. He's not married but I guess he has a few children."

"Is his wife dead?"

"I have no idea, but I've never heard Shiva talk about his having a wife."

Derek pondered that for a moment. "Does he have money? Is he attractive?"

"He's very wealthy, which is probably why my mother is friends with him. And yes, he's handsome, too, even for someone his age."

Derek nodded. "Was the Kama Sutra ever out of your possession during your trip home?"

"No," she said firmly. "We had a three-hour layover in London and I carried it with me at all times. If you've seen it, you know it's priceless. I couldn't let it leave my sight. If nothing else, Brooklyn would've killed me if it were stolen."

I smiled. "What about on the plane? Did you leave your seat at any time?"

"I went to the restroom a few times, but there's no way anyone could've tampered with my stuff and gotten away with it." She seemed to relax even more as she spoke, and now she showed a hint of a smile. "There were two women sitting next to me who would've gone berserk if that happened. They were, you know, yentas."

Derek flashed me a look.

I grinned. "Yenta. It's Yiddish, I think. It means 'busybody.' "

"Dad used to call Mom a yenta," Austin said, and awarded me a crooked smile.

"Right," I said, enjoying the fact that Austin might be letting go of his anger. "Because she was."

"Still is."

It wasn't much, but I took the brief exchange to mean that Austin's feelings were thawing out.

Robin stared at her fingernails, then gazed up at Derek. "Is my mother in danger?"

Derek reached over and gave her arm a consoling squeeze. "I don't see why she would be. But I've alerted my people to check on her, if you don't mind."

"No, I don't mind," she said, sounding relieved. "Thank you. She's a pain in the butt, but she's mine, you know?"

"Anyone for dessert?" Mom called from the kitchen door.

"Can we get it to go?" I asked.

"Oh, my goodness!" Mom cried out in shock. "Oh, my goodness!"

"What is it, Becky?" Dad called from somewhere on the other side of the house.

Austin stood, ready for anything. "Mom, what's going on?"

Derek whipped around. Gabriel looked ready to pull a gun from his pocket.

"The most wonderful surprise," Mom gushed as she pulled open the screen of the sliding glass door. "Robin will be so thrilled."

"We are all delighted," Guru Bob announced as he walked out to the terrace, arm in arm with a tall, beautiful, dark-haired woman.

"Oh, my God," I whispered.

Robin's mouth fell open. "Mom?"

"It's simple really," Shiva said, once everyone had hugged and greeted her. She gripped Robin's hand as we all moved inside to the living room. "While you were visiting, I was reminded of everything I love here at home. Then, after you left, I missed you so much. I decided it was time to take a trip back to Dharma."

"We have missed you as well, gracious," Guru Bob said. "You have been away too long."

"Thank you, Robson," she said, smiling sweetly for her teacher and guru. "It has been such a long time. And yet, now that I'm here, it feels as though I never left."

"That is the nature of true friendship," he said.

She touched her jawline. "Sadly, I've grown into an old woman in the interim."

Guru Bob chuckled. "That is simply not true."

"Thank you, my friend, but I'm feeling my age more and more every day."

"Don't be silly, Shiva," my mom said as she handed her a cup of tea. "You look absolutely beautiful. Not a day older than the last time we saw you, which must be what? Ten years? Good heavens."

"You're sweet, Becky. You look wonderful, too. That gold does lovely things for your complexion."

"Thanks." Mom smiled with pleasure as she gazed down at the wavy gold tie-dyed mandala in the center of the apron she'd sewn and dyed by hand.

"I have a dress those very colors and it makes me feel so happy when I wear it." Shiva's eyes grew soft. "It's a gold silk sari I bought in the Punjab. Now, that was an adventure. Someday I'll share the story with you all."

"But it's so weird, Mom," Robin said, still awestruck by her mother's sudden appearance. "We were just talking about you."

"No wonder my ears were burning," Shiva joked. "Why were you talking about me?"

"It's a long story," Robin murmured. She waited until Shiva was seated on one of my mom's antique lyre-back chairs; then she sat down on the couch. Austin joined her there with a beer in hand.

"Does anyone else need something to drink?" Mom asked, holding a teapot and two cups.

"Thank you, Rebecca." Guru Bob took one of the cups and sat down on another of the lyre-back chairs that faced the couch. I chose the recliner, while Dad leaned against the mantel over the fireplace. Derek and Gabriel had remained outside on the terrace, and I couldn't help but wish I were out there listening to their conversation.

I tried not to stare, but Shiva's beauty was almost mesmerizing. Everyone in Dharma had always loved her, and I could see why. I don't think she'd been back in almost ten years, and I knew she had to be in her fifties, but she looked as young and beautiful as I remembered her from when I was growing up.

She had a star quality that drew all eyes to her, and she showed an avid interest in the people she met. It was no wonder she'd attracted the attention of everyone from the Beatles to the current United Nations secretary, who had recently asked her to serve as one of his goodwill ambassadors for human rights.

Today she wore all black, turtleneck, pants, and boots, with a colorful turquoise scarf wrapped casually around her neck. Her long dark hair was pulled back in a simple ponytail.

Looking from Shiva to Robin, I realized that Robin was just as beautiful as her mother, but she lacked the drama. Thank God.

"It's such a weird story," Robin was saying, "but Derek thinks someone's after the Kama Sutra you gave me, the one you wanted Brooklyn to fix."

"I don't understand. Someone tried to steal it?"

"Not exactly," I said, and gave Shiva the abridged version of everything that had happened since Robin returned from India. I glossed over the grislier details of Alex's death and was gratified when Robin smiled at me for doing so. Maybe she was coming back around.

While I spoke, Derek and Gabriel walked into the room and stood casually on either side of my recliner.

Shiva was visibly shaken by my story. "You think my friend Rajiv hid this thing, this . . . microchip? Inside the book?"

"It's actually a tiny flash drive," I explained, then confessed, "We don't know for sure whether it's in the book or not."

Derek sat on the arm of my chair. "It may have been passed to Robin without her knowledge sometime during her flight home from India."

He met my glance and smiled tightly. I knew he'd said that to mollify Shiva's fears, but I could tell he still didn't believe it.

"You know, that happened to me once," Shiva said. "It was on a missionary flight to feed the refugees along the Uganda border. I was in the Entebbe airport, and frankly, I was so worried about Robin at the time that I wasn't paying attention to my surroundings." She reached over to clutch Robin's hand. "You had the measles, love. What a nightmare I went through, worrying about you while being too far away to do anything about it."

"I don't remember ever having the measles," Robin said, shaking her head.

"Oh, dear, maybe it was the mumps," Shiva said, and a frown marred her unlined forehead. "I'm getting so forgetful in my old age. My point is, I was in such a state that someone was able to slip a small parcel of drugs into my tote bag and I was arrested. I was completely innocent, of course. The State Department and the United Nations had to intervene."

"That's terrible, Shiva," my mom said. "We never heard about it back here."

"No, it was kept very quiet," she said, sipping her tea. "I had just started working with the U.N., and nobody wanted an international incident to erupt."

"That was good of them to clear it up

quickly," Dad said.

"Yes, I would've hated to be stuck in a jail cell when Robin was suffering so badly." She gazed fondly at Robin. "It was the mumps. I remember you describing your chipmunk cheeks to me over the phone."

"Anyway, that's why I'm in Dharma, Mom," Robin said wearily. After taking a deep breath and letting it out, she added, "Brooklyn sugarcoated it on my account, but the truth is, that man was shot in the head and the chest. It happened in my bedroom. There was blood everywhere. Then, two days later, I was viciously attacked on the street."

"What?" Shiva's frantic gaze whipped around from Derek to Austin to Gabriel to me. "No. Who did this?"

I watched Robin as Shiva freaked out over that brief but macabre description of the murder scene. Robin wouldn't meet my gaze. I knew something was going on with her.

"The police are on the case," Derek said. "But in the meantime, we thought it best for Robin to leave the city."

"We'll find out who did it," I said with resolve. "And we'll find that flash drive, too. I'm tired of having my door broken down."

"Oh, my heavens," Shiva said, her normally smooth forehead creased with worry. "But this has nothing to do with Rajiv, I assure you. He is a dear friend and would never hurt me this way. I . . . I'll speak to him as soon as possible about this flash drive."

"It would be helpful if you could," Derek said. "The sooner we get some answers, the sooner Robin will be out of danger."

Shiva's frown disappeared slowly and a shrewd smile took its place. "Well, then, isn't it convenient that Rajiv will be joining me in San Francisco in a few days?"

"Convenient indeed," Gabriel mused under his breath.

"Isn't it?" she asked, her eyes wide and clear and focused exclusively on Gabriel. "He insists he couldn't bear my absence from Varanasi for more than a few days, so he's flying out to meet me in San Francisco. I've promised him a trip down the coast after a few days in the city."

"Sounds like a delightful trip," Gabriel murmured, his gaze never leaving hers.

Shiva laughed, a pure, joyful sound. Was it Gabriel's attentions that made her so happy? I couldn't blame her for that. "Yes, it should be fun. But first things first. I'll arrange a meeting with all of you and Rajiv and you'll see that he's innocent. Will next Saturday be soon enough?"

I looked up at Derek. "Is that soon enough?"

"It's perfect," Derek murmured as one eyebrow arched cynically. "Please convey our thanks to him for obliging us."

CHAPTER 13

I wasn't proud of it, but while cleaning up in the kitchen, I noticed Robin heading toward the bathroom. So I followed her. We met at the bathroom door. "I'm going in there with you."

"That's just weird, Brooklyn."

"I want to talk to you."

She tried to stare me down but finally gave up. "A girl can't get any privacy around here."

I closed the door and locked it. "We used to share this bathroom, remember?"

"Yeah. You, me, and your three sisters."

"Crazy," I admitted. "I don't know how you survived."

"It was cozy. I loved living here with you guys."

I sat on the edge of the tub. "It was pretty much the best time ever for me."

"Yeah." Standing in front of the mirror, she brushed her hair with her fingers. "I don't care what you think of me, Brooklyn. I'm just not ready to go back yet."

"For goodness' sake, Robin, you were attacked and terrorized. I don't blame you for not wanting to go back. We only came up here because I needed your help and you weren't answering the phone. We were worried."

"Sorry. I didn't think about you guys being worried. I was with Austin and . . ." She met my gaze in the mirror. "So, did you get all your questions answered?"

"I'll probably have a million more by the time I get home, but Derek and I will work it out. I'm looking forward to grilling Rajiv. I hope he'll provide more insights."

"I hope so, too."

I stretched my legs out and crossed my ankles. "So what do you think you'll do next?"

"I'm staying up here for a few more days."

"That's a good idea," I admitted. "I can tell you're happier here than you were in the city."

"I am. Austin is . . . awesome." Her smile softened. "So fierce and protective. I love the way he . . ."

I squinched up my face and covered my ears. There are some things a sister should never find out about her brother. "I don't want to hear the details."

She laughed. "Fine. I'm not quite ready to share them anyway."

"I appreciate that." I scooted to the end of the tub and leaned back against the tile wall. "You still worry me, though."

"Why? I'll be fine." She paused as if thinking about what she had just said, and then nodded decisively. Maybe she was finally coming back to herself. I was glad to see it. Still, teasing your best friend is practically in the job description.

"I'm just afraid you'll start wearing overalls and, you know, flannel."

She cringed. "Not while I have a breath left in me."

"You say that now, Robin, but you went hiking and camping."

"Yeah," she said, smiling. "Weird." As she spoke, she touched the skin around her eye experimentally.

"Does it still hurt?"

"It twinges every so often, but it feels much better. It's just ugly."

"Not so much anymore." But I scowled at the memory of crazy Galina. "I can't believe we took that lunatic woman down. I think she was on a mission to kill."

Robin shuddered. "I hope she's still in jail."

"She'd better be. I'll call to make sure when I get back to town." I got up and studied her black eye more closely. "It definitely looks a lot better."

"Austin got some concoction from your mom and it really helped."

"Uh-oh. Was it green?"

"Yeah, why?"

I shivered. "Parsley."

"Oh, right." She pulled a tube of pink lip gloss from her purse and squeezed a small amount onto her lips. "Well, I hate to tell you, but it worked great."

"Stranger than fiction," I said, and held out my finger for a dab of her lip gloss. She complied, and I rubbed it on my lips as I returned to my perch on the tub's edge. "So what are you going to do about your mother?"

Robin found an emery board in a canister on the sink and sat with me. "We talked for a few minutes while you were in the kitchen. She'll stay in Dharma for a few days, visit with Guru Bob and some of her friends, and then we'll follow each other back to the city when she goes in to meet Rajiv."

"She seems happy to be here," I said cautiously. Robin and her mother had a complicated relationship, to say the least.

"I was amazed and excited to see her at

first." Her smile turned acerbic. "But then did you see how quickly she turned everything around and talked about herself?"

"Sort of," I said with some caution.

"Oh, come on. The way she went on and on about getting arrested in Uganda? She tried to pretend it was all because I had the measles and she was worried — and I've never had the measles, but whatever. But no, it was all about her. All about her and the United Nations, all about her and her missionary flights around the world. It's always all about her. Maybe she can't help herself. It's just the way she operates. And maybe I'm just hypersensitive to every little thing she says, but still." She tried to shrug off the negative thoughts, but I could see she was hurting.

"You're right," I said loyally. "When Shiva's around, it's all about her."

"Thank you." She hugged me tightly and I hugged her back, relieved that our friendship was back on more solid ground.

I studied her. "Is that why you got so gross when you described the blood and the vicious attack?"

"Yes," she said sharply. "I just wanted to shake her up a little, get her to realize that I was the one suffering at the moment, not her."

I nodded. "Okay. I think it worked."

"God, do I sound like the world's biggest whiny baby?"

"No, absolutely not," I said, and hugged her again.

"Good." She took a deep breath and it seemed to clear things up for her. "So I guess we'll get back to the city Wednesday or Thursday. And I suppose I'll stay at her hotel with her."

"No, you won't," I said. "I'll have your place completely cleaned and good as new by then. You can go home."

"Are you sure?"

"Absolutely."

She winced, then said, "I still feel bad about having you do the work."

I leaned against her. "I won't be doing the work. I'll call other people to do it. And seriously? Better me than you."

"Yeah, I guess."

"I would've taken care of it already, but it's been a little crazy around my place."

Her smile was soft with regret. "Yeah, no kidding."

"But by the time you get back to the city, it'll be a done deal," I said, standing up to give her a hug and end the conversation.

Derek and I made it back to the city with

barely enough time to shower and change into party clothes. For me, the choice was simple. I owned one black dress and one pair of black heels. I'd worn the dress once before, last month when I had a special date with Derek, but we'd had to cancel due to an inconvenient murder.

His offices were located in a beautiful four-story Mediterranean-style building on California Street near the top of Nob Hill. The party took place in the spacious two-story-high lobby, where a crowd of over one hundred people was mingling, drinking, laughing, and chatting when we walked in. They all seemed to know one another, naturally, which intimidated me a little. But since I was here with the boss, I was determined to be cool.

Derek's office administrator, Corinne, stood near the wide arched doorway and acted as unofficial greeter, so I met her first thing. She was in her fifties, slightly overweight but comfortable with it. Her hair was a beautiful platinum gray bob and her eyes sparkled with wit and good humor. She introduced me to her husband, Wallace, who gave truth to the notion that couples grew to resemble each other with age.

A waiter passed with a tray of champagne glasses and Derek handed me one. I took a bracing sip for courage.

"How are you enjoying San Francisco?" I asked Corinne.

"Oh, we've fallen in love with the city," Corinne exclaimed, her British accent clipped. "The first day we arrived, we spent two hours wandering through Golden Gate Park. We got lost in the Japanese garden. It's exquisite. And your arboretum rivals our Kew Gardens. You've seen it, of course?"

"Yes, it's wonderful," I said. "Do you live near the park?"

"Just a few blocks away," Wallace explained. "We've purchased a lovely flat in the Sunset District."

"I love the Sunset," I said. "One of my brothers lived near Ninth and Judah for a while. You must be fairly close to the beach."

"Oh, yes. We love your beaches. So rough-and-tumble. And the fog is lovely." She patted her husband's arm. "Reminds Wallace of home."

"I'm so glad," I said, smiling at him.

Wallace took a long sip of beer. "Drove up to Mendocino last weekend. Spectacular drive. You Californians have no idea what a paradise you live in."

"Oh, we do," I insisted. "San Franciscans love their city and take it very seriously. No teasing allowed. Not like Los Angeles. Everyone mocks Los Angeles, but here, it's not permissible."

They both laughed and Derek beamed. I took a moment to glance around the spacious lobby, then smiled at Corinne. "The offices are beautiful. I imagine you're responsible for pulling everything together in time for this party."

"Oh, I like this girl, I really do," she said, patting Derek's arm.

"So do I," he said, his eyes twinkling.

A look passed between them and Corinne smiled her approval. Had I just passed a test?

"Hi, boss!" a woman cried, and four attractive women gathered around to greet and flirt with Derek. After a minute of laughing and teasing, he introduced me to all of them. I was determined to remember as many names as possible, so there was Shana, word-processing supervisor; Maris, personal assistant to one of Derek's partners; Liv, accounts supervisor; and Kara, human resources secretary. Liv and Maris had moved here from London, and the other two had been hired locally.

Derek had mentioned the name Maris before. She was the one who was working with the real estate broker to find Derek the perfect home. And why that caused a spurt of jealousy to zing through me, I didn't want to know.

The women were dressed for a night on the town, and I guessed this party qualified. They all described their jobs to me in glowing terms, then mentioned a club they were planning to go to later that night. They seemed friendly and interested in what I did for a living, which was nice. Then Derek saw a client approaching and the women took that opportunity to head for the bar.

Derek introduced me to everyone we encountered as he led me on a brief tour of the offices.

"I can't imagine anything more boring than roaming around a business office," he said, grabbing two more glasses of champagne just before we left the lobby and entered a well-lit hall. "But the views from several of the offices are spectacular."

"This building is beautiful," I said as I peeked inside one large office. "I love the high ceilings and the crown moldings and the windows. How did you find the space?"

He glanced at me as he pushed open another office door for my perusal. "Do you recall our adventures in Chinatown last month?"

I smiled. "I do." We'd been chasing down

a rare book but ran into a dead guy instead, something that was happening more and more lately.

"We drove past this building that day," he said.

"We did?"

"Yes. I noticed the sign and made inquiries."

I was drawn to a wall of books in his partner's office. On closer examination, I saw they were mostly spy novels, which seemed appropriate, given the nature of Derek's business. Graham Greene, John le Carré, Ken Follett, Ian Fleming, Jack Higgins. Hundreds more. An impressive collection.

"So you were considering a move even then?" I asked.

"Yes, a bit earlier than that, actually."

"Really?" I turned and headed for the doorway where he stood. "When did you first start thinking about it?"

He closed the door and we walked arm in arm back toward the lobby. "When I saw you across the room at the Covington Library."

I stuttered to a stop in the middle of the wide, well-lit hall and gaped at him. The Covington Library? Where I found my mentor dying in a pool of blood? Where Derek first accused me of murder? "No, you didn't."

"Yes." He held my arm as he kissed me lightly on the lips. "I did."

I was flustered. Flattered. Flummoxed. And okay, yes, flabbergasted. It was hard to think of something to say.

"I've succeeded in silencing you," he said wryly.

"Yeah, well." My throat was dry as a desert, so I took a big, long sip of champagne. "You really know how to shut a girl up."

He moved in for another slow, simmering kiss that managed to fry my brain. Then he pressed his hand to the small of my back and led me toward the lobby. "I'm afraid I must mingle for another hour or so before we can go."

"Right," I mumbled. "Mingle."

Twenty minutes later, while Derek talked with Paul Maynard, a longtime client, and his wife, I excused myself to get another glass of champagne. I wasn't looking for something to drink so much as for the comfort and security of having something to hold on to. As I approached the counter, I heard laughter bubbling at one of the circular bar tables set up nearby.

"So she's Derek's flavor of the month," a

woman said in a low voice.

"She's pretty."

"But nothing special."

"Do we know how they met?"

"I have no idea."

"You work with Corinne. Can't you find out?"

"Maybe when he was out here for the Winslow exhibit. But I can't imagine what he was thinking when he . . ."

The woman's voice dwindled down to a whisper, and despite my subtle efforts to listen in, I couldn't hear anything else. Moments later, though, there was a burst of laughter. At my expense, no doubt.

Was I being paranoid? I summoned my courage and turned to look at the women. Maris, the prettiest of them all, was staring right at me. Seeing me confront them obviously stunned her, and she blinked and looked away.

I clutched my champagne glass. This felt like a bad sitcom. What had I done to deserve their wrath? Besides snag their wealthy, totally hot boss, that is.

And speaking of the hot boss, if Derek were to overhear their bitchy remarks, I didn't think he'd be happy with them. Just a guess. And how rude was it that they were loudly discussing the woman their boss had brought to the party? Did they care about their job security?

I walked as far away as I could get from the group, to the other side of the room. Because if I had to keep hearing their cackling comments, I would be tempted to poke their beady eyes out with one of these ridiculously tight (but very cute) three-inch heels I was sporting.

And there I went again, getting all violent and bloodthirsty. Still, under the circumstances, who could blame me?

Standing near the wall of elaborately scrolled ironwork windows, I centered my energies, aligned my chakras, and took a moment to admire the view of Huntington Park and Grace Cathedral in the distance.

Then I turned back to observe the well-dressed crowd enjoying Derek's generous spread. Waiters strolled among the guests, serving delectable hors d'oeuvres. There were two full bars in the room, with bartenders pouring top-shelf alcohol. Food stations were placed in each corner of the room and featured the four food groups: Italian, Thai, Mexican, and desserts.

Other than the mean girls, this was a fabulous party and I'd been having a good time. Another burst of high-pitched laughter arose from the women's table, and I watched Derek turn and smile at them with admirable tolerance. They returned his attention with an annoying round of giggling and flirting and — Oh, hell. I was being sulky and petulant, wasn't I? I was letting them win.

But were they correct? Was I Derek's flavor of the month? I hated that term, by the way. And hadn't he just admitted that he'd been thinking about moving here since the first night we met? Didn't that mean I was more significant to him than a mere passing fancy? Was I going to believe some cackling women or the man himself?

"Flavor of the month," I muttered. The fact was, I'd been his "flavor" for almost five months now, although we certainly hadn't dated all that time. To be honest, we'd barely dated at all. Then, all of a sudden, he'd moved into my home. We were living together. I'd turned over half my closet to him. Not that I minded. On the contrary, I loved having him there. I loved the way he kissed and the way he looked at me as though I were the only woman in the world. And I loved doing silly things with him, like racing each other to the corner on the way to the coffee shop, and reading the Sunday paper out loud. I loved talking and laughing with him. I loved . . . him.

"Oh, God, shut up," I whispered. No way.

I whipped around and stared out the window, knowing my inability to hide my feelings. Anyone who looked at me right now would guess how I felt by simply tracking the path of my overly ardent gaze in his direction. My radish-red cheeks would probably give me away, too.

It was time to be honest with myself. Why would I have allowed Derek to move in and live with me and rearrange my closet space if I didn't, sort of, you know, love him?

Still, this couldn't be good. It was a well-known fact that I made bad decisions when it came to love. After all, the first man I was engaged to marry turned out to be gay. Not that there was anything wrong with that, but if I were going to all the trouble of marrying someone, I wanted it to mean more than a lifetime of good fashion advice.

Watching Derek now, in his element, surrounded by friends, partners, clients, and employees, I found it hard not to be impressed with everything about him. He was strong, confident, gorgeous, witty, smart, dangerously sexy, loyal.

"Sounds like a Saint Bernard," I admitted under my breath. Well, except for the sexy part. On the other hand, the man had his share of faults. He could be pushy. And let's not forget he carried a gun, although I couldn't complain about that too much, since he'd used it to protect me in a number of frightening situations. Still, the fact that I was with a guy who owned guns and knew how to use them was an ongoing surprise to me.

Derek came with some currently unidentifiable baggage as well, and I worried that more would be revealed — and not in a good way — in the months to come if we stayed together. For instance, he carried on clandestine telephone conversations on a regular basis, going into the guest bedroom and shutting the door. I knew he dealt with private, often classified matters, but sometimes I wondered if maybe he was in there talking to old girlfriends. It was silly of me, but my imagination was a scary place sometimes. Needless to say, the mean girls' comments were stoking that imaginary fire for me.

Another problem was that Derek left town fairly often. That was fine, of course, and usually he told me where he was going. But other times, he wouldn't say. I knew the nature of his business was often confidential, but I hadn't realized how much information he'd have to conceal from me. It didn't leave me with a warm, fuzzy feeling.

Ah, well, who didn't have faults?

More guffawing from the mean girls' table brought me back down to earth. I didn't want to believe those women were right about me and Derek, but doubts crept in anyway. Was this a pattern of his? Was I being used as a halfway house until he got his bearings and found his own comfort zone in the city?

I mentally arm-wrestled my neuroses into submission, tossed back my hair, and strolled across the room, smiling and nodding and greeting people.

Flavor of the damn month. Hell, as long as I was this month's flavor, I was going to be Triple Caramel Chocolate Cherry Crunch.

When I reached Derek's side, I tucked my arm through his.

"Hello, darling," he murmured close to my ear. "I missed you. Were you enjoying the view?"

"I was." I smiled at him and everyone else faded into the fog. "This is a lovely party."

"It is now," he whispered, gazing at me. Then he turned to the small group he'd been talking to. "Gentlemen, allow me to introduce you to my lovely friend Brooklyn Wainwright."

See? I was his lovely friend. Hmm. Well, it

beat the heck out of being introduced as his flavor of the damn month.

Chapter 14

The next day was Sunday. Derek and I walked to South Park for coffee and a breakfast wrap. We were both anxious to discover whether the flash drive might be hiding somewhere inside the Kama Sutra, so I spent the rest of the morning and most of the afternoon in my workshop, taking the book apart. Derek was there, too, watching, pacing, wishing I weren't being so meticulous, praying I would pick the book up in both hands, rip off the covers, and cut into the leather with a carving knife.

He didn't say any of that out loud, of course, but I knew he was thinking it. I could tell by the way he was breathing in and out. Restless. Impatient. Fidgety.

But he would just have to suck it up. That wasn't the way I worked. I especially didn't work well while being watched. I'd never developed that ability. I tackled each step carefully, deliberately. In solitude.

Derek knew that. I think he hovered nearby simply to drive me crazy. I tried to ignore him as I used my scalpel to pick away at the edges of the endpaper covering the leather overlay. I had to be fastidious in order not to tear the endpaper, because its design was irreplaceable. Frankly, the procedure I was doing presently went against all my personal rules of minimal intervention in book reconstruction. But it had to be done. We needed answers.

As I worked, I took photographs with my digital camera to memorialize the process.

When Derek finally slid his stool even closer to mine to get a better look at what I was doing, it was the last straw.

"You're invading my personal space," I said, with as sweet a smile as I could summon, what with my left eye beginning to twitch and all.

"I didn't think you'd mind." Closing his eyes, he sniffed. "You smell good."

"Yeah, nice try," I said with a laugh. "The dank smell of musty vellum is intoxicating, isn't it?"

He gazed at me. "I'm finding it so."

I shook my head. "Don't you have some guns to clean?"

"They're clean," he said with a smirk. "Besides, I get such a kick out of watching you work."

"You get a kick out of tormenting me."

"An attractive side benefit."

"You just want to be here in case I find the flash drive."

"I do indeed."

"Fine." I waved my hand at him. "But just . . . back up a little. You're making me nervous."

"Intriguing thought." From the corner of my eye, I could see him grinning as he scooted his stool a few millimeters away.

As long as I was distracted, I got up and found the bag of chocolate-caramel Kisses I'd bought, popped it open, and poured them into a bowl. I worked better with chocolate.

After munching two Kisses, I picked up my scalpel and tried my best to ignore him as I made a series of tiny picks along the edges of the endpapers.

"Be careful," he muttered. "You'll slice your hand off."

I eyed him. "Will you relax? A scalpel is a girl's best friend."

"I'd heard it was diamonds," he murmured, but was silent after that as he watched me pull back the thin, hand-painted paper that kept the leather turn-ins in place.

Endless minutes later, the leather edge was exposed from top to bottom. Now I began the systematic scraping back of the leather from the boards. Once I'd peeled the leather off the inside cover, I could see the layers of cotton batting the original binder had used to create the padding.

Padded book covers were a popular binding style in the nineteenth century, but they weren't in favor much anymore, thank goodness. It was time-consuming and tricky to get the batting to lie smoothly and evenly between the leather and the boards. These days, when padding was called for, some bookbinders used sheets of synthetic foam rubber, the half-life of which was still undetermined.

I was careful to keep the batting in place as I peeled away the leather. Otherwise, this would be one hellish job of reconstruction.

Despite the anxiety of the search, I took a moment to revel in the lovely scents that arose as the book revealed itself to me. Aged leather, musty vellum, old secrets, beauty. Had it known treachery? Did it suffer pain? Did a book remember? Did it feel the knife? Did my work destroy or revive? Some of both, I supposed.

"Do you see anything?" Derek asked, stirring me from my deep thoughts. "Can you feel any sort of foreign object stuck in there?"

"Not yet. I have a ways to go." I could feel his impatience again, and I couldn't blame him. I was in a hurry to get answers, too, but I knew I had to take care and do it right. I continued peeling, but after a while, I knew it was useless. Nothing was hidden in the batting. I'd been fairly certain of it even before I started, because the seams of the endpapers looked undamaged and unaltered. But that wasn't necessarily definitive. A reputable bookbinder could've done the job, opened up the book, hidden the item, rebound the book, and made it look pristine.

"What about the spine?" he asked. "They might've tucked it inside there."

"That's where I'm going next."

To get to the spine, I used the scalpel to slice along the inner joint. It wasn't quite as painstaking as the earlier task, and within minutes the inner spine was separated from the text block.

"Nothing." He slid off the stool and walked back and forth with his arms folded across his chest. "Now what?"

"I'm sorry."

"It's not your fault, love. But it's frustrating. I was hoping the book held the key."

"I still have to check inside the back cover."

"Right. Of course. Let's do it."

I repeated the process, but twenty minutes later, we'd arrived at the same outcome. There was nothing hidden inside the Kama Sutra covers that even vaguely resembled a flash drive of any size.

I stared at the sections of book laid out on my table. "Could it be affixed to one of the pages or is it too thick?"

"Too thick," he muttered.

"That's what I figured, but thought I'd better ask, just in case."

Since the pieces of the book were spread out anyway, I tore off a sheet of butcher paper from the roll I kept on the counter and laid it on my worktable. I placed the book's pieces on the paper to help establish the "map" that would be invaluable in putting the book back together. I drew boxes around the spine and bits of leather, boxes around the threads and text block, then wrote names, notes, and details inside the boxes so I wouldn't forget or lose track of anything. Finally, I took more photos of individual items as well as one big picture of the entire tabletop.

I hadn't bothered removing old glue from the inner spine or the boards. That was something I could do once I was alone and back to my day-to-day work. But I pulled out my woodblock press and left it on the worktable in anticipation of really going to work on this book.

Because I was curious, I grabbed my magnifying glass to examine the diamonds that made up the peacock's crest on top of his head.

As I'd already determined, there was no way I could remove them and return them to their original state. Each gem was wrapped in a thin band of gold, then inset into the leather. I would simply remove as much dirt as I could by rubbing everything with a lightly dampened cloth.

"May I see?" Derek said.

"Sure." I handed him the magnifying glass and watched as he studied the cover up close.

"It's a beautiful book," he said after a moment. "I hope our search hasn't caused extra work for you."

"Not really. I wanted to check the batting for mold, so I would've done this anyway." There was nothing else we could do, so I covered everything with a soft white cloth and put my camera away.

As we left the workroom, Derek said, "What time are the cleaners due at Robin's tomorrow?"

"Not until after lunch, around twelve thirty."

"Good. That'll give us a chance to do one more search of her rooms tomorrow morning."

"Us?"

"Yes. After that, we might take a drive over to Alex's apartment and see what we can find."

"We?" I held back a smile.

He turned. "Am I to believe you're not interested in going with me?"

"Absolutely not. I'm just a little astounded that you would include me without my insisting."

"Darling, we're partners," he said, wrapping his arm around me as we strolled into the kitchen. "I wouldn't dream of breaking the law without you by my side."

I brought candy corn for sustenance.

Derek called his office to let them know he wouldn't be coming in at all that day. Since he didn't have meetings to attend or pending crises to deal with, he wanted to spend time trying to clear up Robin's mess. I assured him I would be eternally grateful for his help and he let me know he'd hold me to that promise.

So on the off chance that Alex actually had hidden the flash drive somewhere inside Robin's place, we were going to spend the next two hours searching through every nook and cranny possible. First, Derek gave me some pointers on the fine art of covert searching; then he set me loose in the second bedroom, which Robin used as a sculpture studio. She normally locked this room, because it held her treasured sculptures, so it hadn't been trashed like the others. I knew where she kept the key, so I unlocked and opened the door, thankful that no blood had been tracked inside.

Standing in the doorway, I tried to figure out the best place to start. The bookshelves along one wall were jammed with art books held upright by clay molds of human hands and feet, a cow skull, jars of old paintbrushes. The top shelf was home to more than twenty clamps and a heavy-duty pair of cable cutters.

One long table held sculptures in various stages of completion. Most were heads or busts, but there were also a few torsos. Male and female, all life-size. There were more paintbrushes of every size and shape, many of them standing upright in glass jars filled with clear liquid. Coffee cans held rulers and dozens of tools for carving, shaping, and cutting. A mallet hung from a hook off the side of the table. Everything was splotched with dried liquid clay in shades of beige or sage or gray. Under the table were stacks of rags and ten or twelve plastic buckets of different sizes.

Abstract pen-and-ink drawings were tacked on the wall. Streaked wood pallets were piled precariously next to four large wrapped chunks of clay in a corner. In another corner were her potter's wheel and a sturdy stool. On a pedestal in the middle of the room was a wonderful, life-size sculpture of a dancing goddess.

I'd been in here countless times, but I was struck anew by the odd beauty of all the assembled bits of junk. From any angle, there was a compelling still-life portrait. How in the world was I supposed to find something so tiny in the midst of all this? I decided to get started and see how far I got.

"Are you sure it's a flash drive we're looking for?" I asked as we drove away from Robin's house two hours later.

Derek gave me a sideways glance. "I'm sure."

"Just checking. Because if it's not a flash drive, I'm going to be very annoyed with your informant."

"I'll alert him to watch his ass."

The crime scene cleanup service had arrived, and after letting them know exactly what we needed them to do, Derek and I left them to their dirty work in Robin's apartment and drove across town to Alex's place in the Richmond.

We hadn't found a flash drive in Robin's home, no surprise. But in the interests of leaving no stone unturned, we'd given it our best shot.

Derek turned off the GPS after I suggested we take the scenic route up Market to Portola. We wound around Twin Peaks, catching dramatic views of the city around every turn, then descended into the Sunset District. At 19th Avenue, we turned right and entered Golden Gate Park. Once inside the park, I asked him to turn on MLK Drive, then cut back on JFK so we could enjoy the green.

"It's the long way around," I explained. "But if we stayed on Nineteenth, it would feel like any other busy thoroughfare in the middle of town."

"This city is a constant surprise," he said, gazing right and left as we drove past green meadows and thick groves of trees.

"There's a pretty lake in the middle of the park," I said. "We can go and rent a lazy rowboat sometime."

"Sounds delightful," he said, and squeezed my hand.

We'd both been feeling frustrated and worried about finding the flash drive before Robin got back to town, but the brief change of scenery lightened our spirits.

We exited the park, winding up on 30th Avenue in the Outer Richmond. Alex's apartment was on 26th, three blocks from the gold-domed Russian Orthodox church that served the many immigrants who had moved to this area in the last twenty years after the collapse of the Soviet Union.

Derek had wangled the address from Inspector Jaglom, so we drove slowly past the apartment first, then parked a block and a half away.

"I can't wait to see how you're going to get us inside this place," I said as I shut the car door.

"Watch and learn," he said cryptically, and took my arm.

"Yes, Sherlock." We walked the first block past rows of uniform, three-story Marina-style flats. The architectural style was named for the Marina District where they were first built and proliferated. On this street, each small building had a garage on the ground level, with one apartment each on the second and third floors. Most tended to feature spacious rooms, hardwood floors, and bay windows.

We crossed the street and approached Alex's place just as a woman exited through the gated front entrance, then turned to lock it.

I gasped and whipped around, pulling Derek over to the nearest wall. Using him as a shield, I whispered, "Kiss me, please?"

He obliged. A moment later, he murmured, "Not that I'm complaining, you understand, but why am I kissing you?"

I exhaled in relief that I hadn't been seen. "The woman who just walked out of Alex's place? It's Robin's attacker, Galina."

Derek craned his neck to watch her. "She's going the other way. Just got into a car. Looks like a Jetta."

"What's she doing out of jail?" I groused, mentally kicking myself for not having followed up with the police on her whereabouts. "I can't believe it. She almost killed Robin and now she's walking around as free as a bird."

"She's driving away," he said, and then a few seconds later, "Let's go."

I tried to act casual as we strolled to Alex's entry gate, but my nerves were on red alert. Derek removed some thin tool from his pocket and slipped it into the keyhole. After a moment, he turned the knob and we walked inside.

"That was a little too easy," I said in a low voice.

"No, I'm just that good," he said, leading the way up the steps.

I chuckled and a tiny bit of tension left my shoulders. But I couldn't quite brush off the sense of impending doom. What if Galina returned for some reason? I really didn't want to deal with her.

When we got to Alex's door, Derek worked his magic again and whisked the door open within ten seconds. He took one cautious step inside, and I followed.

"Christ almighty," he swore.

"What?" But he turned and I saw for myself.

"Go." He grabbed my shoulders and pushed me out the door. I went willingly.

"Call the police," he added, drawing his gun from his shoulder holster. "We've got another body."

CHAPTER 15

"You should come with a warning label, Wainwright," Inspector Lee said, then snorted at her own joke. I wasn't laughing. Her comment hit a little too close to home.

It wasn't like I went looking for dead bodies, although I could see how it would appear that way to the police.

According to the passport inside the dead guy's pocket, his name was Stanislav Ostrovsky, a Ukrainian. Not surprising, since he was found inside the place rented by Alex, another Ukrainian. I'd seen only a flash of Stanislav's body before Derek pushed me away, but it was enough to make me sick, and not just in a physical sense. No, this one hurt my heart. He looked too young and innocent to be caught up in all this spy-versus-spy nonsense. For a few moments, I speculated that he might be Alex's younger brother. Otherwise, maybe they were recruiting spies out of high school these days.

What did I know? But I concluded sadly that he had to be involved in the same operation that Galina and Alex were caught up in. Why else would he have been found here in a place Alex used as a cover for his intelligence activities?

The Ukrainian connection fed into Lee's theory that this whole mess was related to the escalating turf war. Once again, Derek and I kept mum, but I wouldn't be able to be quiet much longer. We were withholding evidence, and all those levels of government jurisdiction didn't matter to me as long as Robin was still in danger. If the police knew we were looking for a mysterious missing flash drive, they would freak, and I wouldn't blame them.

I knew Derek wasn't in favor of telling the police. He'd obtained the intelligence on the flash drive from his sources at Interpol and knew there were people at the highest levels of the U.S. government who were aware of the situation and would step in if and when they felt the need to do so.

I didn't share with him that confidence that our government officials would play fairly. Besides, I had a personal relationship with Lee and Jaglom. I didn't want them coming out of this with egg on their faces because their higher-ups didn't feel a need to keep them in the loop.

"At least we saw who killed the guy," I said to Inspector Lee in my defense, lame as it was.

Lee and I stood on the small balcony outside Alex Pavlenko's apartment. She and Jaglom had been first on the scene, beating the uniformed guys and the medical examiner. Now Jaglom and Derek were talking inside while we all waited for the medical examiner and the crime scene specialists to show up. Two uniformed officers were already knocking on neighbors' doors, looking for witnesses.

Lee smirked. "So you're saying you saw Galina Shirkova pull the trigger?"

So that was her last name, I thought, then sighed. "No, I didn't exactly see her do it."

"You hear a gunshot?"

"Okay, no. But —"

"All you really saw was Shirkova walking down the sidewalk and driving away in a car."

"Maybe so, but she was in there," I said, pointing at Alex's door. "Then she left, drove away. Two minutes later, we get up here and, oh, look, there's a dead body."

"Still not good enough."

"Oh, come on," I retorted. "She's a menace who never should've been let out of jail.

I don't know why you're hedging about her. If I'd done the same thing, you'd already have your handcuffs out."

She pulled them off her belt and twirled them around her finger. "That's because you would look so good in these."

I regarded her askance. "Okay, that's weird."

"Yeah, maybe," she said, chuckling as she slipped the handcuffs back in place.

It had been a little tricky at first, explaining to the police what we were doing at Alex's apartment. I'd attempted an elaborate explanation with justifications and details, but Lee interrupted rudely, shutting me down, telling me I was the worst damn liar on God's green earth. That was when Derek had stepped in to offer a semblance of the truth, saying we were merely curious to see where Alex lived, but when we saw Galina leaving, we felt duty-bound to check things out.

Now, desperate to change the subject away from murder, I asked, "How's your mom doing?"

"Hey, she's doing okay. Thanks for asking." Lee leaned her elbows on the porch rail. "No sign of cancer after the surgery and the tests, so she'll be coming home from the hospital tomorrow."

"That's great news. Does she have someone staying with her, helping her get around?"

She made a face. "Oh, hell, no. She's too damned independent for that. But she's got good friends and neighbors, so I've secretly organized them all to take turns checking on her, offering to pick stuff up at the grocery, that sort of thing."

"You're a good daughter."

"What're you gonna do?" She lifted both hands in surrender. "I can't be there around the clock, so this is the next-best way to make sure she's being looked after."

We kibitzed for twenty more minutes until the medical examiner arrived. Then Derek and I took advantage of the distraction and left the scene.

In the car, Derek gave me some bad news. "Inspector Jaglom believes the victim was shot sometime yesterday."

"What?" I cried. "But Galina was just there. She had to have shot him during those few minutes before we got there."

"I'm sorry, darling. Nathan will call with the medical examiner's findings, but he's fairly certain, based on rigor mortis, that the man was shot at least twenty-four hours ago."

I punched the seat cushion. "So they

won't even question Galina."

"They'll certainly question her if they can find her."

"Yeah, that's the problem. Where is she?"

It was after five o'clock, too late to get back to Robin's place before the cleaning service clocked out for the day. I called Tom, the lead guy, on my cell and he assured me they'd be back to finish the job tomorrow morning, bright and early. For someone who cleaned up the dirtiest consequences of violent death, he was remarkably affable.

Too tired to cook, we parked the car in the garage and walked to Hama, my favorite hole-in-the-wall sushi joint two blocks away. Laughing and arguing about what to share, we finally settled on a mixed platter of sushi, sashimi, and tempura. We ate the whole thing, finished off a small bottle of sake, and were in bed and asleep by ten o'clock that night.

The next day, Derek was up early and I joined him for coffee before he left for the day. Seeing him dressed for work in a beautiful dark gray suit, white shirt, and swirly navy-and-gold tie that by itself probably cost more than all the shoes in my closet, I was reminded of the mean girls from the office party. At this point, I didn't even care about the flavor-of-the-month comment. What bugged me all over again was that they could talk so rudely and vocally about a woman their boss was obviously dating and cared for enough to bring to the party. It showed disrespect for Derek, and I hated them for that.

As my father says, sometimes people just suck.

After Derek left, I took a shower and dressed, then went to work. There was so much to do on the Kama Sutra, but first I wanted to get little Tyler's beloved book finished and back to him.

So I spent the next three hours working on *Where the Wild Things Are,* separating the text block from the cover, resewing the signatures, and reinforcing the spine with a strip of heavy card stock. I replaced the endpapers with a thicker piece of stock that would strengthen the joints. Then I slid sheets of Mylar in between the front and back endpapers and the text block and glued everything down.

After that, I slipped the book between two pieces of wrapped plywood to keep it secure, then placed it in Big Betty, my heavy-duty antique brass book press, and clamped it securely. The book would remain there for twenty-four hours so the glue could dry, then be good as new for Tyler.

At eleven, I drove over to Robin's to meet the cleaning crew. Yesterday I'd suffered a twinge of uneasiness when Derek and I left them alone to work in her apartment. But I'd been assured that the company employees were fully bonded, and besides, they'd come highly recommended by Inspector Jaglom. That had to count for something. Now, walking through the apartment with Tom, the head guy, I was happy to see that my trust had not been misplaced.

I learned two things from Tom that I'd never realized about crime scenes before. The first was that when blood was spilled, the scene became a biohazard site. Robin had tracked Alex's blood from the bedroom to the bathroom and across the floor of her living room. These cleanup guys took their job seriously; they dressed head to toe in disposable hazmat gear.

The other thing I learned was that crime scene cleanup was covered by Robin's homeowner's insurance, so Tom wouldn't take my check. Go figure.

But back to the biohazard issue. Not only had the guys cleaned and wiped down every surface where all that creepy fingerprint dust had scattered, but they'd also disinfected every square inch of the floors and walls surrounding the bed where Alex had died. They had stripped and disposed of the bloody linens, only to discover that the mattress itself would have to be thrown out.

I cringed when Tom told me that, knowing it meant that Alex's blood had seeped through the sheets and into the mattress. I asked them to dispose of the box spring, as well, knowing Robin would never want to sleep on any part of a bed where Alex's blood had been spilled so violently.

But in the midst of all the negative vibes, there were Tom and his team. Compassionate and respectful, they left Robin's place sparkling clean and smelling as fresh as springtime. I couldn't thank them enough for the work they'd done.

On the way to the mall, I had a long telephone conversation with Robin, who let me know she wanted the exact same super-deluxe mattress she had before. So I spent the afternoon buying her a mattress and box spring, then shopped for sheets, two new pillows, a down comforter, a duvet, and some cheerful mix-and-match throw pillows. I made sure everything I bought was the most beautiful and most expensive I could find. I knew my finicky friend well enough to know that that was exactly what she would've done.

■ ■ ■ ■

That evening, I decided to experiment with making a shepherd's pie. I had warm memories of my mother's version, and I wanted comfort food after spending time with Robin's crime scene cleaners.

Derek called to let me know he was running late, so once dinner was in the oven, I took the opportunity to work on the Kama Sutra. The only French dictionary I'd found at the mall that afternoon was for children, so I didn't know how much help it would be, but I would consult it anyway. I'd also bought *The Knucklehead's Guide to the Kama Sutra,* thinking it might come in handy. And I booted up my computer in case I needed to find references online.

I picked up the text block and turned at random to one of the middle pages and began to read, translating as I went along. I lost track of time as I studied the romantic French phrases and meticulously wrote out the English translations in my notebook. I had progressed from the chapter that emphasized sharing love and mutual commitment to the beginning of the section on the sixty-four elements of sexual loving, but now I struggled with one line.

The lingam soothes the fire in the yoni, and their union appeases . . . Appeases what? I couldn't make out the French words.

Yesterday, I didn't have a clue what a lingam was, never mind a yoni. Now I blushed whenever I came upon the words, but at least I knew what body parts they referred to. I had managed to translate another page when the front door opened and Derek walked inside.

"Hello, darling, are you still working?" he said as he strolled over and kissed me. Then he noticed what I was reading and a slow smile formed. "Ah. Do you need help with that?"

I met his smile with one of my own. "I do. I'm sure you must know twenty different languages, but how are you at reading Old French?"

"Do you believe the book is that old?" He placed his briefcase on the desk and took off his jacket. "I'm no expert, but didn't Old French fade out with the bubonic plague?"

I chuckled. "No, the book isn't that old, but I'm wondering if some of the archaic language was chosen deliberately."

"Let's find out, shall we?"

I slanted the page so he could read it and pointed to the sentence I'd given up on a little while ago. "It's this word that's giving me trouble. *Arracher.*"

He squinted at the word, then glanced up. "*Arracher.* To extract. To pull out."

"Right." Why did it sound so sexual when he said it? "I did a Google search and found this 1887 French dictionary. Its first definition is 'to pluck out.' But in context with the sentence . . ."

" '*Arracher la mangue meür,*' " he read, finishing the phrase. "*La mangue* is mango, of course. But I don't recognize *meür.*"

I scanned the 1887 dictionary. "Here it is. That spelling is out of use. The modern word is *mûrs,* which means 'ripe.' "

"Ah, that makes sense. 'Pluck the ripe mango.' " He raised one eyebrow. "Lovely visual."

"Um . . . yes." Was it getting hotter in here or what? "I guess I was overcomplicating the phrases."

"What else have you translated?"

Pointing to a previous illustration, I said, "I've got this one worked out. It's, um, 'ride the wild stallion.' "

"Stallion." He nodded, fighting back a smile. "Of course. Go on."

"They're a little obsessed with animals in here," I muttered, my throat suddenly dry. I turned the pages and pointed to the various animals I'd translated. "Here's a cow, a dog, a crab, a cat, a goat, a crow."

"The crow is not to be missed."

"Well," I whispered, then coughed to clear my throat. "Maybe we've seen enough."

"Hardly." He turned the page and we both gazed at a couple enjoying a position as old as time. Beneath was a phrase I hadn't yet translated.

"Ah, 'driving the nail home,' " Derek translated easily, and shot me a lopsided grin. "An old favorite of mine."

My vision was starting to fog up, making it difficult to write in my notebook. "I really should check on dinner."

"How about that one?" he asked, pointing to a picture on the opposite page.

"You're taunting me, right?"

"Yes." He shifted closer, lifted my hair, and planted kisses on my neck.

I groaned, then focused my energies on my three highest chakras in order to keep from melting into a pool of lust on my clean floor. Fine. Two could play at this game, right? But it was getting harder to concentrate. I turned reluctantly and read the French words under the rather graphic illustration he'd pointed to. "That one is known as 'trapping the snake.' "

He nuzzled my neck as he reached for the

top button of my shirt. "And exactly what are they doing there?"

I didn't have to look too carefully at the drawing of two people, one on top of the other, lying in opposite directions. I'd already spent way too much time studying it. "Each person holds on to their partner's feet. The movement is more of a rocking motion. It's supposed to be . . . more pleasurable for the woman."

"I'm in favor of that," he whispered in my ear, causing a few of my synapses to snap and fire.

"Yeah, me, too." Did I really say all that out loud? Were we having a conversation? Why wasn't he tearing my clothes off and driving the nail home? But wait. Dinner was cooking in the oven. Oh, God.

He'd finished with my buttons and was pushing my blouse off my shoulders. "Do I smell something cooking?" he murmured against my skin as his mouth traveled along my jawline.

I barely heard him through a fog of pleasure. "What?"

His deep chuckle reverberated as he raised his head and gazed into my eyes. "I said, I'm going to kiss you again. Then I'm going to pick you up and carry you to the bedroom, where we'll conduct research for your book."

"Oh, yes, research," I said, smiling up at him. "But dinner . . ."

"I'll turn off the oven."

Much later that night, long after we'd had dinner in bed and conducted more *research,* Derek shifted his pillow and sat up. "I had to fire two employees today."

"I'm sorry," I said. "That can't be easy."

"On the contrary, it was the easiest thing I did all day." He tilted his head to make eye contact with me. "Why didn't you tell me about those women at my office party?"

"What?" I blinked a few times, then rolled over and sat up. This was not a conversation I'd imagined having in bed. In fact, this was not a conversation I ever thought we'd be having at all. I guessed I was hoping the problem would just go away.

"Corrine told me," he said.

"So you've known about it for days?"

"No, I just found out this morning. However, Corinne has known for days. She heard them talking and saw your reaction. She expected you to tell me and thought that at any moment I'd storm in and fire the women. When I didn't do anything, she finally brought it up. Why didn't you say something to me?"

I sighed and adjusted my pillow to get comfortable. "I'll admit I was hurt by their words, Derek, but I wasn't going to whine about it to you. They were just women being . . . you know." I wasn't about to call his employees *bitches,* but I could tell by his frown that he got the gist. "Believe me, my biggest problem wasn't with what they said about me, but the fact that they were so disrespectful to you. But even so, I still didn't feel I could say anything. They work for you, they're loyal to you, and I assumed you trusted them. For all I know . . ." I stared at my hands.

"For all you know, they were speaking the truth." Troubled, he reached out and brushed my hair back from my forehead, then cupped my cheek with his hand. "They weren't."

"I'm glad."

He nodded, then gritted his teeth and said, "Can you put yourself in my shoes for a moment and imagine my reaction when Corinne told me what she'd heard? I felt . . . ill, absolutely sick to my stomach, that people I thought I could trust would betray me by hurting someone I care so deeply about. I was furious. I didn't want to simply fire them. I wanted to throw them into a dungeon somewhere and leave them to the dogs."

I smiled forlornly. "That would teach them to cross you."

"Indeed." He grimaced. "Sadly, Corinne pointed out that I have no dungeon here in the States, so my only remedy was to fire them."

"I'm so sorry."

"Yes, so am I, because it wasn't nearly as satisfying. On top of that, I could only fire two of the women. Corinne reminded me of all the red tape we had to go through to get the other two transferred over here from London, so they've been sent to different departments, put on probation, and had their security clearances revoked."

"Wow, don't mess with Mr. Stone."

"No," he said tightly. "Don't."

I didn't feel like gloating, but I didn't feel guilty, either. I flashed back to the way I felt when I heard the four women cackling about me. I was hurt, confused, and angry. I remembered how it made me doubt Derek and his feelings for me. "I'm sorry I didn't say something sooner."

He searched my face — looking for what, I wasn't sure. Finally he said, "Do you trust me, Brooklyn?"

I was taken aback. "Of course."

"Then trust me when I tell you that I'll never hurt you — No, wait. Let me rephrase that." He pulled me closer and wrapped his arms around me. "I will never knowingly hurt you. I know the work I do sometimes worries you, and I'll try to be more open about it when I'm able. But trust me when I say there is nothing I wouldn't do for you. If you ever have a doubt or a concern about anything I say or do, or *don't* say or do, I want us to talk about it. Will you promise me?"

I nodded and rested my head on his shoulder. "Yes, I promise."

His hold tightened. "I trust you, too, Brooklyn," he whispered, and kissed my temple.

A gasp closed my throat and tears sprang to my eyes. His simple statement overwhelmed me. I could feel his heart beating in rhythm with my own and it filled me with joy. I almost blurted out how much I loved him, but I hesitated. The time wasn't quite right. We'd come so far so fast, it was probably best to wait. Right now, all I wanted to do was savor this moment in his arms.

The following morning, I found myself moving a little slower than usual and chalked it up to all the Kama Sutra research

Derek and I had undertaken the night before. That's right, I was calling it *research,* and that was the end of the discussion. A warm shower, a hot cup of coffee, and two aspirin fixed me right up.

After Vinnie popped in to feed Pookie, I left the house and drove to Robin's neighborhood. My first stop was a florist's shop, where I bought a bouquet of red tulips. Then I couldn't resist running into the bakery and buying two red velvet cupcakes as a welcome-home gift. I drove to Robin's place and waited for the deliverymen to bring her new bed. After the movers had put it all together, I made up the bed for her, then placed the tulips on her dining room table with a note welcoming her home and letting her know there were cupcakes in the refrigerator.

That afternoon, Inspector Lee called to let me know they'd picked up Galina and brought her in for questioning. I was happy they'd found her, but it concerned me that Inspector Jaglom thought she might be innocent, based on the time frame when that young man, Stanislav, was killed. If Galina didn't do it, then who did? Who else was involved in this espionage fiasco?

But looking on the bright side again, at

least Galina was in custody and unable to attack Robin or me.

Nevertheless, I felt anxious and antsy, so I buried myself in work. Fortifying myself with three kinds of chocolate, I began the actual restoration of the Kama Sutra.

I started with the leather cover, wiping it with a specially treated cloth that wouldn't hurt the leather but would clean away any grime that had been caught in the seams and around the embedded gems. When I got to the elaborately gilded edges of the leather, I pulled out my magnifying glass to study the dentelles more closely.

As I stared at the intricate design, I recalled the information Rajiv sent me that indicated that the book had been created sometime between 1840 and 1880. I had accepted that time frame, not only because his papers said so but because some of the designs and the precision of the tooling was typical of French bookbinding methods during those decades.

But forty minutes later . . . good grief, I didn't know what to think. Was it feasible? I couldn't wrap my mind around the possibility. I rolled my shoulders and combed my hair back with my fingers. It couldn't be true. Could it? I popped another Butterfinger ball in my mouth and grabbed my magnifying glass.

"What's going on?" Derek said.

I jolted slightly. "Where did you come from?"

"I've been standing here watching you for the last five minutes."

"You have? I didn't see you."

"I know. You're so wound up, you're shaking the table. What I can't figure out is whether you're trembling with happiness or anger. Or perhaps it's excitement. Have you been peeking at the pictures without me, love?"

I looked at the book, then smiled at him. "Never."

"Good," he said, prowling toward me. "But something's captured your attention. What is it?"

I hadn't realized my left knee was shaking like crazy. I pressed my palm down against my leg to make it stop.

"Tell me what's got you so tickled," he said, as he dragged another stool over and sat next to me.

"Okay." Where to begin? I wondered. "At first I thought this book was a nineteenth-century work, but now I think that's wrong."

Derek focused in on me. "Are you saying it's a forgery?"

"No," I said quickly. "Well, yes, actually.

At least insofar as the information goes that I received from Rajiv. But if my theories are correct, he's wrong. I can't say whether he deliberately told me something different or if he's simply unaware of what he has. I guess I can ask when we meet him."

"Of course you can."

"Right. But my point is, I believe this book is almost a century older and infinitely more valuable than I originally thought. Look at this."

He scooted his chair closer. I placed the back cover in front of him and handed him the magnifying glass. "See these tooled and gilded designs on the leather here? Near the edge of the endpaper?"

"Here?" He pointed, then glanced at me. "Where it's been ripped apart?"

"Oh." I frowned at him. "I did that the other day when we were looking for the flash drive. But don't worry. I'll fix it when I put the book back together."

Derek chuckled. "I'm not worried. You know what you're doing."

"Yes, I do." Taking a deep breath, I exhaled slowly. I was nervous, I realized, and there went my knee, shaking again. I shifted in my chair and rolled my shoulders to realign my energies. "Anyway, this mark on the leather is called a dentelle, and it —"

"What's a dentelle?"

I rewarded him with a beaming smile, as though he were my star pupil. "Good question. It's a specific pattern made in the leather by a gilding tool. Here, it gives the effect of a lacy border along the inside cover. Can you see?"

"Yes." He bent closer and focused the magnifying glass. "Looks a bit like a snowflake."

"Exactly," I said. "Sometimes they're simple, sometimes more elaborate. I think of it as the crown molding on a book. It softens the border and distracts the eye from the hard edges where leather and paper meet."

"Yes, I see what you mean."

"Here's what I'm excited about. It's common for different binderies to create their own signature dentelles. Sometimes the pattern is simply repeated by the hand of the binder, and sometimes they design a pattern in metal and form a plate. That plate is placed over the leather and the design is etched into it; then gold sheets are rolled or worked into the indentations."

"Fascinating."

"I know — it's complicated. Anyway, some experts can open a book and state unequivocally that the book was created at a certain bindery, based wholly on the dentelles. I'm not a true expert, but I know enough to have given a few lectures on the subject."

He patted my knee. "And I know they were riveting."

I laughed. "Of course they were. Anyway, call me cuckoo, but I'm almost certain that the particular pattern of this dentelle is identical to the pattern used by the bindery of Jean-Pierre de Garme."

Derek leaned over with the magnifying glass and stared at the gold tooling for another moment, then sat back in his chair. "Well, that's lovely, isn't it?"

"Lovely?" Laughing again, I took the magnifying glass back. "You bet your sweet ass it's lovely. But I don't think you grok the true significance of what I'm saying."

It was his turn to laugh. "Apparently not, so why don't you explain it in simple English. Speak slowly. I'm still a little weak from your complimenting of my ass."

"Sorry. That was rude." I clutched his arm. "But this is an emotional moment for me."

"Clearly," he murmured, and pushed a strand of hair away from my cheek. I think it was his way of calming me down with his touch. "Tell me."

I took another breath and let it escape slowly. "Jean-Pierre de Garme was one of the royal bookbinders to Louis the Sixteenth of France."

"Ah. Well, that is monumental."

"Yes!" I choked on a sudden laugh. "Yes!" Unable to sit still another moment, I jumped up and paced a few steps in either direction, then shrieked and raised my arms in victory.

"It's incredible," I cried. "If it's true, this book was made sometime in the late seventeen hundreds, which makes it well over two hundred years old. Which also explains why this translation doesn't follow the Burton text, of course."

He stood as well and pushed his chair in. "Because Burton didn't begin his translation of the Kama Sutra until the late eighteen hundreds."

"Yes." Tapping my fingers on the back of the chair, I calculated. "And that brings up an entirely different issue. This translation could very well be the first evidence that someone else in the Western world discovered the Kama Sutra almost a century before Burton."

"A stunning possibility," Derek said.

"But I can't even think about that right now. Not until I've done more research."

"I have every confidence in your ability to find the truth."

"Thank you. That means a lot." I kissed him lightly on the cheek. "Just think, Derek. This book might've been commissioned by the king of France." I grinned at him, then frowned. "Was Louis the Sixteenth known for his wild sexual pursuits? Do you know if he and Marie Antoinette were, you know, players?"

Derek laughed. "I doubt it. They were too busy evading the guillotine."

I laughed with him. "Right. It doesn't matter. Jean-Pierre is the key."

"Good point." He whirled me around and planted a hot, hard kiss on my lips.

"Wow," I whispered. "What was that for?"

"You," he said, and bent to kiss my neck, causing shivers to zip up and down my spine. "I'm very proud of you and your discovery. But, darling, if we're not going to look at the naughty pictures, I've got to get back to my phone calls."

I smiled and touched my cheek to his. "Okay, I'll be working here a while longer. Oh, I should call Ian at the Covington. He's going to die when he hears this."

"Do send him my regards."

A day later, Robin and Shiva arrived back

in the city around noon. Robin called me first thing to let me know that the flowers were beautiful, the cupcakes were delectable, and the bed was spectacular. I couldn't help but breathe a sigh of relief that I'd nailed it. You just never knew about such things.

"It's like it never happened, Brooklyn," she said.

I recognized her tone, so I dropped my scalpel and moved to my desk chair to sit and talk. "You almost sound sad about that."

"It is a little sad, don't you think? All trace of him is gone. Don't get me wrong. I'm glad they cleaned everything up. But they cleaned it up so well that there's not even a vibe of Alex left."

"I'm sorry, honey," I said gently. "But that's kind of what those guys get paid to do."

She chuckled softly. "And I appreciate it. I guess I thought I'd walk in and feel his presence somehow. And I don't."

"And you wanted to?"

She thought for a moment. "No. I really didn't. I'm just in a weird place. I'm still flipping out to think that I chose to go out with someone so duplicitous. So now shouldn't I be questioning my choices?

Shouldn't I wonder about my feelings for Austin? Is he really the right man for me?"

I picked up a pencil and drummed it on the desk surface. "Yes, he is."

"It's that simple?"

"Yes," I said. "You've loved him for more than half your lifetime. This isn't an impulsive decision, Robin. It's nothing at all like the situation with Alex. And Austin finally realizes he feels the same way. Are you really going to question that? Do you know how rare it is to find real love?"

"I guess."

"Austin is the real thing," I said. "Alex was a blip on the screen. A bump in the road. A misstep. A wrinkle in time."

She laughed. "Enough with the metaphors."

"Really? Because I have more. A leaf blowing in the wind."

"A ship passing in the night?" she whispered.

"Um, well," I said, and decided to shut up.

"Anyway," she said, changing tones again, "the bedding is beautiful. I'm still in shock that you showed such good taste."

There was the Robin I knew and loved. "Wait till you see the bill."

"Worth it at any cost," she said. "Thanks."

"No worries. So, did your mom get a chance to talk to Rajiv yet?"

"They spoke last night. He's in New York right now and won't be in San Francisco until Saturday morning. She set up the meeting for the afternoon."

"Okay, I'll tell Derek."

"Great. I think we should all be there."

"I do, too." I grabbed a pencil and pulled out my desk calendar. "Oh, crap-a-doodle."

"What's wrong?"

"We promised Jeremy we'd go to the Castro Street Fair to see his street performance."

"That's right." Robin groaned. "I forgot all about it."

"Rats." I sighed. "I'll tell him we can't make it."

"Oh, but that's my favorite street fair," she said. "There's a great local sculptor who always has a booth there. And I might get some of my stuff in there, too."

I thought about it. Truth was, I loved the Castro fair, too. All those cute boys in their leather chaps. And the food stalls were always top-notch. And Jeremy had been so excited about having us all show up to watch him perform.

"Maybe we can set up the meeting for later in the afternoon," I said. "I think

Jeremy's on at one o'clock."

"Yes, okay," she said. "We can watch Jeremy, then meet Rajiv at the Cove Cafe maybe around three or four."

The Cove was your basic American diner, but it wasn't greasy, the waiters were great, and it was located on Castro Street. We wouldn't have to walk too far after Jeremy's performance.

"And Shiva will love the street fair," Robin added. "It'll remind her of the bazaar in Varanasi."

"Minus the Ganges," I said, laughing. "Okay, if she's up for it, that would work out perfectly."

"She's up for anything I say she's up for," Robin murmured.

"It's like that, is it?"

"Oh, yeah. She kind of flipped out once she heard what I'd gone through. She came by Austin's place twice a day just to check up on me. It's weird having her around, doting on me."

"I think it's nice that she's worried about you." After all the years of benign neglect, it was good to know Shiva actually cared about her daughter.

"We'll see how long it lasts, now that we're living in the same space for the next few days."

"Yeah, good luck with that," I said. "Listen, Derek's going out with clients Friday night, so I'm having a girls' night. Margaritas and tacos. If you and your mom don't have plans, why don't you come over? It would be interesting to introduce Shiva to Vinnie."

"Sounds like fun. We'll be there."

Tyler stared at the book. He turned it over and scanned the back cover. Then he opened the book, checked the last few pages, and leaned in close to examine the inner hinges. Finally, he closed the book and gazed up at me. "Is this my book?"

"Tyler," his mother said, "of course it's your book."

"But it's different."

"It's all fixed, just as you wanted," Lisa said, and shot me a look of embarrassed confusion. "Miss Brooklyn sewed the pages back together and glued the covers so it would be like new."

He was sitting up on his knees at their dining room table, so I sat down in the chair next to him. He had both elbows on the table now, and his expression was so serious, I had to smother a grin. "Look in the front of the book, Tyler. You signed your name, remember?"

"Oh, yeah," he muttered, and turned the book over. On the flyleaf, he had written his name in block letters, in heavy pencil. He studied the signature minutely, then looked up at me, still suspicious. "That looks like my name."

"It is your name. And do you remember where you colored the beast orange?"

His eyes widened and he flipped through the pages. He nodded rapidly and tapped his fingers on the page. "It's mine, it's mine."

"Do you like it?" his mother asked.

He rubbed his fingers over the crayon scrawling and tiny orange flakes came off on his skin. He nodded again. "Good. It's . . . good. Mine."

"So you're happy with it?" Lisa said, prompting him to be polite.

"Yes, it's mine. It's good." He stroked the page, then looked up at me. "Thank you, Miss Brooklyn."

I'd had more effusive praise from my clients, but there was something honest and pure about the six-year-old's approval. "You're welcome, Tyler."

Without warning he threw himself at me and hugged me as best he could, considering he was sprawled between two chairs. "How did you do it? You made it new. It's like . . . magic."

I laughed. "It is magic, but someday I'll show you how to do it."

He sat back in his chair. "Yes. I want to see how you did it."

"I'll teach you, if it's okay with your mom."

"Can I, Mommy?"

It was the first time I'd heard him call her Mommy, so I knew this was important. We both looked at Lisa, who smiled and nodded.

"Yes, yes." Tyler rubbed his hands and bobbed and wiggled in his chair.

"Tyler, isn't there something you're forgetting?" Lisa said, and touched the pocket of her jeans.

"Oh." He reached into his pocket and pulled out five wrinkled one-dollar bills. He straightened them, then handed them to me. "This is for you, Miss Brooklyn. You earned it for a job well-done."

Pookie wasn't eating.

It was early afternoon on Friday, and I could see the reason in her eyes. She'd been here long enough. It was so unfair that she had to stay at my place while Splinters, the sick cat, was allowed to luxuriate at home with Vinnie and Suzie at his beck and call.

What had Pookie done to deserve this banishment? Why did she have to be the one to live with me, the human who almost forgot to feed her?

It happened only once, but I wasn't off the hook yet. Probably never would be. Cats held grudges; I saw that now.

Naturally, Pookie didn't say any of that out loud, but it was apparent every time she looked at me. She wore her contempt for me like a second fuzzy skin. She was the prisoner; I was the jailer. She let me know with each swift swish of her tail that she would despise me to her dying day.

Or maybe that was just my imagination.

The fact is, I love animals; I really do. But I was never very good with pets. While I was growing up, there were always animals in the house. My brothers had dogs and my baby sister had a cat. There were hamsters and gerbils and little white mice, but none of them were mine. At age seven, I finally insisted on getting a pet of my own, but my mom drew the line at another furry beast. I could have a goldfish, she told me.

I was thrilled. Goldfish were so pretty and shiny. I could have a fishbowl in my room and decorate it with colorful pebbles and fake seaweed and a ceramic treasure chest. At the pet store, I picked out the one fish I thought had the best personality in the tank. Shiny and bright orange-gold, she wasn't the fastest swimmer, but she seemed to like me. And I liked her. I'd already named her in my mind. Goldie. Undulating back and forth near the side of the tank where I stood watching, she seemed to stare back at me, reaching out, calling my name. *Take me home, B-B-B-Brooklyn,* she seemed to say in her bubbly little voice. *I am your fish.*

Who could've known that Goldie had a weak gill? It was so unfair. That was why she undulated. That was why she wasn't a fast swimmer. I came home from school and found her dead, bloated, floating on the surface of the water in her pretty little bowl. I'd had her only two weeks.

I took Goldie's death personally. It broke my spirit and destroyed my confidence as a pet owner. Fear and guilt were my new watchwords. I could never ask for another pet after that. For goodness' sake, I couldn't take care of a fish. How could I be trusted with a mammal?

And Pookie knew it.

I called Suzie to tell her the cat wasn't eating and she hung up on me. Twenty seconds later, she was knocking on my door.

"Thanks so much for coming over," I said as I closed the door and led her into my living area.

"No worries, kiddo," Suzie said as she followed me. "Hey, are you okay? Looks like you're limping."

"What? No." Oh, God, I'd pulled a muscle in my leg the other night when Derek and I were doing research, but I wasn't about to let anyone know. "I . . . bumped into a chair. I'll be fine."

"Hope so, but if it keeps hurting, Vinnie's got a poultice that'll set you right."

"Thanks. I'll be fine."

Pookie came skittering across the floor at the sound of Suzie's voice.

"There she is," Suzie said, picking up the cat and hugging her. "She's only got two more days left here. Splinters's medication is finished, but we have to wait until Saturday before the cats can be together again."

"She must feel like she's in solitary confinement over here," I said, then couldn't help but smile as Pookie draped herself over Suzie's shoulder, a boneless, furry lump of love.

"No, no," Suzie said as she scratched the cat's ears. "She likes it here."

"Nope. I think she's had it with me," I muttered. "She's ready to go home."

"Don't be cracked," Suzie said, stroking the cat's fur. "She loves you. Don't you,

Pookers, don't you? Yes, you do. Yes, you do."

Suzie's normally tough-chick voice shot up three octaves as she continued crooning to her cat. "Yes, you do. Yes, you do."

Pookie's purrs of sublime love radiated through the room. I could feel her blissful vibrations from several feet away. She never vibrated around me. Of course, that was probably a good thing. Still, seeing the love generated between the two left me feeling bittersweet. Maybe it was time I found an animal of my very own to love.

"Hello, darling."

I lit up like a Christmas tree at the sound of Derek's voice. As he crossed the living room, I ran to greet him. "You're home early. I'm so happy. What's going on?"

He wrapped me in his arms and whispered, "Maybe I just missed you."

"Oh." I hugged him back, loving the masculine scent of him. Hmm, who needed a cat?

Suzie sighed. "Sweet."

"Hello, Suzie," Derek said over my head.

"Hey, Derek. Just visiting my baby, here."

"She's a lovely cat."

"Yes, she is," Suzie murmured, then repeated it straight to Pookie. "Yes, you are. Yes, you are."

I chuckled. There was a whole lot of love going on in here. I looked up at Derek. "Does this mean you'll be here for girls' night?"

"Are you serving Cornish pasties, by chance?"

"God, no," I said, wrinkling my nose.

"Then, sadly, I can't make it," he said, smiling wryly. He eased back to check his watch. "I'll be heading out in a while to meet Clive and his partners at Gary Danko."

"Wow, how'd you swing that one?" Suzie said, putting the cat down. "It takes three months to get a reservation there."

With a brief shake of his head, he said, "Corinne takes care of these things."

Suzie snorted and winked at me. "I'll give Corinne a call next time I'm in a jam."

Pookie wandered over to her bowl of mashed salmon and began to nibble.

"She's eating," I marveled.

"My work here is done," Suzie said. "I'll be back at seven for margaritas."

"Thanks so much for coming over."

"She just needed a little Suzie love," she said, grinning. After bending to give the cat one more affectionate scratch behind her ears, she stood up and punched my arm. "See you later, gator."

As soon as I heard the door close behind

Suzie, I looked at Derek. "How long before you have to leave?"

"Long enough," he said, grabbing hold of my arms and backing me toward the couch.

I laughed. "What are you doing?"

"I should think it would be obvious." He yanked off my sweater in one brash move. I shook my hair back and watched him watching me, his dark eyes glittering with intent.

"You're awfully dressed up," I said, fingering his tie. "Aren't you afraid you'll wrinkle your suit?"

"No."

My knees hit the couch and I fell backward. He followed. I pressed my hand to his chest. "What if I told you I'm not in the mood?"

"I'd have to call you a liar."

CHAPTER 16

Earlier that day, I'd made the margarita mix and chopped up all the ingredients for the tacos. Good thing, because Derek had put a wrench in my schedule, so to speak. I wasn't complaining. On the contrary, I felt like bragging, but I'd never been that kind of girl. No, our afternoon interlude would be my little secret. I hoped so, anyway. Knowing Robin and her big mouth, the whole world was likely to hear the full details if I wasn't careful. I made a mental note to avoid eye contact with her.

The only thing that had dampened my pleasure was that just before Derek left for his evening out, we heard from Inspector Lee that Galina had been questioned and released. Despite my protests, Lee stood firm. Galina had an alibi for the actual time of death, and her story had checked out. But they would be watching her, Lee assured me. I reminded her that Robin was back in town, and if Galina was free, then Robin was in danger. Lee again insisted they'd keep an eye on her.

Her word should've been enough to ease my worries, but it wasn't. I would be sure to warn Robin to be on guard.

The doorbell rang and I ran to the front to answer it. Robin and Shiva smiled as I pulled the door open. Then Robin's eyebrows shot up in surprise — and a touch of admiration, I'd like to think.

"Somebody got lucky," she murmured.

"Shut up," I whispered, then quickly smiled at Shiva as they both walked inside.

As Robin passed me she winked, and we both knew that she knew and wanted me to know she knew. Twisted, but that's a best friend for you.

Shiva stepped into my studio and gazed around the room. "Brooklyn, this is wonderful. A truly professional space. You have come so far since your days as Abraham's pupil."

Pleased, I gave her another big smile. I really had worked hard to get where I was now. Nice that someone noticed. "Thank you, Shiva. I'll give you a quick tour in a minute, if you'd like."

"Yes, I would like that very much." She walked around the worktable, trailing her hand along the smooth wood counter as she took in everything. "Abraham was so proud of you."

"Oh, that's sweet," I said, beaming. "I really appreciate hearing that."

"Mom," Robin said as she slipped off her coat, "let's get a margarita and relax."

"Of course." Shiva stared at the shelves as she circled the table.

"Mom?"

"What?" She blinked, then smiled. "Yes. Margaritas. Goodness, what are we waiting for?"

"Let me hang up your coats," I said. "Then we can go to the kitchen."

"I love this room," Shiva said as I opened the closet door and hung up their coats. "So much creativity. I can feel your energy in here. What are in those cupboards up there? Oh, is this Rajiv's Kama Sutra? Oh, my."

I turned in time to see that she'd lifted the white cloth to peek underneath. Wincing, I said, "I'm sorry it's in pieces, but that's the best way to clean and resew it. It'll be as good as new when I'm finished; I promise."

She nodded but seemed not to have heard me as she stared at the book.

I'd always tried to avoid having my book-loving clients observe my work or witness their property in this broken condition. It was stressful seeing their favorite book taken apart and strewn out over my table. I liked to compare it to seeing a loved one in surgery, although I supposed that was a slight exaggeration. Still, the point was that, intellectually, you might understand what was happening, but in reality, you just didn't want to have to see it with your own eyes.

Shiva continued to gape in rapt fascination. She touched the red leather cover tentatively, felt the padding, then started to reach for one of the pages.

"Mom," Robin said, jerking her head toward my living area, "Margaritaville is this way."

"All right, dear." She joined us and laughed gaily. "I don't believe I've had a margarita in at least three or four years. I think my mouth is watering."

"How did you ever last that long?" I asked.

She laughed again. "I have no idea."

"Oh, here's Pookie," Robin said as she entered the living room. "Hello, my feline friend."

Pookie wrapped her body around Robin's legs and purred in happiness. Apparently, I remained the one human being in the world Pookie had no use for at all.

"She likes you a lot," I said with a sigh.

"That's because I love her," Robin crooned, and lifted the cat onto her shoulder. "She took good care of me."

"Robin, what are you doing?" Shiva said. "You don't like cats."

"I do now," Robin said, her voice muffled by Pookie's fur in her face.

"My goodness, you never wanted a cat," Shiva said, looking confused. "I think I'll take that drink now."

I couldn't blame Shiva for her reaction. It was sort of a shock to me, too. Robin had turned into a cat person in her short time living here with me and Derek and Pookie.

While Robin was staying here, Pookie had seemed to recognize that she was in pain. The cat had comforted her, curling up on the couch next to her and sleeping in the guest room with her. I loved the cat for her natural empathy, even if she barely acknowledged me.

"Do you think you'll get a cat now?" I asked her as I took the pitcher of margaritas out of the fridge and filled three salt-rimmed glasses.

"I've been thinking about it," she said, grinning at the irony. It used to be that whenever one of us broke up with a boyfriend, we would tease each other about buying a cat to keep us company. Now it seemed at least one of us was seriously considering the idea.

There was a knock at the door. "That should be Suzie and Vinnie. Be right back."

"Hello, Brooklyn," Vinnie said when I opened the door. They walked in with armfuls of bags that they dumped on the kitchen bar.

I looked inside the bags. "What's all this?"

"Wine and some Thai food leftovers for you," Vinnie whispered, pointing out the appropriate bags. "And Suzie made guacamole for tonight."

"Ooh, yummy," I said, grinning from ear to ear at the thought of those leftovers.

"And I brought you a poultice for your bad hip."

Robin frowned. "You have a bad hip?"

"No."

"She was limping earlier," Suzie said.

"Really?" Robin said, her lips quivering as she tried not to guffaw.

I ignored her and turned to my neighbors. "Do you both want margaritas?"

Suzie grinned. "Does a polar bear shi—"

"Shush, Suzie, you are not to be uncouth," Vinnie said. "Brooklyn has company."

"Company?" Suzie spread her arms wide. "Well, what am I, chopped liver?"

"She is in a state," Vinnie said, rolling her eyes.

Robin grinned. "Suzie and Vinnie, this is my mother, Shiva Quinn."

"Oh, hell, sorry," Suzie said, slapping her forehead. "I'm feeling a little frisky tonight." She reached out to give Shiva's hand a rousing shake. "Vinnie's right; I'm a toad. But it's great to meet you. Robin's world-class."

"Thank you," Shiva said, her eyes sparkling with humor. "It's lovely to meet you, too."

Vinnie nodded her head respectfully. "I am Vinamra Patel, and I am so pleased to meet you. We love your daughter very much."

"Oh, my goodness," Shiva said. "You're Indian."

"Yes, madam."

Shiva touched her chest with both hands. "I live in Varanasi."

Vinnie smiled as she nodded again. "Yes, Robin has told us all about you and your beautiful home overlooking the Ghats."

Shiva blinked, then whipped around to find Robin. "You never told me you had Indian friends."

"I'm sure I mentioned Vinnie and Suzie."

"But I thought Vinnie was a . . . Never mind. Really, Robin, you should've told me." She turned back and smiled. "It's my pleasure to meet you, Vinamra."

Vinnie's laugh was melodic. "Please call me Vinnie. I'm so looking forward to hearing about your wonderful life in my homeland."

"I would love to share some of my memories with you."

I poured two more margaritas and passed all the glasses across the bar. "Here you go."

"Awesome," Suzie said, and took care of passing the other drink to Vinnie, who sat at the dining table with Pookie on her lap. Shiva sat next to her and they chatted quietly. I grabbed my own drink and walked around the bar to join the group in the dining area.

"Cheers and welcome," I said, and we all clinked glasses and sipped. I looked at Suzie. "So, why are you feeling so frisky?"

"Oh, dude, wait'll you hear." She wiggled her eyebrows at Vinnie.

"Wait. Do I really want to know?"

"Yes." Vinnie laughed again. "Suzie and I have taken the grand prize in the Stanislaus County wood arts festival."

"Hey, that's fantastic," Robin said, and toasted them with her glass.

"Wow, congratulations." I set my drink on the dining room table and gave first Suzie, then Vinnie a big hug. "That's wonderful. Was this for the flying pyramid?"

"Yes."

"Told you that piece was a winner," Suzie gloated with glee.

"Congratulations," Shiva said politely.

Vinnie smiled at her. "Thank you."

"What is it you do?" Shiva asked a moment later.

Robin grinned. "Chain-saw sculptures, Mom."

"Oh, my."

As I moved back into the kitchen to grab the bowls I'd piled high with chips, salsa, and Suzie's guacamole, I described the sculpture to Robin and Shiva: a massive wooden pyramid with wings, eight feet tall and nearly as wide, carved from one piece of wood.

"The detail in the wood is astounding," I said. "You can see each individual minute feather that makes up the wings."

"Sounds awesome," Robin said.

I continued to describe the base of the pyramid, where animals, humans, saints, and angels gamboled among the trees and flowers growing up the sides of the pyramid. The apex was crowded with iconic symbols and figures. It should've been a train wreck, but instead it was glorious.

I was pleased that they'd taken their inspiration from photographs I'd brought back from Rosslyn Chapel outside of Edinburgh. The chapel walls and wide stone columns were famous for their intricate carvings depicting the lives of saints and sinners, musical instruments, stars, and flowers. I'd visited Rosslyn a few months back with my parents and Robin while attending the Edinburgh Book Fair.

"I had a miraculous experience in Rosslyn Chapel," Shiva said, and began to relate what happened when she was confronted by the ghost of William Wallace.

"Mom, did I mention they sculpt with chain saws?" Robin said quietly.

Shiva blinked, then blushed. "I'm doing it again, aren't I?" She laughed. "Robin has informed me that I have a tendency to bring the spotlight around to myself, so I do humbly apologize. Please go on with your little story, Suzie."

"But I would very much enjoy hearing what William Wallace said to you," Vinnie asked politely.

"It was nothing," Shiva said with a wave of her hand. "Tell me all about these chain saws you use. They look so powerful and deadly. Aren't they dangerous?"

"Yeah," Suzie said, enjoying Shiva's reaction. "They could cut your arm off."

"Good heavens," Shiva said, and shivered in horror. "And where did you find a piece of wood big enough?"

Suzie smiled with pride. "We've got a forest ranger pal up in Klamath who calls when she finds a good fallen tree."

"We do not believe in using living trees," Vinnie elaborated. "This way, we imbue the dead trees with new energy to share with the world."

"That's lovely," Shiva said. "How do you —"

The doorbell rang loudly.

Shiva flinched. "What in the world?"

"Sorry," I said, touching her arm. "That'll be my neighbors Jeremy and Sergio. I told them to drop by if they got home early enough."

"Oh, I'll get the door," Robin muttered, set her drink on the bar, and disappeared down the hall. A moment later she led them into the room and quickly introduced them both to her mother.

Jeremy took Shiva's hand in his. "I certainly see the resemblance, but I can hardly believe you're Robin's mother. You are both absolutely beautiful."

Robin caught my glance and rolled her eyes, but I couldn't help smiling. Jeremy was gushing, yes. But I could see that he meant it. And why not? It was true.

Shiva wove her arm through Jeremy's and led him over to the window, where he could tell her in more precise detail how beautiful she was. Robin met my gaze again and we both laughed.

Sergio held out a sturdy white shopping bag. "Tonight's dessert."

"From your restaurant?" I said, my eyes growing bigger.

"From my home kitchen," he said, grinning.

"Even better." I took a quick peek into the bag. "You made flan?"

"It's actually a thick custard, but we're calling it flan tonight." He waved his hand deprecatingly. "It seemed the most appropriate accompaniment to tacos."

"You rock," Suzie said, punching his arm.

"I'll drink to that," I said, taking a sip of my drink. "Oh, sorry. Let me get you a margarita."

"The perfect payment," he said. "There's whipping cream in the bag, too."

"I think I love you." Moving into the kitchen, I put Sergio's bag in the fridge and pulled out the various bowls and containers of taco makings. Vinnie took charge of the margarita pitcher and filled everyone's glasses.

"Brooklyn, you're rubbing your neck," Vinnie said. "Are you in pain?"

"No, no," I insisted, and rolled my shoulders self-consciously. "I took a long, um, walk today and must've tweaked something."

"Something got tweaked," Robin muttered, then snorted.

"Now, you'll all be coming to the street fair tomorrow, won't you?" Jeremy cried as he and Shiva joined us. "I go on at one o'clock, and my performance is going to wow the crowd."

"We will be there," Vinnie said, and turned to top off Shiva's glass. "Are you going, Shiva?"

"I wouldn't miss it for the world," she said.

"Wonderful," Vinnie cried. "Our friend Wingo has a booth that will feature several of our latest sculptures."

Robin whipped around. "Are you kidding? I know Wingo. He has three of my torsos."

Elated, Vinnie grabbed her hand and shook it. "We will be showing in the same booth. This is very exciting and should be toasted appropriately."

"I'll be in the buff," Jeremy crowed. He held up his glass to clink with the others.

"We'll all be showing our best pieces."

Sergio snorted as everyone laughed.

"You really going buck, Jeremy?" Suzie asked.

He winked at Robin. "I'll be wearing some lovely accessories."

"I can't wait," I said, placing the bowl of hot shredded beef at the far end of the bar. "Okay, vegans on the left, heathens on the right. Let's eat."

The next morning, Saturday, I rose early, made coffee, then took a full cup into my workshop and continued my work on the Kama Sutra. Today I concentrated on the batting used to pad the covers. I'd discovered bits of mold in the cotton material, so I would have to replace all of it after all, just to be safe.

Meanwhile, Derek spent the morning in my second bedroom, where he'd set up an office, making phone calls to England and working on some files he'd brought home. At ten, we met back at the coffeepot, both in need of a refill.

I took in Derek's outfit as I filled our two cups, then poured a splash of cream in mine. He wore a pair of worn Levi's that fit him to perfection, topped with a thin black cashmere sweater that was so soft, I wanted to curl up in his arms and stay there all day. As I considered making my move, Derek's cell phone rang.

"Who's calling you on a Saturday morning?" I asked, feeling a little grumpy about the distraction.

He glanced at the screen. "Jaglom."

I grimaced. That was not the answer I'd expected to hear. For the past few hours, I'd managed to forget we were still embroiled in the throes of a vicious murder spree, still searching for a flash drive that too many people seemed ready to kill for.

And suddenly I remembered that Galina was free and Robin was in danger. Goose bumps covered my skin and I was chilled to the bone.

Time slowed as I watched Derek run his hand through his thick, dark hair in frustration. He said very little, leaving me to wonder what in the world Inspector Jaglom was telling him.

Derek ended the brief call. "They tracked down Galina again."

"Good," I said, encouraged by the news. "I hope they threw her back in jail."

"No. Unfortunately, they found her dead."

Chapter 17

"At least I wasn't the one who found the body this time," I muttered, then wanted to swallow my tongue. I rubbed my face in disgust. "That was a self-centered, awful thing to say, wasn't it?"

Derek slipped his hand around my neck and pulled me close. "Understandable, though, love. Don't beat yourself up about it."

"But a woman is dead, and that's terrible. And we're no closer to the truth than we were a week ago." I buried my face in his shoulder briefly, then looked up at him. "But I'm still glad I didn't find her body."

"You do have an odd habit of attracting police attention, so it's perfectly natural that you'd be relieved in this case."

"I'm just tired," I said, enjoying the feel of his soft sweater against my skin.

"You ladies were up late last night."

"Sergio was regaling us with restaurant

horror stories."

"Did Shiva enjoy herself?"

"I think she did." I was grateful for the change of subject. "She and Vinnie hit it off, which I knew they would. And Robin kept interrupting her whenever she tried to launch into one of her fabulous stories."

"Why?"

"Because Robin thinks Shiva is a narcissist. She brings everything back to herself. Robin's heard all the stories and didn't want her to be the only center of attention. It's an ongoing mother-daughter thing for them."

Derek nodded. "I suppose that's somewhat normal, but was it uncomfortable for you?"

"Not at all," I said. "Shiva was on her best behavior and even made a little joke of it. And she was captivated by my workshop, so that was fun. She wanted to see inside every cabinet and kept marveling about how well organized everything was. Wanted to know every aspect of how I'd taken the Kama Sutra apart, which was a little weird. I never like to reveal that stuff to anyone. We must've spent an hour in the workshop. Sergio and everyone finally went home and Robin dozed on the couch until Shiva was ready to leave."

His eyes narrowed. "It's nice that she took such an interest."

"It was. To be honest, I was surprised that Shiva came with Robin in the first place. They have never been close."

"You said she was somewhat neglectful of Robin while you were growing up. Perhaps she's making up for lost time."

"Maybe. I think the attack on Robin really shook up Shiva."

"Yes," he said. "It must've shaken her badly for her to leave her home in India and come all the way back here."

I studied him carefully. "You almost sound sarcastic."

"Me?"

"Yes. I don't like that look on your face."

He gave me a twisted smile. "I'm sorry, darling, but it's the only face I've got."

"And it's a very pretty face," I said, patting his cheek. "But the expression on it has me curious."

"You mean this one?" He made an exaggerated frown that added lots of wrinkles to his forehead.

"Yes, that one," I said, laughing again. "What was that for?"

He merely smiled.

"Wait. Now I get it. You don't trust Shiva?"

He held up both hands in a gesture that indicated he was weighing all the facts.

"What are you thinking?" I asked.

"We've been assuming that Rajiv has all the answers, but Shiva had a hand in this, too." He considered for a moment, then said, "She gave the book to Robin, packed inside that satchel, right? Can you show it to me again?"

"Sure." He followed me out to my workshop, where I opened the cupboard and pulled out the bag I'd stashed there.

We sat at the worktable as Derek searched every inch of the leather satchel again, running his hand carefully along the long strap and delving into the outer pocket. As he turned the bag inside out, he said, "Tell me again about the night Robin came to see you with the Kama Sutra."

"Again?"

"We're missing something." He sat back in the high chair. "I'd appreciate it if you would go through that evening step by step."

Intrigued now myself, I went through it all again. "She came inside, she brought wine, and I ordered pizza. The delivery guy came. We had pizza and wine and talked. She told me about Alex. Then we went to my workshop so she could show me the book. I took it out of the satchel and unwrapped it, and there it was in all its glory."

"Did you do any work on the book right then?"

"No."

"Did you leave it somewhere?"

"I left it out on the table." I laid my palm down. "Right here."

"Did anyone else see it?"

I had to stop and think. It had been two weeks since Robin first brought me the book. So much had happened since then. "I remember you came home from Kuala Lumpur the next day."

"Yes."

"Robin's date with Alex was that night. And very early the next day, she showed up here all bloody."

"I remember that, of course. But before that, did anyone else see the book? Did you take it out of the house to show Ian? Or someone at the book arts center, perhaps?"

"No. Ian saw it later, but . . . Oh, wait. Jeremy and Sergio stopped by the night Robin was here. Sergio brought cookies."

Derek lifted an eyebrow. "I'm surprised you didn't remember the cookies sooner."

"Me, too. They were really good cookies."

"Yes, I've tried them. Heavenly. Continue."

"I showed them the book and we all giggled at the pictures. Sergio was interested, but Jeremy was . . . Jeremy wanted . . ."

"What did Jeremy want?"

"Crap."

"Crap?" he prompted.

"Damn it. Jeremy wanted something to wear for his performance. He took the scarf."

"What scarf?"

"The scarf. The scarf the book was wrapped in."

Derek grabbed my shoulders. "What scarf? What wrap?"

"You're going to kill me."

"I couldn't do that. I'd miss you too much. But if you don't spit it out right now I'll —"

I broke away and paced. "Jeremy wanted some crazy accessories for his street fair performance and we gave him . . ." I blinked, turned to Derek.

"You gave him . . ."

"The scarf. A long, flowing Indian scarf that Shiva wrapped the book in."

"But it would be impossible to disguise the flash drive in a scarf."

"No, no. It had these big fat beads and chunks of mirror and little animals and sequins sewn into the material and hanging off the fringes. It was very ethnic, and frankly, it was an ugly mess. Robin thought it was awful, but Shiva had told her —"

"What happened to the scarf?"

"Jeremy has it."

He took a deep breath. "I interrupted you. What did Shiva tell Robin?"

I had to stop and breathe, too. "She told Robin to give the book to me and keep the scarf for herself. But it wasn't Robin's style. It was old and dirty and . . ."

"And . . ." he encouraged.

I buried my head in my hands. "And a tiny flash drive could easily be sewn into it or hidden inside one of the brass beads."

I ran to the kitchen and grabbed my house key. After I locked the front door, we ran down the hall to Jeremy's place. Derek pounded on their door, but there was no answer.

I checked my watch. "It's after eleven. They must have left for the street fair."

"Let's go."

On the way to the Castro District, I called Robin, trying to keep my tone casual. "Is your mother there with you?"

"Yeah, do you want to talk to her?"

"No, just wanted to make sure she had a

good time last night."

"She had a blast. She was so wired when we got home that she couldn't sleep. She made a bunch of phone calls to her friends, then went out for a long walk. It was well after one o'clock and I was a little worried, even though my neighborhood is safe. I fell asleep and don't even know what time she got home."

"Interesting." I aimed a glance at Derek. "She's still coming to the street fair, right?"

"Of course she's coming," Robin said. "She's excited about it. What's up?"

"I'll tell you in person. We're already on our way."

"Parking is going to be a nightmare. Be prepared to leave your car a few blocks away and walk. We can meet at Falafel Eddie's."

I checked my watch. "Okay, we'll meet you there at noon. Bring your cell phone. I'll call if I don't see you."

"You sound a little tense, Brooklyn."

"Derek has some ideas about who might've killed Alex."

She was silent for a moment, then said, "I'll see you at noon."

I hung up and looked accusingly at Derek. "You didn't trust Shiva from the start."

"I wouldn't say that," he said, evading the issue.

"When, then?" But I thought for a moment and had my answer. "No, it was right from the start. I never asked you why you stayed outside talking to Gabriel when Shiva first arrived at my mom's house."

"He thought she looked familiar, but he couldn't place her."

"Of course she would look familiar to a guy," I said cynically. "She looks like a well-aged Angelina Jolie."

"That's not why," he said, grinning wryly. "I simply thought it was suspicious that she showed up so soon after Robin ran into trouble."

"Everything is suspicious to you," I grumbled.

He shrugged but said nothing, confirming my statement.

I sighed. "I guess I should be glad about that, seeing as how you're usually right. But I still can't believe Shiva would deliberately put her own daughter in jeopardy. I also don't believe she's capable of murder, for God's sake. There has to be some logical reason for all of this. Maybe her friend Rajiv instigated the whole thing."

"Maybe."

But then something hit me. I told him the full conversation I'd just finished with Robin, specifically the part where Shiva had gone out walking late last night. Derek listened without commenting, but it was clear what he was thinking.

Galina was killed sometime last night.

It was quarter to twelve when Derek found a place to park. Before leaving the car, he called Inspector Jaglom and told him his suspicions. He asked if they knew Galina's time of death. "Sometime around two o'clock this morning?" he repeated for my benefit.

My shoulders slumped. That was around the time Shiva had been out "walking around," or so she'd told her daughter.

"This is all circumstantial and may lead nowhere," Derek warned Jaglom near the end of their brief conversation. "But I'd appreciate some police presence."

A moment later, he ended the call. Reaching across me and into his glove compartment, he pulled out his gun and checked that the bullet thingie was good to go.

"What is that thing called?" I asked, morbidly fascinated.

"This is a magazine," he said, holding it up. "It contains bullets. It goes right in here." He shoved it into the handle. Then he pulled out a cylindrical piece of metal. "This is a suppressor. We don't want to cause a panic with any loud gunshots."

"Oh, hell, no," I said, rolling my eyes. But then I put my hand on his knee to get his attention. "Derek, you're not actually planning on using that in this crowd, are you?"

He touched my arm. "Darling, you know I would never endanger an innocent bystander."

I met his gaze. "I know you wouldn't. Just had to, you know, check. Guess I'm a little freaked out."

"With good reason." He slipped the gun into the holster he wore under his jacket, shoved the suppressor in his pants pocket, then winked at me. "Let's go to the fair."

Because of the mass of people, it took us more than fifteen minutes to make it to Falafel Eddie's halfway down Castro Street, right in the heart of the fair. As we walked, Derek used his cell to call Inspector Jaglom and tell him what was going on, letting him know that we would be at the performance-art platform within the hour.

Robin was standing on the sidewalk, using both hands to finish one of Eddie's specials. "Sorry. I was starving, so I went ahead and ate."

"Where's your mom?" I said.

She glanced around. "She went to make a phone call. I guess she's calling Rajiv."

Derek and I peered through the crowd, trying to find Shiva, but she was nowhere in the area.

"Oh." Robin laughed in delight. "We ran into Jeremy, by the way. He looks great!"

"You did? Was he wearing the scarf? Did your mother see it? What happened?"

"Easy, girl," Robin said, after polishing off her meal. "Yeah, she saw the scarf. I think she was a little miffed that I gave it away, but I tried to explain that I only loaned it to him. So please don't mention that I thought it was butt-ugly."

"I won't." I looked at Derek. "We have to find her."

"What's going on with you two?" Robin tossed the falafel wrappings in a nearby waste bin. "You're both acting weird. You said you knew who killed Alex. Tell me."

"We need to find Jeremy," Derek said, taking hold of her arm gently. "Where is he performing?"

Robin frowned at him, but pointed in the direction of Market Street. "He said he'd be down at that end of the street. There's some kind of performance stage."

As we walked, I wondered why they bothered with an actual stage when there was a performance every few feet along the way. At one point, we passed a stunning man wearing nothing but a black leather studded G-string and work boots. He was dancing with a sailor who looked perfectly normal except that a strategic section of the backside of his sailor pants was missing.

I told Robin what our thoughts were, being careful not to accuse Shiva of anything. The woman might not be my favorite person, but she was my best friend's mom, and I didn't want to hurt Robin any more than she'd already been hurt. I ended up casting the blame for everything on Rajiv.

"Mom's usually not that gullible," Robin said, contemplating everything I'd just said. "Rajiv must've really done a number to trick her into sending the book home with me."

"Must've," I echoed.

"Oh, my God," Robin said suddenly. "Do you think Rajiv's the one who killed Alex?"

"We don't know," I said. That was my honest answer. Because even if Shiva had been responsible for sending the flash drive with Robin, she wasn't in the country when Alex was killed. And besides, Shiva wasn't a killer. She might've been a pain in the ass and a bit of a narcissist, but she was a humanitarian. She'd always been devoted to peace and love. So someone else had to be responsible for the deaths of all the Ukrainians and the Russian man who died in my apartment.

But why would Shiva go for a walk late last night, around the same time Galina was killed? It was all too coincidental, and I'd learned during the last few murder cases I'd been involved with that nothing was coincidental.

"Oh, there's Jeremy," Robin cried.

I saw him at the same moment. He stood on a wide pedestal at least four feet off the ground and he was loving life. Painted white from head to toe and wearing only a jaunty loincloth and the motley scarf, he would've looked like an alabaster statue except he was waving his arms and moving his stomach like he was some kind of belly dancer. Was this really his homage to the homeless? It looked more like his homage to the funky chicken. But maybe I was just a peasant when it came to performance art.

The whiteface looked cool, though. And Shiva's scarf stood out in colorful, sparkly contrast to his pasty white head.

"We're going to have to interrupt his performance," Derek said in a businesslike tone.

"Oh, too bad," Robin said. "He looks so happy."

I glanced at Derek. "We've got to get that thing now."

"Oh, there's Mom," Robin declared, pointing toward Jeremy's stage. I turned and saw Shiva, looking smart in a crisp white blouse, black stretch pants, and boots, climbing the steps leading to the wide platform where Jeremy was performing.

Robin took off jogging in that direction.

"Run!" Derek shouted, and I tore after him. We reached the stage just as Robin began to climb up after Shiva.

"Mother!" she cried. "Jeez, I'll get the scarf back! Leave him alone."

Shiva hit the top step and rushed toward Jeremy.

"What's she doing?" I cried.

A gunshot cracked the air and a few people in the crowd screamed. Most didn't even seem to recognize the sound. Maybe they thought it was a firecracker, but I knew what it was.

"Look," Derek said, pointing at the stage.

I turned and saw Shiva clutch her shoulder as blood began to seep through her fingers. Someone had shot her!

I scanned the crowd as some people scattered. I didn't see any police, but I didn't see a gunman either.

"Brooklyn, stay down!" Derek shouted, and took off in search of the gunman.

Another shot rang out.

"Derek, no!" I yelled.

A high-pitched shriek arose behind me. I spun around in time to see Jeremy bobble as a splotch of red gushed from his arm. Tottering in panic, he took a flying leap off the stage and ran toward Market Street, wearing only the loincloth and Shiva's scarf fluttering in the breeze behind him.

People in the crowd began running after him, laughing and hooting, thinking it was all part of the performance. Shiva, looking tense and determined, hobbled down the stairs on the opposite side of the stage from Robin and ran after Jeremy.

Robin had just reached the top of the stage. She stopped and yelled, "Mother, what're you doing?"

"Robin, get off the stage!" I shouted. Didn't she see people getting shot up there? I ran over to the stairs to drag her off, if necessary. As I started to climb up, I was jerked from behind. I fell backward, and twisted my body so I wouldn't fall on my back. My arms shot up to protect my head and I landed on my left side, smacking my left elbow on the blacktop and shaking me up so hard that I saw stars.

I moaned, then rolled over to see what had happened. A dark-skinned man in a black suit, obviously the one who'd pulled me off the stairs, was storming up to the stage toward Robin.

"Stop him!" I yelled, but my voice was gravelly. I struggled to stand, just as the man grabbed Robin and held a gun pointed roughly under her chin.

Then he shouted, "Shiva!"

Was that Rajiv? Was he the one who shot Jeremy and Shiva? And now he held Robin hostage. Why?

More people screamed and ran for cover. The area in front of the platform emptied as everyone scattered and hid. Three police cars screamed to a halt fifty yards away, just beyond the barricades used to hold back traffic. Several cops jumped out of the cars and drew their guns.

Before I could think straight, Derek came running over, knelt down, and wrapped me in his arms. "Christ, are you all right? I saw what he did. I'll kill him."

"I'm good; I'm fine," I said, patting his back. Everything inside me hurt, but I was okay. "Help Robin. Be careful. Don't get shot."

"I'll be careful," he muttered, then pressed his lips to mine. He helped me to my feet, then kissed my right cheek and my left. "I love you. Now stay out of the way, for God's sake."

"Okay," I said in a daze. Had he just said what I thought he said? I'd have to think about that later, I thought as I watched him crouch under the stage and weave his way around the scaffolding to the back of the platform.

At that moment, I was distracted by the sight of Jeremy, who had circled back around to Castro Street. The cops didn't seem to be bothering with him. Their eyes and rifles were trained on the stage, where Rajiv held Robin at gunpoint.

Shiva caught up with Jeremy at the corner of Market and tackled him onto the sidewalk, barely twenty feet away from where I was standing. The crowd in front of the Twin Peaks bar spread out to give them room to fight and began cheering for one or the other.

Shiva ripped the scarf off Jeremy's head and he grabbed it right back, clutching it to his chest as though it were a precious treasure. Shiva pushed herself up to a standing position. Then, turning to shield her actions from the police, she pulled a small gun out of her pocket and pointed it at Jeremy.

"Shiva, no!" Rajiv shouted.

"Mother!" Robin cried.

At the shouting, Shiva's gaze darted toward the stage, and Jeremy kicked her in the knee. She fell and the gun went skittering down the sidewalk. She scurried back, popped Jeremy in his bloody arm, and grabbed the scarf.

"Shiva!" Rajiv pushed Robin away and went running toward the stairs. Derek jumped onto the platform and raced after him.

I waited at the bottom of the stairs, and as soon as Rajiv reached the ground, I whipped around and kicked him in the groin, just like my brothers had taught me. I'd never had a chance to use the move, but it worked really well. The guy dropped like a rock and groaned like he was dying. His gun flew into the crowd and more people screamed. The police came forward then and grabbed him.

Derek stood on the stairs, shaking his head at me as I grinned proudly. Every muscle in my body was screaming in pain, but right at that moment I was pretty pleased with myself.

"Mother!" Robin shouted.

I whipped around in time to see Shiva running toward Market Street holding the scarf. Robin jumped off the platform and raced after her. She caught up with her quickly, grabbed her blouse, and spun her to the ground.

Derek helped me hobble over to assist

Robin. Shiva's shoulder was still bleeding, but Robin wasn't showing her much sympathy.

"What did you think you were doing, Mother?" Robin demanded.

Shiva sighed. "This really isn't a good time, Robin."

"Mother, did you kill Alex?"

"Don't be silly."

"Oh, I'm the silly one? I don't think so."

"Dear, please get off me. You're wrinkling my blouse."

"Oh, screw your damn blouse. The blood has ruined it anyway, thanks to your buddy Rajiv. And in case you didn't notice, he's the one who was holding me at gunpoint a few minutes ago. You really hang with a classy crowd."

Shiva grabbed Robin's hand. "Whatever happens, just know that I'm sorry, honey."

"Sorry isn't cutting it right now, Mom."

"Fine," Shiva snapped. "But when you get to be my age, you might have a little more sympathy. A woman has to take care of herself in this world, and that's all I was doing."

"By threatening to kill my friend? Nice try, Mom."

That was when I realized Robin was crying. I couldn't blame her, since I was tearing up a little, too. I still wasn't one hundred percent clear on Shiva's role in this nightmare, but it was obvious that she'd pulled a gun on Jeremy. Was she willing to kill him for that flash drive?

I stared across the street at the man still writhing on the ground, the one I'd successfully kicked in the groin. So that was Rajiv, Shiva's so-called buddy? Had he gone insane? What in the world was going on here?

Two more police cars and two ambulances screeched to a stop a few feet away. I watched a crowd of handsome men in everything from leather chaps to suspenders and Speedos take off running in the opposite direction. There was chaos all the way up Castro.

Then two black SUVs pulled up and four men in suits stepped out. These had to be the feds. Homeland Security? FBI? I guess we'd find out soon enough.

A few yards away, Derek had helped Jeremy over to a bench and held a cloth to his bleeding arm. I had an absurd thought that, for assassins, everyone's shots today were way off the mark. I said a little prayer to Buddha, Yahweh, Allah, and all the saints in heaven to thank them for that small mercy.

■ ■ ■ ■

Jeremy was whisked away to the hospital. The bullet was removed safely from his shoulder. I heard from Sergio five hours later that Jeremy had been allowed to go home and sleep in his own bed. I assured him we would visit later.

"He's wide-awake and surrounded by our friends," Sergio told me, and I could hear the relief in his voice. "He can't wait to read the reviews of his performance in tomorrow's papers."

"Send him our love," I said, and was laughing when I hung up. But the good humor faded fast.

Robin, Derek, and I had been stuck at FBI headquarters for the last five hours, answering a battery of questions, first from the local police, then the FBI, and then a few shadowy government characters Derek seemed to know pretty well.

The local police gave us the most grief. Inspector Lee seemed to take it personally that we hadn't told her about the flash drive and the book.

"Here I was carrying on about a stupid turf war," she griped, "and you all were playing *The Spy Who Shagged Me.* Not fair,

Wainwright."

"I'm sorry," I said, mostly meaning it. "I barely knew what was going on."

"Yeah, I'll believe that when pigs fly out my ass."

So I guess this meant she wouldn't be coming over for wine anytime soon. But I liked her and refused to give up on her now. I'd allow her a few weeks to sulk, then invite her again.

Shiva, meanwhile, had already made a deal with the feds to reveal everything she knew in exchange for immunity. Given her special status with the United Nations, the authorities agreed rather than risk international embarrassment. Now she was singing like a birdie.

Thanks to Derek's spooky contacts, more of the story was emerging. All those years when Shiva was traveling for so-called humanitarian causes, she had been a spy for the U.S. government. For the most part, anyway. Once in a while, her loose scruples allowed her to play for the other team.

When Robin heard that, she whispered, "No," and I felt her shudder at the news. It wasn't every day that you found out your mother was a scumbag double agent playing fast and loose with your own life.

"It's all right, sweetie," I said, hugging her

as she began to cry. I watched Derek get up and find a box of tissues for her to use. My hero. I grabbed a few myself.

When Derek sat down again, he took the chair next to Robin. Both of us held her hands as his Interpol buddies spilled the rest of the background they'd collected on her mother.

Recently, Shiva had come into possession of information so inflammatory that its disclosure could embarrass and topple the Russian government. She'd worked with Galina, the Ukrainian agent, before, so she devised a scheme to sell the volatile information to Galina and rake in millions.

Knowing the Ukrainians were positioning themselves to barter a new oil deal with Russia, Shiva knew Galina's people would want to get their hands on the information. Shiva figured she'd make enough money to retire to an island off the coast of India and live in splendor for the rest of her life.

She placed all the particulars — racy phone call transcripts between high-level married diplomats, incriminating e-mail, texts, and a number of documents — onto a tiny flash drive that she stuck inside a miniature brass elephant, and then she sewed the brass doodad into the old scarf. She called Galina and asked for four million dollars in exchange for details of when the flash drive would be carried into the United States via her daughter, Robin.

The money was deposited into her account while Robin was visiting her. Talk about convenient timing. Robin shuddered when she heard that.

But once Robin got back to San Francisco, things went very wrong. It seemed to Galina that either the Russians or the Americans were thwarting the Ukrainians at every turn. Alex, who'd been Galina's superior as well as her part-time lover, was dead now. Galina had managed to track down the big Russian man, and when he admitted to killing Alex, she shot him. Then she dropped him off in front of Brooklyn's apartment, where she knew Robin was staying. She hoped the police would accuse Robin of killing the man, but didn't realize that Robin was already out of the city.

Shiva had admitted that Galina wasn't the brightest crayon in the box, but the young operative had her uses. But then Galina contacted Shiva in Varanasi to complain about the screwups. She was furious that Alex had been killed and blamed Robin. She accused Robin of paying the Russian to kill Alex as a way to double-cross her mother.

That was when Shiva decided she'd better get on a plane to the Bay Area and take charge of the operation. While she was there, she would spend time consoling her daughter, Robin. And, if necessary, she would rough up a few of her friends.

CHAPTER 18

Three days later, after Pookie went home and some of the dust had settled on what I'd taken to calling the Kama Sutra Caper, the three of us, Derek, Robin, and I, drove back to Dharma. On the phone, Mom had whispered that Guru Bob had asked her to perform a banishment ceremony, but she wasn't sure she had the heart to do it in front of Robin. I suggested we wait and gauge the state of Robin's *prakriti,* or mind-body-soul constitution, before deciding.

Sitting in my parents' living room, we shared the sordid details of the downfall of Shiva Quinn with Mom and Dad, Austin, Gabriel, and Guru Bob. Austin sat on the love seat holding Robin as close to him as he could get her.

I found myself focusing on my brother again. It was as though he had truly grown up while I wasn't looking. Yes, I'd always known he was good-looking, but a sister tended to forget a brother's mere cuteness in the face of age-old sibling rivalries. But watching him now with Robin and seeing the way he gazed at her and laughed with her, I couldn't be happier that they had finally found each other.

He was a wonderful man — and lucky, too, because Robin was a delightful, talented woman with a fantastic sense of humor and a wide-open heart. The fact that her own mother had never recognized Robin's amazing qualities was Shiva's loss — and one more big black eye for her, as far as I was concerned.

I was going to get weepy in a minute if I didn't shake off those thoughts. Glancing around the room, I could see the stress and confusion in everyone's eyes. Except Gabriel's. Nothing seemed to surprise Gabriel, including the pain of betrayal.

It was Guru Bob whose reactions wrenched my heart the most. I couldn't remember a time when I'd seen him express negativity. Ever. But watching him now, I could see anger and great sadness mar his features as the details of Shiva's duplicity emerged.

We had Derek's Interpol friends to thank for filling in a number of blanks in Shiva's story. For instance, the big man who died in my home was Yuri Borkov, a Russian operative who had received a tip early on that there was highly embarrassing information on the market that could disgrace people at the top levels of the Russian government. He'd had no choice but to follow every lead.

Shiva later confessed that she'd been the one who leaked the flash drive information to the Russian. She wanted a kickback from their side as well. And why not? She needed the money. She wasn't getting any younger, and wealthy men were starting to lose interest in her. When she realized she couldn't count on her wealthy lovers to keep her in the high life much longer, she took matters into her own hands.

When Robin heard that, it was the last straw. I agreed it was a pathetic, arrogant, and egotistical excuse for doing what she did, but it was the closest Shiva had come to revealing the true motivation for her actions.

"I still can't believe it," Robin said, her tone a mix of bewilderment and scathing anger. "I know she didn't do the killing herself, but she set everything in motion, and a lot of people died just so she could line her own pockets. And I saw her pointing that gun at Jeremy. She was so desperate, who knows if she would've gone ahead and used it, just to get her hands on that butt-ugly scarf and the stupid flash drive."

"Oh, sweetie," Mom said, "I'm so sorry. I'm having a hard time believing it myself."

"I know, Becky," Robin said, and sniffed a few times. "My own mother was a double or triple agent. It's so bizarre. It's like I stepped into the Twilight Zone or something. I mean, Shiva was never what you'd call maternal, but still . . . I keep expecting someone to jump out and tell me it's all been a giant misunderstanding, that she was actually one of the good guys and . . . I never really knew her, obviously."

And that was Shiva's fault, not Robin's, I thought, angry all over again at her mother's treachery. Robin insisted she'd given up years ago on ever being close to Shiva, but I knew it wouldn't be easy for her to overcome this major revelation.

The other night, after we'd left the FBI building, Robin had begged to come home with me and Derek. Once again, her own place had a stigma attached to it. Shiva had stayed there. She'd probably searched the place while Robin was sleeping, made phone calls, maybe arranged a murder or two. Robin didn't have the heart to return there just yet.

While at my house, Robin had spent hours on the phone with Austin, filling him in on the latest news and discussing their future. Later, she told me that Austin wanted her to move to Dharma, but she wasn't sure she wanted to right away. He had offered to buy her a store or office on the Lane in town, where she could sell her sculptures and operate her small tour company. I was impressed with my brother's offer; the Lane was currently the cynosure of wine-country chic. Fancy shops, restaurants, and wine bars attracted people from all over the Bay Area and the country.

But along with the offer of a fashionable place to do her work, Austin had offered himself. He wanted to marry her.

Through misty eyes, I had assured her that it all sounded wonderful, and while I would miss having her living so close to me in the city, she would be only an hour's drive away.

It was a lot for her to think about on top of her mother's betrayal, so Robin was still debating her next move. Seeing her with Austin today, realizing again how perfect they were together, I had a feeling her decision would come soon.

"But wait. Shiva's story is not over yet," I said to the group.

"Then keep going," Dad said with the air

of a man who wanted all the story out in the open so they could deal with it and move on.

"Okay, so guess what." I looked around the room at everyone's expectant faces. "It was all bogus."

"Bogus?" Dad said, his eyes narrowing. "Explain."

I nodded at Derek to take over, because he told the story so much better than I did. I think the British accent helped.

"It was Shiva's old friend Rajiv Mizra," Derek began. "He was the one who set the whole operation in motion in order to snare Shiva in a trap."

"Wait a minute." Dad shook his head as though his ears were plugged. "Her friend set her up?"

"Yes." I sat forward and gave Robin a sympathetic look. "It was all a sting to catch Shiva."

"Rajiv has always been one of Mom's oldest and dearest friends in Varanasi," Robin explained. "But it turns out that he's really an agent for the Indian government. He's been watching her for years. But she's always been so devious, it was impossible to catch her until now."

"Whoa," Mom said. "Now, that's bizarre.

This is starting to sound like a bad spy movie."

Dad stood. "Does anyone want more wine?"

"Oh, yeah," I said, needing a breather. "I'll help pour." I pushed myself up off the couch and walked carefully around the room, filling glasses for everyone.

"You're moving kind of slow, sweetie," Dad said. "You got a hitch in your get-along?"

I was relieved that, for once, I didn't have to feel guilty about my aches and pains. "That guy Rajiv pushed me off the steps and I fell on the blacktop. I'm still a little achy."

Dad froze; then his hand tightened around the bottle's neck. "For that alone he should serve twenty to life."

"Thanks, Dad."

Derek continued the story. "Rajiv used various channels to feed the fraudulent information to Shiva, then gave her the means to smuggle it all into the United States. Namely, the book, the Kama Sutra. He knew her well enough to know that the very subject matter would intrigue Shiva. He also knew that Robin visited her mother at least once a year, so he'd been monitoring her activity and had timed everything to her arrival."

"Don't I feel special?" Robin said, shaking her head in disgust. Austin squeezed her hand reassuringly.

"Unfortunately," Derek said, "while Rajiv informed some top officials in the Ukrainian state department that he was running a sting operation, he didn't inform the Russians. He cared only that Shiva would eventually act on the information she got, and when she did, he would make his move."

"Wow," Dad said, scratching his head. "Becky, this isn't a movie. It's more like a Ken Follett novel."

Derek smiled. "Shiva's contact was Galina, because they'd worked together before. She suggested to Galina that the Ukrainians might use the information to barter a better oil deal with Russia. In a classic case of the right hand not knowing what the left was doing, the sting information never filtered down to Galina and Alex, and those two never told their superiors what they planned to do. Mainly because they were promised a kickback from Shiva if they retrieved the flash drive in record time."

"Amateurs," Gabriel muttered.

"They probably thought they'd get a big

bonus for capturing the information," I surmised. "But instead, they both died gruesome deaths."

"For nothing," Robin said grimly. "I should blame Rajiv for their deaths, since he started the ball rolling, but I don't. I blame my mother. She was at the center of it all. She lied to everyone from day one, and the worst part is, she did it for money. Why? She had plenty of money, but she wanted more. She could've killed Jeremy! I'll never forgive her for that."

Guru Bob, sitting in the chair next to Robin, reached out and took her hand in his. "Forgiveness will remove the weight of guilt from your shoulders, gracious. Allow me to suggest that you learn to forgive, but do not ever forget. Do not forget her lies. Do not forget her true nature. Do not forget that her beauty cloaked the snake within. That is the lesson I will have to take with me, as well. For I, too, and all of us were deceived by the woman."

Robin gripped his hand. "I'm so sorry."

"You have a lovely heart," he said. "You have done nothing wrong, gracious, and I want you to remember that always." Then he smiled at her so sweetly that I felt tears spring to my eyes.

"Thank you," she whispered.

After a solemn moment, Derek picked up the story. "Shiva had told Yuri Borkov, the Russian, about the flash drive hidden in the scarf. And since Robin was staying with Brooklyn, he broke in to search for it. He didn't get very far before we returned and he had to run."

"I don't know what would've happened if he found the Kama Sutra," I said. "But thank God he didn't."

The book was now in the safe hands of Ian McCullough and the Covington Library. Ian assured me that Minka had been fired — again — so I would finish my work on the Kama Sutra in one of their on-site workshops.

Rajiv had received a slap on the wrist for his part in the fiasco. He'd shot both Jeremy and Shiva, but he said he'd meant only to scare Shiva into backing down. He also insisted he'd grabbed Robin only to make her mother toe the line.

Rajiv had been so guilt ridden by the outcome of his sting that I was able to coerce him into donating the Kama Sutra to the Covington Library. He would receive credit as the donor, of course, and I would receive credit for discovering the book's connection to Jean-Pierre de Garme, royal bookbinder to the French court of Louis

XVI. A small win-win in a sea of tragic losses.

"Indeed, it was a good thing Yuri didn't find the book," Derek said. "But his day got worse when he was unknowingly spotted by little Tyler, Brooklyn's neighbor. Once the police got a workable sketch from Tyler's description, Galina was able to use a connection she had inside the police department to track down Yuri. Based on Shiva's admissions, we believe Galina is the one who killed Yuri, because he admitted to her that he killed Alex."

"So who killed the young one, Stanislav?" Dad asked.

Derek leaned forward, his elbows resting on his knees. "We don't know. My money is on Rajiv, but I'm not sure we'll ever know."

"And who killed Galina?" Mom asked.

Derek struggled not to smile as he and I exchanged glances. Mom and Dad were hanging on to every word of the story.

"Again, we're not sure," I said. "Rajiv and Shiva have denied killing her, even though both of them had the means and motive. But now that Galina is out of the picture, it becomes a matter of 'he said, she said' between Shiva and Rajiv. We may never know what truly happened unless one of them breaks their silence."

"So many deaths," Mom whispered.

"It's all an ugly mess," Robin said. She took a deep breath and let it out slowly before she continued. "They let me see Shiva before they took her away. You know what she said to me?"

"What, honey?" Mom said.

Robin sniffed. "She said I should forgive her because she didn't do anything to hurt me."

I gasped, then covered my mouth quickly.

Robin glanced at me. "I know; it's unbelievable. She used me as an unwitting mule. I was drugged. Viciously attacked. A man was killed in my home. My friends were almost shot. I could've been killed by any one of those silly agents, not to mention that jackass Rajiv, and she wouldn't have given a damn. As long as she got her money."

Guru Bob took her hand again. Austin held her other hand tightly. I got up and knelt before her. Mom and Dad came around the back of the love seat and touched her shoulders.

"You are loved, gracious," Guru Bob said. "You are strong. Your mother was weak."

"We love you, honey," Mom said, and squeezed her shoulder.

"Sure do," Dad said.

I slipped Robin a tissue as tears trickled down her cheeks.

Guru Bob stood. "We will not speak of her again."

"Right on, Robson," Dad said, and raised his fist in solidarity.

Derek kissed my forehead and gave me a tight hug, and I sighed with relief that it was all over.

"Rebecca," Guru Bob said, turning to my mother, "I suggest you perform one of your charming purification ceremonies to rid us of the negativity that the woman has wrought upon us all."

"Super idea!" Mom said, clapping her hands. "I've been working on a cleansing chant that's a guaranteed humdinger."

Robin laughed, and it was the loveliest sound I'd heard in days.

BROOKLYN'S GLOSSARY

Parts of the Book

Boards — Usually made of stiff cardboard (or, occasionally, wood) and covered in fabric (cloth, paper, leather).

Covering — Cloth, paper, or leather fabric used to cover the boards.

Endband — Small ornamental band of cloth glued at the top and bottom of the inside of the spine, used to give a polished finish to the book (also called a headband or tailband).

Endsheets — The first and last sheets of the textblock that are pasted to the inside of the cover board; the pastedown.

Flyleaf — First one or two blank pages of a book, not pasted to the inside of the cover board. These pages protect the inner pages of the textblock.

Fore edge — The front edge of the textblock opposite the spine edge. The edge is usually smooth but may, on occasion, be rough, or deckled. The edge may be gilded or, in rare instances, painted. Fore-edge painting gained popularity in the seventeenth century when religious or pastoral scenes were painted onto the foredge to embellish the book's content. The painting was invisible until the pages were fanned in a certain direction.

Grain — The direction in which the fibers are aligned in the paper. When grain direction runs parallel to the spine, the paper folds will be straighter and stronger and the pages will lie flat.

Head — The top of the book.

Hinge — Inside the book cover, this is the thin, flexible line where the pastedown and flyleaf meet and is the most easily damaged part of the book.

Joint — Outside the book at the point between the edge of the spine and the hard cover that corresponds with the inside hinge. Its flexibility allows the book to open and close.

Linen tapes — Strips of linen sewn onto the signatures and used to hold the signatures together. The tapes run perpendicular across the spine edge and are pasted down between the cover boards and the endsheets.

Pastedown — *See* Endsheets.

Signature — A gathering of papers that are folded and sewn to make up the textblock or the pages of a book.

Spine — The back edge of a book, where the pages are sewn and glued.

Swell — Term that indicates the way paper lies after folding. Generally, the folded edges of a stack of paper will be thicker than the outer edges. Consolidating and rounding the textblock will reduce swell and allow the book to lie flat and even.

Tail — The bottom of the book, where it rests when shelved upright.

Textblock — The sections of paper sheets or signatures sewn through the fold onto linen tapes.

Other Bookbinding Terms

Conservation — The care and preservation of books, often at a total resource level — that is, a library or the archives of an institution. Conservators will take into consideration the damaging effects of age, use, and environment (including light, heat, humidity, and other natural enemies of paper, cloth, and leather) and strive to apply their knowledge of bookbinding, restoration, chemistry, and technology to the restoration and protection of the collection under their care.

Consolidation — Once the textblock is sewn and pressed, the spine should be consolidated (that is, compressed, in a press) and coated with adhesive (PVA). When consolidation is completed (the glue is dry), the textblock is rounded by pushing and pounding against the sections, first one side, then the other, with a bookbinders hammer.

Kettle — The kettle actually refers to the first and last holes (usually found at each end of the page) where the stitching together of the signature pages begins and ends (or reverses back to the beginning). The kettle stitch refers to the stitch used to sew one signature page to the next, linking the next page to the previous one, as well as binding the linen tapes to the textblock.

Restoration — The process of returning a book to as close to its original condition as possible. A book restoration specialist will pay close attention to the materials and techniques in use at the time the book was first made, and will attempt to follow those guidelines in terms of resewing, rebinding, and reconstructing the book. This is in contrast to book *repair,* which does not encompass restoration or conservation but focuses strictly on bringing a book back to its basic functional level (which may or may not involve duct tape).

Rounding — The process of hammering or manipulating the textblock spine into a curved shape after gluing and before backing. Rounding diminishes the effect of swelling and helps to keep a book standing upright on a shelf.

Some Basic Bookmaking Tools

Awl — Used for punching sewing holes in folded paper.

Bone folder — A tool used for making sharp creases in folded paper and smoothing out surfaces that have been glued. It is generally made of bone and is shaped like a wooden tongue depressor.

Bookbinders hammer — Used for rounding the spine of a book, a bookbinders hammer is smaller and lighter than a carpenter's hammer, with a large, flat, polished pounding surface.

Book press — There are various types. One small type of wood press can be used to hold the textblock while gluing. With a newly finished book, a large brass press will help strengthen, straighten, and fuse the book together.

Punching jig or Punching cradle — A V-shaped piece of equipment with a slim opening at the bottom for cradling signatures in order to punch holes in them.

PVA (polyvinyl acetate) — Preferred adhesive in bookbinding, it is liquid and flexible and results in a permanent bond. It dries colorless and is pH neutral, so it is recommended for archival work.

ABOUT THE AUTHOR

A native Californian, award-winning writer **Kate Carlisle** worked in television for many years before turning to writing. A lifelong fascination with the art and craft of bookbinding led her to write the Bibliophile Mysteries featuring Brooklyn Wainwright, whose bookbinding and restoration skills invariably uncover secrets, treachery, and murder. Kate lives and writes in Southern California and loves to visit readers online at katecarlisle.com. You can also find her on Facebook and at her group blog, http://romancebandits.blogspot.com, where she blogs monthly.

We hope you have enjoyed this Large Print book. Other Thorndike, Wheeler, Kennebec, and Chivers Press Large Print books are available at your library or directly from the publishers.

For information about current and upcoming titles, please call or write, without obligation, to:

Publisher
Thorndike Press
10 Water St., Suite 310
Waterville, ME 04901
Tel. (800) 223-1244

or visit our Web site at:

http://gale.cengage.com/thorndike

OR

Chivers Large Print
published by AudioGO Ltd
St James House, The Square
Lower Bristol Road
Bath BA2 3SB
England
Tel. +44(0) 800 136919
email: info@audiogo.co.uk
www.audiogo.co.uk

All our Large Print titles are designed for easy reading, and all our books are made to last.

We hope you have enjoyed this Large Print book. Other Thorndike, Wheeler, Kennebec and Chivers Press Large Print books are available at your library or directly from the publishers.

For information about current and upcoming titles, please call or write, without obligation, to:

Publisher
Thorndike Press
10 Water St., Suite 310
Waterville, ME 04901
Tel. (800) 223-1244

or visit our Web site at:

http://gale.cengage.com/thorndike

OR

Chivers Large Print
published by AudioGO Ltd
St James House, The Square
Lower Bristol Road
Bath BA2 3SB
England
Tel. +44(0) 800 136919
email: info@audiogo.co.uk
www.audiogo.co.uk

All our Large Print titles are designed for easy reading, and all our books are made to last.